ONLY LIES REMAIN

VAL COLLINS

This is a work of fiction. Names, characters, places and incidents are products of the author's imagination or are used fictitiously and are not to be construed as real. Any resemblance to actual events, locales, organisations or persons, living or dead, is entirely coincidental.

THE MAIN CHARACTER in this book is Aoife. This is a very common Irish name and is pronounced "Eee-fah".

Two minor characters are called Tadhg and Cian. Both are common Irish names. Tadhg is pronounced like 'Tiger' without the 'er'. Cian is pronounced 'Key-en'

If you would like to hear these names pronounced, check out the video on my Instagram page here: *http://bit.ly/Aoife-Tadhg-Cian*

ONE

THE NEWS ENDED, but the murderer didn't notice. The room grew dark and the mug of tea cooled. At last the murderer rose and began pacing the room, muttering, 'Could I have misheard? No, of course I didn't. After all this time! What am I going to do? They can trace DNA in ways that weren't even imagined fifteen years ago. What if they find a hair, or saliva or whatever else it is that they examine? Will the police arrest me? A good solicitor could convince a jury that DNA evidence is unreliable, couldn't he? I can't spend the rest of my life in prison—and, hell, I shouldn't have to. It's not like I wanted to kill him. These things happen. But nobody would ever understand how it was. They'd never believe it wasn't my fault. People need someone to blame. But the truth is some tragedies are nobody's fault. He didn't want to die, I didn't want to kill him, but it happened anyway. It was fate. His and mine. You can't fight fate. You just have to accept it.'

TWO

IT WAS THE same each time. The minute the house came into sight, it started. 'Breathe in…hold…breathe out,' Aoife muttered to herself. She really needed to get a grip. It wasn't like she was expecting a confrontation. Maura wouldn't say anything. Aoife knew that. But the very fact that there was bad feeling between them sent Aoife into a minor panic every time they met.

By the time she reached the front door, Aoife's heartbeat had almost returned to normal. She rang the doorbell and waited. Amy's light feet raced across the wooden floor, and a moment later her little nose pressed against the narrow glass panel that ran the height of the door.

'Mama!'

'Hi, sweetie.' Aoife waved at her.

'Mama! Mama!' Amy turned and bolted down the corridor, shouting, 'Nana!' A few seconds later she returned alone, wailing, 'Mama!', her tiny fists banging on the glass panel.

Aoife searched her bag for the key she hadn't used in almost six months.

'Mama!' Amy leaped into her arms.

Aoife swung her around and Amy screeched with laughter.

'Where's Nana!'

'Nana sick.'

'Sick! Maura?' She put Amy on the ground and headed for the kitchen. Amy raced ahead of her.

Maura met them at the doorway. 'Sorry, Aoife. I was just coming.'

Her face was pale and had the wretched look that only came from bitter tears. Toys, which Maura normally stored in the playpen, were strewn all over the kitchen floor. Amy was rooting through them, flinging them in all directions.

'What are your toys doing on the floor?' Aoife asked.

'Man. Big man.'

'What man?'

'Moaney,' Amy said.

'Moaney? What's going on, Maura? Are you okay?'

'Detective Moloney called earlier. He gave Amy some toys to play with while we talked. He had some upsetting news.'

'Detective Moloney!' Aoife gripped the countertop. 'Was he looking for me?'

'You've spoken to him? Of course, you met him when you worked in DCA. He was the detective who handled the murder investigation, wasn't he? I'd forgotten you knew each other. Why didn't you say anything, Aoife? Things may be difficult between us, but I didn't deserve to hear news like that from a stranger.'

Amy pushed between them and thrust a book at Aoife. 'Book.'

'Not now, sweetie.'

'Book. Now!'

Aoife picked up Amy and put her in the playpen. 'Read a story to your dolls. I have to talk to Nana.'

Amy's face puckered. Aoife had never put her in the play-pen before.

Aoife opened the book and placed it on the floor of the playpen. 'Wouldn't your dollies love to hear about the beautiful princess?'

Without waiting for an answer, she took the teabags from the cupboard and filled the kettle. A glance showed Amy lining up the dolls in readiness for her words of wisdom.

'What did Detective Moloney tell you?' she asked, putting two mugs on the glass table.

'Only the basics. They found him somewhere in the city centre.' Maura reached for the mug, then shoved it to one side. 'You probably know more than I do.'

'I haven't spoken to Detective Moloney in over six months. Who did they find?'

'Oh God! Well, I suppose you'll find out sooner or later. I'll have to tell the boys tonight.'

'Tell them what?'

'Their father. He's dead.'

'Oh no! Oh, Maura, I'm so sorry. He'd come back to Ireland?'

Maura shook her head.

'Jason will be devastated. I know he always says he hates him, but deep down I think he hoped his dad would get in touch someday. If only so he could scream abuse at him for abandoning you.'

'But that's the thing, Aoife. Danny didn't abandon us.'

'He may have sent you money, Maura but he still disappeared without a word.'

'Not willingly. He was murdered.'

'What! When?'

'Fifteen years ago. Remember a few weeks back, a body was found in the grounds of that old house in the city centre? They just identified him as Danny.'

'But—I don't understand, Maura. How could Danny be dead for fifteen years? I thought he sent you money every month.'

'So did I.'

⤺

Aoife was filling Orla in on the news when she thought she heard a noise.

'Hang on a sec.' She stood at the bottom of the stairs and listened. 'Sorry, I thought I heard Amy moving around.' She settled back on the sofa. 'What did you ask me?'

'Who found the body?'

'Some guy working on a building site. The house had been deserted for years. Something to do with a disputed will, I think. Then there was some problem with planning permission, but a few months back it was sold to a developer. There was a bit of land around it, so he decided to knock down the house and build an apartment block. They'd been working on the site a few days before they found human bones.'

'Do they know how he died?'

'He was stabbed in the back.'

'They can be that precise after fifteen years?'

'The knife nicked the spine. Apparently damage to bones leaves a permanent mark that can be identified even centuries later.'

'Why would someone stab him? He wasn't into anything illegal, was he?'

'I don't know, Orla. I doubt it. He worked in a bank.'

'It must have been awkward, having to talk to Maura when she was upset.'

'A bit. It's been a while since we had a proper conversation. I felt sorry for her. I think she feels she let him down.'

'Her husband? How?'

'By believing he'd run off and left her. Other families go on the radio and TV and make sure the whole country knows about the missing person. If Maura had done that, Danny's body might have been found years ago.'

'Far better for her that it wasn't.'

'Huh?'

'If they'd found her husband years ago, Maura wouldn't have received that money every month. How would she have managed?'

'That's another thing, Orla. Who would send her money?'

'Someone in the family? Didn't you say she wasn't in contact with her husband's family? Some big row?'

'I'm not sure what happened. Jason says they never spoke.'

'So presumably she wouldn't have accepted money from them. Someone in the family probably pretended the money was from Danny so she would take—' The doorbell rang. 'Oh, that's Robbie. We're off to the new club I was telling you about. I have to go.'

Aoife could hear a deep voice in the background. She had no idea who Robbie was, but Orla's conquests came and went so quickly there wasn't much point in remembering their names.

'When did you say your next interview was, Aoife?'

'Tuesday.'

'Great, let's meet for lunch. You can tell me the whole story then. Bye.'

❧

Aoife knew it wouldn't be long before Jason arrived, but when she heard his key in the front door, she felt a flash of irritation. How many times did she have to ask him not to use that key?

She shook her head. What was wrong with her? Her husband was going through a crisis and she was worrying about keys.

Jason walked into the kitchen, head slumped.

'Sweethear—Jason!' She put her arms around him and he buried his head in her neck. 'I'm so sorry.'

She could hear his muffled sobs. 'Come on, sit down and I'll get you a drink. Did you bring the car?'

Jason nodded.

'You can leave it here. I'll drive you home.' She had the whiskey waiting on the worktop. 'Drink this.' She took the seat opposite him.

'I hated him.'

'You thought he'd abandoned you.'

Jason didn't appear to hear. 'But now when I think back on it, I can't understand why I felt that way. He was a good dad. He spent all his spare time with us. We had everything we needed. He didn't drink or waste all our money, and I can't remember him ever losing his temper. How could I go from loving him one day to hating him the next? Why didn't I give him the benefit of the doubt?'

'You were a kid, Jason. You were angry that somebody you loved could turn his back on you.'

'It wasn't just anger. It was so much stronger than that, and Dad hadn't done anything to deserve it.' Jason took a gulp of the whiskey and had a fit of coughing. 'I know this is daft, Aoife'—he struggled to catch his breath—'but I have a picture in my head of Dad sitting in some other world looking down at us. He's got this expression that's halfway between hurt and anger, and I know what he's thinking. He—Aoife, if I could never see you again, it would destroy me. But if you hated me as well—how could we do that to him?'

'If your dad is looking down on you, he understands. Anger is part of grief. I know that from my own experience.'

'You don't know, Aoife. You can't even imagine the effect something like that can have on a young kid.' Jason sipped the whiskey and grimaced. 'You never thought your parents abandoned you. You always knew how they died. When Dad left, it killed something in me.' He took another sip and coughed again. 'This is awful. Don't you have any wine?'

'I thought you'd need something stronger.' Amy took a bottle of wine from the wine rack, wiped the dust off the screw top and poured him a glass.

'Thanks.' Jason took three large gulps. 'Even at ten, I knew nothing would ever be the same. I never really trusted anyone again. Not even Mum. For years I came home from school expecting to find she'd left us too. And even when I was older— it's the reason we split up, isn't it?'

Aoife nodded. It wasn't the time to point out that Jason's fear of abandonment was only part of their problems.

'Can I stay here tonight?'

'I'm not sure that's a good idea, Jason.'

'I'll sleep in the spare room. Please. I can't go back to Mum's. She spent the whole evening talking about what a great husband and father Dad was. I can't listen to any more. I feel guilty enough.'

'Of course you can stay.'

THREE

Aoife sat in the basement of Fallon & Byrne's in Exchequer Street. Her book was propped in front of her as she sipped her soup. Most people Aoife knew preferred the upstairs restaurant. Orla practically lived there. Even Aoife's Mother & Toddler group trekked all the way from Kildare every few months just for a special lunch. Aoife preferred the basement. For one thing, it was cheaper. Normally she avoided basements because she found the lack of natural light depressing, but the thing she loved about the basement in Fallon & Byrne was the long wooden tables. Everybody sat together, so even when you were alone, you never felt uncomfortable, and there was so much chatter you could have quite personal conversations without worrying you would be overheard.

'Sorry I'm late.' Orla put her tray down on the table and flung her fur-lined aviator jacket on the back of her chair. 'How was the interview?'

'Terrible. I don't know what's wrong with me. I was never great at interviews, but at least I could give the impression of being reasonably articulate. These days I'm not far short of a babbling idiot.'

'It's stress. After—'

'Is that your phone, Orla?'

Orla pulled the vibrating iPhone from her Gucci backpack. 'Hi, Tanya… No, not today. I'm meeting Aoife for lunch…. Okay, bye. Sorry Aoife, I just have to take it off silent.' She fiddled with the phone for a few seconds, then stuffed it into the backpack, which she shoved under her chair. 'Where were we? Oh yeah, you're just stressed. After all, you barely survived your last job. Who could blame you for being nervous about working again?'

'Well, I'm going to have to get it together soon. I'm worried Jason will stop giving me child support now he's moved back in.'

'What?'

'Oh, I'm sure he'll pay the bills and give me money for housekeeping, but I don't want us falling back into old habits. I need to be financially independent.'

'You didn't tell me you were back together.'

'We're not. Jason was so upset the night he found out about his father that I said he could stay. I thought it would only be for one or two nights, but at the weekend he moved his things into the spare room.'

'And you let him?'

'I said he couldn't move back into the house without even asking me. He said he wasn't moving back. He was only staying for a few days until his mother got herself together.'

'How long is that going to take?'

'I don't know. She seems fairly okay to me. Jason says she puts on a brave face in public but cries the rest of the time. He says he can't cope with her.'

'He's not going to learn to cope from your house. Tell him it's time he went back to Maura's and learned to deal with it.'

'He's still my husband, Orla, and he's not coping either.

He's barely eating and he paces the house half the night. I can't make things harder for him.'

'One of his brothers can put him up.'

'Ryan's the closest and he lives in Navan. It would be a two-hour round trip every time he wanted to see Amy.'

'Do you want Jason living in your house, Aoife?'

'I don't know. I mean, I think I want us to get back together again but—'

'You think?'

'I know I want the marriage I thought I had. But that only existed in my head. I don't want Jason to move back if we're going to continue the way we were before, and I'm not convinced he can change.'

'Didn't the marriage counselling help?'

'I don't know. The counsellor said I have to understand that Jason doesn't mean to be controlling. He's afraid I'll leave him, just like his dad deserted him when he was a kid.'

'Didn't you already know that?'

Aoife nodded. 'I knew. It didn't make it any easier to cope with his behaviour.'

'Did Jason learn anything?'

'He says he accepts he was too controlling. But I see the way he looks at me when we're around other men. He doesn't say anything anymore, but I'm pretty certain he's the same Jason underneath.'

'Maybe not saying anything is the first stage. The next stage might be to not let it bother him.'

'Do you think?'

'I really don't know, Aoife. Ask the counsellor.'

'We had to stop going. She was so expensive. Maybe when I get another job we can think about having a few more sessions.'

'And in the meantime Jason lives with you?'

'I'll wait until Maura's feeling better, then I'll ask him to leave. Him living with us can't be good for Amy. She was too young to understand when he moved out, but she'll soon expect to see him in the house every day.'

'All the more reason to tell Jason his mother needs him and he can't desert her right now.'

'He says she has Evan.'

'If Evan's like most teenage boys, he won't be much help.'

'That's another problem. I can't leave Maura to cope with this on her own. If Jason won't help, I'll have to.'

'Can you do that?' Orla fished under the chair and pulled out her bag. She gathered her long blond hair in one hand and rooted in the bag with the other. She removed a pencil and used it to pin her hair into a loose bun. Every man in the restaurant watched her.

'I'll have to. Our relationship can never be what it was, but if the situation was reversed, I know Maura would be the first to offer help.'

'Well, as your lawyer—okay, I'm not qualified yet, but I'm assuming you'd want your oldest friend to take care of your affairs. So, as a law student and your lawyer to be, I'm advising you to tell Jason you want him out of your house by tomorrow. Letting him live with you is asking for trouble.'

'It's not that simp—'

'It is that simple, Aoife. Either you and Jason are a couple or you're not. If you're not, it's madness letting him live in your house. Getting rid of him will solve your problem with Maura. It's Jason's responsibility to give Maura the support she needs, not yours.'

'I know, but Jason is in no state to help anyone.'

'Aoife, Maura has five sons. If you don't step in, someone else will have to fill the gap.' She paused. 'Tell me it's none of my business if you like, but you did sort out your financial affairs with Jason, didn't you?'

'Yes. After we separated we went through all the accounts, but there wasn't much to settle. Jason's well paid but most of it never reaches his bank account. He came to an agreement with the credit card company, and three quarters of his salary goes straight to them each month.'

Orla picked up her sandwich. 'You do know it's not your responsibility to pay off his credit card debts?'

'It's a joint responsibility, Orla. We both ran up the debts, and when we separated, Jason paid off my debt so I'd have a credit card to use in an emergency.'

'How did an accountant ever run up such high debts in the first place?'

'I'm not sure. I was still trying to cope with Mum and Dad's death at the time and I wasn't in any state to worry about our finances. I imagine most of the money went on renovations. Ask anyone who's ever bought a house, particularly an old one like ours. You wouldn't believe how quickly the bills mount up.'

'Well, at least make sure Jason gives you the same amount of money each month whether he's living with you or not. Otherwise, before you know it—' A young man tapped Orla's shoulder and she turned around.

'Hi.' The man straightened his tie and grinned. 'I'm David. You're a friend of my sister, right?'

Orla flashed him a brilliant smile. 'No, I think you've mixed me up with someone else,' she said and turned her back on him.

The young man hesitated, then slinked back to a table filled with men in business suits, all of whom were greatly enjoying his humiliation.

'Men!' Orla sighed. 'They don't give you a minute's peace.' Her eyes lit up. 'Not that I'd want them all to leave me alone.

Did I tell you about the guy I met last weekend? Oh, Aoife, he's so gorgeous. Where's my phone?'

Aoife glanced at the photos of a guy who could have been a fashion model. Maybe he was. She couldn't concentrate on Orla's prattling.

FOUR

THE SUN STREAMED through the windscreen for what was probably the first time this year. Any sign of spring normally put Aoife in a great mood, but it wasn't working for her today. Jason had been living with her and Amy for a full week now, and Aoife suspected he'd had no contact at all with his mother. Anytime she asked how Maura was coping, Jason would mutter 'fine, fine' and change the subject. Visiting Maura was the last thing Aoife wanted to do. The previous week had been the first time she'd set foot inside the house in over six months. Jason's behaviour was forcing her into closer contact with his mother. She was making a real effort not to resent that.

'I wanted to make sure you're okay. I can go away, if you'd like, Maura.'

'Of course I don't want you to go away. Come in, please. Where's Amy?'

Aoife followed her into the kitchen. 'Alison next door is looking after her for an hour. She has a five-year-old who loves to play babysitter.'

'I'm glad you came by. I'm expecting Detective Moloney any minute and I could do with some support.'

'Maybe it would be better if I came bac—'

The doorbell rang.

Aoife took a few deep breaths, put on the kettle and was taking milk out of the fridge when Maura led Detective Moloney into the kitchen.

'I believe you know my daughter-in-law.'

'Indeed. The DCA case, I believe.'

So the steely-eyed stare wasn't reserved for murder suspects.

'Tea, Detective?'

'Thank you, no. Mrs Walsh, I fully understand you weren't in any condition to be interviewed the last time we spoke. Do you feel up to going through the details now?'

'I think so.' Maura pulled out a kitchen chair for him and took the seat opposite. Aoife busied herself making tea.

'When was the last time you saw your husband?'

'Saturday around noon. He usually took the boys to his mother's on Saturday, but that week he went alone.'

'Why?'

'The older boys were invited to a party. I said I'd take them. Danny's mother hadn't been widowed long and she looked forward to his visits.'

'How did he get there?'

'Usually he took the car, but I needed it to get the boys to their party, so he took the train to Dublin and cycled from there.'

'Where did his mother live?'

'The Grange Road in Rathfarnham.'

'What did he do there?'

'The things his dad took care of when he was alive—gardening, DIY, any heavy lifting. His mother wasn't fond of driving, so he usually did the weekly supermarket shopping as well. Most weeks he had supper at his mother's and left shortly afterwards. The police said he left her house around five p.m. that day.'

'Who was in the house?'

'You'd have to ask his mother. The youngest, Elaine, was still living at home then, but she was in college and rarely around.'

'How was he earlier that day? Did he seem upset or stressed?'

'No. Everything was very normal.'

'Had you been fighting?'

'No. Danny was very easy-going. It was almost impossible to fight with him.'

'Did he have any enemies?'

'None that I know of.'

'What did you make of his disappearance?'

'At first I was worried sick, but once the money arrived, I figured he didn't want to be found.'

'And you were okay with that?'

Maura frowned. 'Of course not. I was devastated and really angry, but I believed he'd chosen to desert us.'

'Even though there had been no arguments and he had no reason to disappear? It never occurred to you that there might be some other explanation?'

'Maybe it should have. Poor Danny. He deserved a wife who had more faith in—' She covered her mouth with her hand.

Aoife picked up the two mugs of tea that were cooling on the countertop. This was none of her business. She placed one of the mugs in front of Maura. Tears were gathering in Maura's eyes, but Aoife looked away. Maura was not her responsibility. She would wait a few minutes, make an excuse and leave.

'Detective Moloney.' Why was she speaking? 'Men leave their families every day. When Maura received the money, of course she thought her husband had deserted her. Where else could the money have come from?'

'That's a very good question.' The detective turned to Maura. 'Tell me about the money.'

Maura gripped the mug. 'Two weeks after Danny disappeared, an envelope arrived. It had a London postmark. There was five hundred inside. The following week eight hundred arrived. The envelopes were erratic at first, but I've been getting one every month for the past twelve years.'

'Were the envelopes addressed by hand?'

'There were always two envelopes. A small one with cash, inside a larger padded envelope. There was no writing on the smaller envelope. In the early days, the padded envelope was handwritten in capitals. I spent hours examining the writing, but it didn't bear any resemblance to Danny's. About ten years ago, the handwriting was replaced with a printed label.'

'Why didn't you tell the police about these envelopes?'

'I did.'

'Who did you tell?'

'I forget his name. The detective in charge of the investigation into my husband's disappearance.'

'You told him you were receiving envelopes of cash every month? There's no record of that on the file.'

Maura shrugged. 'I definitely told him.'

'When did you receive the latest envelope?'

'Almost a month ago.'

'Did you keep it?'

'No. I threw it away.'

'How much was in the last envelope?'

'Four thousand.'

'In cash?'

'Yes.'

'Sterling?'

'No. Euros.'

'Why would someone living in England send you cash in euros?'

'I assumed Danny felt so guilty about abandoning his family that he was trying to make things as easy as possible for me.'

'We'll need the bank statements showing the lodgements you've made over the years.'

'I only started lodging it in the last five years.'

Detective Moloney raised his eyebrows. 'You received forty eight thousand euros every year for twelve years and you didn't lodge any of it until five years ago?'

'Do you have kids, Detective?'

The detective hesitated. 'One.'

'Then you know that four thousand euros a month doesn't go far when you have a mortgage and five sons to raise. Anything left over went on the mortgage. I wanted it paid off as quickly as possible so we'd have somewhere to live if the money suddenly stopped.'

'Why would it stop?'

'I figured a man who could walk out on his family without a word was capable of cutting off their income at any time. I repaid the mortgage five years ago and I've been saving the surplus ever since.'

'I noticed a new silver Volkswagen parked out front. Is that your car?'

Maura nodded.

'It must have cost at least twenty thousand euros, right?'

'Thereabouts.'

'How did you pay for it?'

'Cash.'

The detective raised an eyebrow. 'You kept twenty thousand euros in cash in this house?'

'I know it sounds mad, Detective. I'm not one for buying a

new car every year. So long as they get me from A to B, I don't care how old they are. Every time I bought a new car, I put two hundred euros aside each month until I had enough to buy the next one. I thought about banking my savings, but it was comforting knowing I had cash I could get my hands on in an emergency. And with five kids, I was never short of emergencies.'

'I see. That's all for today, Mrs Walsh. If I have more questions, I'll be in touch.'

⁂

'He doesn't believe me, does he?' Maura asked Aoife when the detective left.

'I don't think so.'

'Great! Couldn't their questions wait until after the funeral? I've enough on my plate right now.'

FIVE

Aoife was waiting at the front door when Maura pulled up. She closed the door quietly so as not to wake Jason and Amy. Jason had refused point-blank to visit his grandmother but, presumably to make up for it, he offered to take the day off to look after Amy.

'Thanks for coming with me, Aoife.'

Now she had decided to get involved, she might as well be gracious about it. 'You take Amy any time I have an interview. I'm glad of the opportunity to return the favour.'

'I'm not doing you a favour, I love having Amy. I was terrified you wouldn't let me see her after—' Maura glanced at Aoife, then looked away. 'Anyway, looking after Amy is a pleasure. I promise you, you're not going to enjoy meeting Bridget.'

'She can't be that bad.'

'She's always hated me. She's of the generation that thinks any girl who has sex before marriage deserves to be burned at the stake.'

Aoife laughed.

'Okay, maybe I'm exaggerating. She tolerated me while Danny was alive. When he disappeared, she accused me of having an affair. Her Danny would never desert his family unless I'd done something dreadful. I had sex with a man who wasn't my husband once, she said. What was to stop me doing it again?'

'That's horrible. As if you weren't upset enough.'

'By then I was furious. It was bad enough abandoning me, but the boys too? And I was livid with Bridget for not telling me where Danny was. I figured if Danny was sending me money, he was definitely talking to his mother. We had a huge fight.' She smiled. 'It's ironic, isn't it? Neither of us believed he would walk out on the other without a word, and it turned out we were both right.'

'Did Bridget have a big family?'

'There was a gang of them, but they all emigrated. She'd be on her own now if it wasn't for Jack.'

'Jack?'

'He's kind of like family. He grew up next door to Bridget. His mother was a widow and had to go to work. There was no childcare in those days—well, not unless you could afford to hire staff. Bridget's family looked after Jack when he was little. They were like his second family. Bridget was a good bit older, but she and Jack became like brother and sister.' Maura turned off the main road and slowed considerably. 'Jack went into the priesthood. He lived abroad on and off over the years. When he came home for good, Bridget was widowed. He spends more time in her place these days than he does in his own.' Maura was now driving at a snail's pace. 'It's somewhere in the middle of this road. Why can't they put numbers on the houses like everyone else?' She pulled up at the kerb. 'We'll have to get out. I need a closer look.'

In the midst of housing estates and apartment blocks were ten small whitewashed cottages, remnants of the time when Rathfarnham was considered the countryside. As they walked down the road, Maura peered at each house. 'It's either the one with the red door or that—Jack!'

A plump man in his seventies hurried down the path. The wind blew his few remaining wisps of grey hair into his eyes and he brushed them aside. He smiled at Maura and enveloped her in a bear hug.

'It's so good to see you again, Maura.' He pulled away to look at her. 'Although I wish it could have been under different circumstances. You're looking well. How are the boys?'

'They're fine. This is my daughter-in-law, Aoife. She's Jason's wife.'

'I'm very pleased to meet you, Aoife.'

Aoife smiled and extended her hand. Was it her imagination that he hesitated before accepting it?

'How's Bridget?'

'She's coping.' Jack pulled on the glove he had removed to shake hands, shivered and zipped his jacket to the neck. 'That kind of news would be a shock to anyone and at her age it takes time to adjust. Have the police bothered you again?'

He put his arm around Maura and they chatted away as they walked up the narrow path. Aoife trailed behind.

✺

Jack showed them into a small, stuffy sitting room. An elderly woman was using a shovel to gather coal that had fallen out of the grate. She looked up as they entered.

So this was Jason's grandmother. Aoife wondered if she had dressed up for the occasion. The grey fitted trousers and red jumper seemed a little formal for hanging around the house, and who tied a scarf around their neck to lounge by the fire? The surprisingly trim woman ground the heel of a grey suede boot into the embers glowing on the marble fireplace and settled back into her armchair.

'Sit,' she said, pointing at a lumpy couch half covered in newspapers and magazines.

'Bridget, this is Jason's wife, Aoife.'

Bridget nodded, her eyes on Maura who was gathering up the papers strewn all over the couch. Jack rushed over, took the papers from Maura and threw them on a dark oak dresser that occupied most of the room. 'What have you been doing to the place, Bridget? It was spotless a few minutes ago.'

'I haven't moved out of this chair. And what do you mean it was spotless a few minutes ago? It's spotless now. Are you saying my house isn't clean enough for the likes of them?'

Maura pressed her lips together but said nothing.

'Jason's wife, is it?' Bridget turned to glare at Aoife.

'Eh, yes.'

'I haven't seen him since my Danny died.' She jerked a thumb in Maura's direction. 'That one over there wouldn't let me see any of my grandchildren.'

'You know very well that's not true, Bridget. It was your decision to have nothing to do with me. How did you expect to see my children?'

'Now, Bridget. We want to make our guests welcome.'

'Don't talk to me like I'm a four-year-old, Jack. You're the one who invited them. You make them welcome.'

'We talked about this. It's time to heal old wounds. Danny wouldn't want you two arguing.' He pulled off his coat and gloves. 'Give me your coats and I'll make us all a nice cup of tea. We can sit down and talk everything out.'

Bridget ignored him. She leaned across, grabbed Aoife's arm and pulled her closer. 'I pity you with that one as a mother-in-law. My Danny was miles too good for her. The worst mistake I ever made was letting him marry that floozy. He was only a teenager. I should have talked him out of it. But I was thinking of my grandchild.' She turned her head to glare at Maura. 'And then she wouldn't even let me visit him. If I'd known then—'

'I never said you weren't welcome in my house, Bridget. It was your own decision to stay away.'

'It isn't your house. It's my Danny's house, and you wouldn't even have a house if it wasn't for Jack.'

'Let go of the girl, Bridget. You're hurting her.'

Bridget glared at Jack, but she sat back in her seat. Aoife resisted the urge to rub her arm.

'Maybe we'd better get straight to the funeral arrangements.' Jack pulled a small notebook out of his pocket. 'Maura, I've spoken to your local parish priest. The church is booked for Monday and Friday, but we can have Tuesday, Wednesday or Thursday of next week. Which would you prefer?'

'I want it on Thursday,' Bridget interrupted.

Maura sighed. 'Fine.'

'Okay, and afterwards I thought we'd go to a hotel near you. What about—'

'After the funeral, everyone will come to this house. The neighbours have all offered to bring food, and we're going to put a big table in the kitchen where people can help themselves.'

Maura stiffened. 'Bridget, you can invite anyone to your home that you wish, but first we are all going to a hotel for a three-course meal.'

'We are not. Danny would want everyone to come here.'

'Danny would want his wife and sons somewhere they would feel comfortable. You and your family are more than welcome, but we are going to a hotel and that's final.'

'You little tart. It's not enough that you killed him, you

have to ruin his funeral as well. You disgust me. Do you think I don't know—'

'Killed him? What are you talking about? You know I had nothing to do with Danny's death. You can't still believe he walked out because I was having an affair.'

Bridget struggled to get to her feet. Jack rushed over to help, but Bridget waved him away. 'Get that floozie out of here. She is never to set foot in my house again.'

Maura rose. Aoife went to follow her, but Maura stood her ground. 'You know how Danny died. It had nothing to do with me.'

Bridget, now on her feet, advanced towards Maura. Her face was twisted with hate, and saliva gathered at the corner of her mouth. 'Do you think I don't understand what that detective was hinting? I might be old but I'm not stupid. It's your fault my Danny's gone. I'm as certain of that now as I was the day he disappeared.'

SIX

'WHAT DOES THAT mean?' Maura demanded, but Jack had stepped between them. He took Maura's arm and led her into the hall. 'What was she talking about?'

'Don't pay any attention.' Jack opened the front door and ushered her outside. 'It was my mistake suggesting you meet. I thought we could sit down together and have a civilised conversation about the funeral arrangements.'

'What did the detective say to her?'

'I'm sure he didn't say anything. Bridget gets weird ideas in her head these days and there's no shifting them. She wants to believe you were somehow in the wrong. That way she doesn't have to blame herself for never getting to know her grandchildren.'

'She could get to know them now. Evan doesn't even remember her. And if she wasn't so stubborn, she'd have a chance to know Danny's granddaughter.'

'I'll talk to her. Maybe I can make her see sense.' They reached the car and Jack pulled Maura into a hug. 'It was great seeing you again, Maura.' He held the car door open for her. Aoife let herself in the passenger door. 'Goodbye, my dear.' Jack gave her a peck on the cheek. He nodded in Aoife's direction. 'Bye.'

❧

'I don't think he likes me.'

'Don't be silly, Aoife. He doesn't know you. Jack's one in a million, but he's spent his whole life around men. He's not comfortable with women. It took him ages to get used to me too, but we're great friends now and Danny thought the world of him.'

'What did Bridget mean when she said you wouldn't have a house without Jack? Did he give you money?'

'Where would he get money? No, Jack came home shortly after we married. He'd been working in Africa for years. He found us living in a dump in the city centre. Damn! The whole road layout has changed.' Maura stopped, waiting for a break in the oncoming traffic. Eventually a man stopped to allow her to change lanes. Maura acknowledged him with a wave. 'Where was I? Oh yes, when Jack came home. Well, that was the middle of the last recession. In some ways it was even worse than it is now. It seemed like half the country was unemployed. All Danny could get was odd shifts in a local bar. Jack fixed everything. The Church had very strong connections back then. Jack was only home on a short visit, but in three weeks he managed to get Danny a job in the bank and talked the bank manager into giving us a mortgage. I don't know what we would have done without him.'

❧

The house was quiet when Aoife got home. The radiators were cold. Jason must have taken Amy out early. Good. She hoped they went someplace nice. They had little enough father-daughter time.

Aoife looked around the kitchen. Two saucepans, two frying pans, four dishes, three mugs, two plates and an assortment of kitchen utensils littered the countertop. Inches of something she couldn't identify was glued to the bottom of the saucepans, and the frying pans were covered in congealed grease. The floor looked clean, but she could feel something sticking to the soles of her shoes. All Jason had to do was give Amy her breakfast. How could he make such a mess?

Three hours later Aoife had cleaned the kitchen, tidied away the clothes and toys strewn all over the house, hoovered, gone through a mound of ironing and prepared a casserole. She was peeling potatoes when she heard a key in the front door.

'Hi, Aoife, how was the dragon?'

'That's what you call your grandmother?'

'We did when we were kids. Mum hated it. Was it dreadful?'

'Pretty bad. Where's Amy?'

'Alison's looking after her.'

'What! I thought you were taking her for the day.'

'I couldn't. I had a work emergency.'

'Oh, Jason! I wish you'd told me. Alison will know I'm home. What will she think of me leaving Amy with her for hours? I'm already behind in returning the favour, and she won't let me pay her.'

'Sorry, I didn't think. They couldn't find one of my files at work. There was this huge drama. I had to go in and I couldn't take Amy with me.'

'Why not? I would have taken her to your grandmother's. And I only went there because you refused to go.'

Jason frowned. 'You think I'm not pulling my weight. Maybe you're right. It's so hard. I can't concentrate on anything.

That's why I put the file in the wrong place. And I'm under so much pressure at work. When they phoned and said they couldn't find the file, I just panicked. All I could think of was I had to get in there and—'

'It's okay. I'm sorry, Jason. I shouldn't be nagging you at a time like this. Why don't you go next door and get Amy? I'll finish making the dinner.' She took a bottle of wine from the fridge. 'Give this to Alison. I'll go around later and apologise.'

'That's the wine I bought yesterday. Don't you have anything cheaper?'

'I'm not giving Alison our cheapest wine.' She looked at the bottle. 'How expensive was this? What about our debts?'

'It was an extravagance, I know, but I thought it would make me feel better. Of course I'll give it to Alison.'

Aoife sighed. 'Don't worry. Drink your wine. I'll go next door and thank Alison. Heat up the oven, okay?'

'Of course I will, darling. Thank you. You're the best.'

Fifteen minutes later, Aoife returned with Amy. Jason had taken the wine into the sitting room and was watching TV. He had tossed the corkscrew into the sink, cork still attached. The oven had reached the required temperature, and the casserole Aoife had prepared was sitting on the countertop. The half-peeled potatoes lay beside them.

'Jason, I think it's time you moved back home. I spent the entire day with Maura and she's coping quite well.'

Jason looked up from his iPad.

'I am home.'

'You know what I mean.'

'I've been thinking, Aoife. I want to stay here. I'm twenty-five. I don't want to live with my mother.'

'It's only until we sort out our relationship.'

'How is that going to happen if we never see each other?'

'Okay, we'll make arrangements to meet once every week. How about date night? Every Friday we'll go to dinner or the movies, just us. I'm sure Maura will be happy to take Amy.'

Jason smiled. 'That's a great idea. A few weeks of that and we'll be back to normal.'

'I didn't mean—'

'Let's start tomorrow. Everybody's talking about this new restaurant near the office. The food is supposed to be amazing. You could meet me after work and we'll go straight there. It's always easier to book the early sitting.'

'We can't afford that.'

'I know, but this is a special occasion. The hell with the cost. Let's enjoy ourselves for once. Everything's been so miserable lately.'

'But—' Aoife was terrified of getting further into debt. Then again, some things were more important than money. Jason was going through a dreadful time. Didn't he deserve a special night? 'Oh, all right,' she said at last, 'but we need to talk about our living arrangements.'

'It's not worth my while moving out if we'll be getting back together in a few weeks.'

'Jason, we—'

'Of course we can talk about it, Aoife, if that's what you want. But not before the funeral, okay? I'm not up to dealing with anything else right now.'

SEVEN

FRIDAY MORNING, AOIFE had to force herself to get out of bed. Amy had woken her several times the previous night, but exhaustion was the least of her problems. Today was her weekly Mother & Toddler group. Aoife never missed a session. They were essential for Amy's development. She needed to be with kids her own age, and she adored tearing around the room with the other kids or playing in Barbara's massive garden. Aoife detested every second.

It had all started so well. In January, Aoife had signed up for a Parent & Toddler group at a local play centre. It got them out of the house during the cold weather, was reasonably priced and parents were given a voucher for a free cup of coffee. Trained staff amused the kids, and Aoife got to know one or two of the mothers. Everything was going great until the play centre closed. Aoife was devastated, and more than grateful when Lucy, one of the mothers she had become friendly with, told her that another mother was starting a Mother & Toddler playgroup in her own home. Enter Barbara.

Barbara wasn't exactly unpleasant. She was a little judgemental and occasionally showed hints of impatience, but her most unforgiveable quality was her perfection. A mother of five, Barbara lived in a big house just outside Kildare town. The house hadn't always been big. Barbara had inherited a small two-bedroom cottage from an uncle, but her husband, Daniel, was an architect and their new home was evidence of his extraordinary skill.

The original two-bedroom house now occupied a small corner of the building. A glass corridor linked it to an enormous extension, and a second glass corridor linked it to the playroom. When Aoife had first been shown into the sitting room, she had grasped Amy's hand tightly, terrified the child would mark the cream walls, cream carpet or white leather furniture.

'This is where the kids play?' she'd asked.

Barbara laughed. 'No, no. This room is strictly for us adults.' She brought them through the glass corridor to a large square room with wooden floors and shelves lined with toys. 'The toys on the bottom two shelves are for the playgroup.'

A friendly middle-aged woman approached. She gave a wide smile and held out her hand to Aoife. 'Hi, I'm Greta. This must be Amy. I have just the toy for you, Amy. Come along.'

Amy grabbed Aoife's leg but let go the moment she saw the beautifully crafted colonial-style wooden doll's house. Every door and window opened, and there were tiny lace crochet blinds that pulled up and down. Greta removed the back so Amy could play with the furniture. Everything was exquisite, from the hand-carved miniature furniture to the flower-strewn porch swing.

'That's so beautiful,' Aoife said. 'Aren't you worried the children will destroy it?'

Barbara shrugged. 'Daniel can always make another. Greta, remember the children must eat their snacks in this room. I don't want them in the kitchen again.'

Greta turned out to be Barbara's live-in nanny. She ran the child entertainment section of the morning while Aoife sat with the other mothers in the all-white sitting room, trying not to spill tea on the heavily polished furniture.

Most of the conversation centred around children.

'My Ethan is so bright. I'm worn out from reading to him. He can't speak yet, but I think he can read already. He turns the page of every book at exactly the right moment.'

'Davy's such a sweet-tempered child. But it's all due to routine. I have strict bedtimes and we only eat organic food. It's all in the parenting.'

'Katie never gives me a second's trouble. I don't understand what people mean by the terrible twos. Katie's an angel.'

Aoife rarely spoke. She was the youngest in the group by at least eight years. Lucy had returned to full-time work after two sessions, and a few months later, she and her family had relocated to Kerry. The other mothers were even more intimidating than Barbara. None of them had nannies but they all had perfect hair and makeup, dressed in the latest fashions and had at least two children. Aoife wondered where she was going wrong. She struggled to find a clean pair of jeans, her hair hadn't been cut in over a year and she was always the last person to arrive.

Today Amy was clutching Aoife's mobile phone when they reached Barbara's house. Two of the mothers gasped. 'You let that poor child play with a phone! Don't you know how dangerous those things are?'

'She only plays with the kids' apps,' Aoife explained. 'It distracts her if she's crying or wants something she can't have.'

'But that's totally the wrong way to handle the child.' Olive covered her mouth with both hands. 'If Amy wants something she can't have, you simply explain why you can't give it to her. Children are a lot more intelligent than most people realise.'

'I can't rationalise with her. She's not old enough to understand. Amy's not even two yet.'

'Nonsense. When Tristan was that age, he understood everything I said. I never let him near electronic devices. Honestly, Aoife, it's practically child abuse.'

'I think you might be remembering that incorrectly,' Claire said, and Aoife felt a surge of affection for a woman she had barely noticed previously. 'My Albert is only two and there wouldn't be much point in explaining anything to him yet.' Aoife gave her a grateful smile. 'I always think the important thing is for us mothers to provide a safe, loving, happy family environment. If Albert cries, I pick him up. It always calms him. Just being near me is enough to soothe him. You must try it, Aoife. No child should ever be allowed near a mobile phone.'

Greta arrived to collect Amy, but the conversation about mobile phones and negligent adults who relied on electronic devices to parent their children continued. Aoife tried not to listen. She didn't believe holding a mobile phone for a few minutes would hurt any child. But why didn't Amy stop crying when she was held? Wasn't she as good a mother as Claire? Hadn't she bonded enough with Amy? Was she doing everything wrong?

It was a few moments before she realised Barbara was speaking to her.

'Sorry?'

'I asked if there was any news about your father-in-law's murder.'

'No, we haven't heard anything. It was so long ago, the police will probably never find out who murdered Danny.'

'It's absolutely appalling!' Olive had her hands over her mouth again. 'A young family man. Someone with a good job in the bank. And this was always such a quiet town.'

Barbara nodded. 'That's exactly what Cian Mannion said the other day. You know Cian, don't you, Olive?'

'The bank manager's son? Not really. I think he was in the same year as my sister, but we never spoke.'

'Well, he and Daniel have collaborated on a few projects. I'm not sure what he does. An accountant, maybe? I know he works from home. Have you seen his house?'

'No, where does he live?'

'He's still in his parents' home. He inherited it when his father died.'

'That house is still lived in? It's a dump! His business can't be doing very well.'

'I don't know about that. It's doing well enough for him to hire a secretary. I ran into him at the K Club last week. I was taking Mum to lunch for her birthday and Daniel was interviewing this appalling woman. We had a good laugh about her after—'

'Cian Mannion is looking for a secretary?'

Aoife spoke so rarely that all the mothers turned to stare.

'Yes. Aoife, you've never seen anything like the outfit that woman was wearing. And the hair! She—'

'So he hasn't actually hired anyone yet?'

'No. You're not looking for a job, are you, Aoife?'

'Yes, I am. I'm a single mother now. Amy and I can't survive on social welfare.'

Olive's hands were heading for her mouth again. 'But, Amy—'

Barbara quietened her with a glare. 'Heaven forbid any young woman should have to survive on that pittance. Aoife, I'll ring Cian Mannion and I'll tell him you will be perfect for the job.'

'Really! That's great, Barbara. Thank you.'

'And I'll make it clear that if he doesn't hire you, he'll have me to deal—did you hear that? Greta! How many times do I have to tell her not to let those kids into the kitchen?'

Barbara stormed out of the room and the conversation

returned to the group's favourite topic—the raising of geniuses. Aoife stopped listening.

※

The elegant grandfather clock chimed twelve and Aoife had to stop herself from jumping to her feet. This was better than being let out of school. She had endured the torture so Amy could have an enjoyable morning, but now she was free. Their escape could not be fast enough.

She should have known it wouldn't be that easy. Amy threw a tantrum at being forced to leave Barbara's playroom. Aoife didn't dare hand her the phone, so she was forced to carry a screaming child the entire way to the car. The other mothers stood by, hand in hand with their perfect, well-behaved, open-mouthed children. Aoife caught the exchanged glances. Clearly, they all believed she was an unfit mother. Maybe they were right.

Aoife could feel tears running down her cheeks as she drove out the long driveway. Five minutes later, she pulled over and handed the phone to Amy. Peace was restored but Aoife felt worse than ever. The mothers were right about one thing. She couldn't handle her own child. No other child in that group ever threw a tantrum. If she couldn't manage a toddler, how was she going to cope when Amy was a teenager? She resolved to put time aside each day to read parenting books.

※

The rest of the day was fairly routine, but by 7 p.m., Aoife was wearing the only dress that still fit her from her pre-baby days. She had found ten minutes to blow-dry her hair and even managed to apply a little make-up. She felt like a real person again. She looked around her. The restaurant had a vaulted ceiling and wooden panels, which seemed a little dated for a new restaurant. Maybe they were trying for the retro look? Aoife didn't care. Her table had a linen tablecloth, and there were linen napkins, Newbridge cutlery and crystal wine glasses. Best of all, she was surrounded by adults. Her happiness dimmed a little when she read the menu.

'When we've paid off our debts, we should do this every Friday,' Jason said.

'Better stock up on the lotto tickets, then. Have you seen the prices? We can't afford this, Jason. Let's go somewhere cheaper.'

'Don't worry about the cost. Mum's paying for it.'

'What?'

'It's okay. She gave me money for my birthday. Didn't you notice we're two hundred in credit at the end of each month?'

'It's a couple of months since I checked the statement.'

'Well, that money is for me to spend on anything I like, and I want to spend it on this meal.'

Aoife smiled. 'Thanks, Jason. It's good of you to share your present with me.' She leaned back in her seat. The restaurant was warm and the lights dim. There was a quiet murmur of voices in the background. She closed her eyes and was nodding off when Jason nudged her with his foot.

'Remember me? The person you wanted to spend more time with?'

'Sorry, it's just so comfortable here, and Amy woke me four times last night.'

The waiter approached. 'Are you ready to order?'

Aoife smiled at him. 'Yes, please. I'll have the mussels for the starter and turbot for the main course.'

'Ah, a girl after my own heart.' The waiter grinned. 'There's nothing like fresh fish, and ours was only caught this morning.'

'Really? That's marvellous. I've never had fish that fresh. Where—'

'Yes, you did, Aoife,' Jason interrupted. 'Remember when we were on our honeymoon? You had fresh fish every evening.'

'I meant I'd never had fish that fresh in Ireland.'

'What about the time—'

'Jason, would you like to order?'

'Oh, I'm allowed to speak, am I? Good. I'll have chicken wings and steak.'

The waiter reached for his pad. 'How would you like your steak cooked?'

❧

'I see he didn't compliment me on my choice,' Jason muttered as the waiter left.

Aoife hesitated. She put down her wine, leaned towards Jason and whispered, 'I want you to enjoy your birthday present, and I'd hate us to fight when you're having such a bad time, but one more comment like that and I'm leaving.'

'What are you talking about?'

'That waiter was doing his job. He was being pleasant and polite. Nothing more.'

'I was just reminding you about the fish you ate on our honeymoon. What's wrong with that?'

'I'm not discussing it, Jason. I don't want to leave you here alone, but if you do that again, I'm gone.'

'Aoife, I honestly have no idea what I said wrong. Everything seems to be annoying you today. Why are you in such a bad mood? Don't you feel well?'

'I'm not in a bad mood. Don't try to make this about me. I've been in perfectly good form all day.'

'You glared at me when I said we'd be late for the restaurant.'

'I did not!'

'And you yelled at Amy when she wanted more ice cream.'

'I may have raised my voice, but I didn't yell. She was trying to pull a glass bowl down on top of herself. I didn't want her to get hurt.'

'It's okay, Aoife. I understand. It's not easy being a single mother, but I'm here now and I want to help. Why don't I take Amy out tomorrow morning for some father and daughter time? You can have a lie-in.'

'That would be nice, but—'

'You could do with a rest, right?'

'Of course, but—'

'That's settled, then. You'll have the house to yourself until lunch. That will give you a nice break. Oh, here are our starters.' Jason smiled at the waiter. 'Thank you. This looks delicious. So, Aoife, tell me about your interview next week. Is there any way I can help you prepare?'

EIGHT

It had been a long day. Yet another interview had ended in disaster. Aoife pasted a smile on her face as she rang Maura's doorbell. Using her key would signal that everything was the same between them, and that could never happen. The lines of their relationship were already blurred. She needed to remember that Maura was not her friend, and she certainly was not her mother. Maura was related to her through marriage. That was it.

'Any luck today?' Maura asked when Amy had stopped jumping on Aoife and was gathering up her toys.

'They said they'd be in touch, but I don't expect to hear from them again.'

'You'll get a job, Aoife, I'm sure of it. The more experience you have of interviews, the better you'll get.'

The doorbell rang. Amy dropped her toys and raced to the glass pane.

'Moaney! Hiya, Moaney.'

Maura and Aoife exchanged glances. 'What does he want now? Do you think Bridget's right? Do they think I murdered Danny?'

'Of course not. Bridget's a bitter old woman. Ignore her.'

'The spouse is always the main suspect, Aoife.'

'My guess is they're interested in the money. I mean, getting envelopes of cash from a stranger is pretty unusual. They're bound to ask questions. But nobody could seriously think you were involved in Danny's death.'

'If the detective just wanted to ask questions, why not phone me?'

'I don't think that's the way they operate. Don't worry, Maura. Everything will be fine. I'll let him in.'

When Aoife went into the hall, she found Detective Moloney crouched down at the glass panel. She had always thought "Moaney" a particularly astute nickname, but it didn't seem appropriate today. The detective's tie was hanging over his shoulder, his long fringe had fallen into his eyes and he was pulling faces at a giggling Amy. He straightened the moment he spotted Aoife. When she opened the door, the detective's tie was in place, the fringe had been brushed back and the steely glare had returned. The slight flush of the detective's pale skin and his refusal to look Aoife in the eyes were the only indication anything unusual had happened.

'I need to speak to your mother-in-law.'

≈

Aoife turned on the Cartoon Network and Amy sat glued to the screen.

Detective Moloney placed a padded brown envelope on the table and removed a smaller envelope stuffed with cash. 'We've been monitoring your post. This arrived last week. We kept it for forensic examination. As you can imagine, we didn't find anything useful on the letter that's been through the postal service, but we found one fingerprint on the smaller envelope.'

'Really!' Maura's expression brightened. 'Have you been able to identify it?'

'We discovered the envelope was posted in Hounslow in London. It's a mainly Indian neighbourhood. Do you know anyone who lives in that area?'

Maura shook her head.

'Have you identified the fingerprint?' Aoife asked.

'Yes.' Was that pity she read in his expression?

'Who does it belong to?'

'Your mother-in-law.'

NINE

'YOU MUST BE mistaken. How could Maura's fingerprints be on the envelope? How do you even have her fingerprints?'

'I gave them to him,' Maura said. 'But I have no idea how my fingerprints could be on an envelope I've never even seen.'

'I think the explanation is very obvious. You posted the envelope to yourself, didn't you?'

'What! You can't be serious. I haven't left the country.'

'Did you ask someone to post the envelope for you?'

'Detective, this is ridiculous.' Aoife put a hand on Maura's arm. 'Why would Maura send herself money? It doesn't make any sense.'

The detective ignored her. 'Do you want to tell me why you posted an envelope full of cash to yourself, Mrs Walsh?'

'I didn't.'

'Very well. I'll have to ask you to accompany me to the station.'

'You're arresting her?'

'No. I'm asking her to voluntarily accompany me to the station for questioning.'

'Can I come with her?'

'If you wish, but it's no place for a child.'

Maura's face was white. She gripped the table and held on to it a little longer than necessary as she got to her feet. 'Helen next door will take her, Aoife.' She turned to the detective. 'I'll go with you to the station, but there's nothing I can tell you. I don't know who's been sending me money, and I have no idea how my fingerprints could be on an envelope I've never seen.'

⊰

'I don't know what to do, Orla. I've been waiting in the station for over an hour. Would they tell me if they arrested her?'

'I don't think they'll arrest her yet, but it might be time she hired a lawyer. I'll get you the name of somebody good. I presume she's entitled to legal aid.'

'I've no idea. Maura!' Aoife jumped up, tossing the phone on her chair. She picked it up again. 'Orla, I'll ring you back.'

Maura looked exhausted as she sank down on the seat beside Aoife.

'Did they say you could leave?'

Maura nodded.

'What were they doing all this time?'

'They asked the same questions over and over. Who were Danny's friends? Where did the money come from? What did Danny do every minute of every day of the last week he was at home? How am I supposed to remember that? I didn't know he was going to disappear. It's not like I was taking notes. And it was fifteen years ago. Can you remember what you did every minute of every day fifteen years ago?'

'Of course not.'

'I need to get out of here, Aoife, and I need to speak to Jack.'

⊰

The taxi pulled into the North Circular Road. The driver peered at each tall red-bricked building as they drove up the street.

'There you are, love.'

Aoife walked up the long narrow drive while Maura paid him. They climbed the ten steps to the front door and rang the bell.

'What is this place?' Aoife asked.

'I'm not sure. Jack said he runs two charities around here. One is a halfway house for men coming out of the prison system and the other is for boys transitioning from foster care.'

'I thought the State paid an allowance to kids who were in foster care.'

'Only if they fulfil certain criteria. I don't think anyone is going to answer, Aoife. Is there another door?'

Under the steps, to the left, was a door which had probably once been the servants' entrance. Maura rang the bell twice. They were ready to give up when the door opened. A young man of about eighteen held a sandwich between his teeth and balanced three books, a mobile and a mug of tea in one hand. He was slightly taller than average, but it was his face that caught Aoife's attention. It was the most perfect face she had ever seen. His hair was the colour of wheat and his eyes were such a deep blue that Aoife wondered if he was wearing contacts. Judging by his age, and the fact that she had difficulty believing anyone so beautiful could be a criminal, Aoife figured this must be the halfway house.

'Mmm?' he said.

Maura smiled. 'I hope we didn't come at a bad time. We're looking for Fr Jack Byrne.'

The young man waved at them to follow him. They entered a large, very untidy kitchen. Seven young men were seated around an oval table strewn with empty crisp packets and half-eaten sandwiches. All talk stopped as they entered. The young man placed his sandwich on the countertop. 'What's the matter with you? Never seen a woman before?'

'Not in this house,' a young man with glasses said.

'Anyone seen Jack?'

'He was in the office earlier.'

'Come on.' The young man led them up a narrow, dark stairs. 'I'm Tadhg, by the way. Are you friends of Jack's?'

'We're family,' Maura said.

'Really?' He gave Maura a broad smile. 'Jack's a great guy. If it wasn't for him, most of us would be on the streets.' He peeked through the office window. 'There he is.' After a brief knock he opened the door. 'Jack, some people to see you.'

Jack was barely visible above the pile of papers that covered both sides of the large, ugly desk.

'Maura!' He stood up. 'Come in, come in. What are you doing here? Oh, hello, Aoife.'

'I've just been interviewed by the police. They think I killed Danny.'

Jack paled. 'Good God!' He plopped down on his chair. 'Well, we know you didn't kill anyone, so there's got to be some way to prove it.' He got up, shoved some files off a battered armchair and motioned for Maura to sit down. 'What did the police ask you?' he asked, pushing boxes off a yellow fold-up kitchen chair and pulling it forward for Aoife.

'They wanted a list of all Danny's friends. They kept going over and over it, asking if I'd forgotten anyone. Then they started reading names off a list and demanded to know when I'd last spoken to them.'

'Who were they?' Jack and Aoife both asked.

'I've no idea. I don't think I've ever heard of any of them.

And everything I said they harped on and on about it. They must have asked me the same questions a hundred times.'

'What questions?'

'Oh God, Jack, I don't know. Everything. What have I been living on all these years? Did I ask someone to post money to me? What did I do every minute of the week before Danny disappeared? Why did I ring Stephen Mannion at the bank on a Saturday?'

'Who's Stephen Mannion?'

'The bank manager,' Jack said. 'He was Danny's boss. What was he doing at work on a Saturday?'

'His wife was sick. She died not long afterwards. Stephen had to take a lot of time off for hospital appointments, so he often worked weekends. Danny was filling in for him during the week. Usually they talked on the phone on Saturday morning, but once Danny went into the bank to sort something out. I thought he might have stopped there on his way home.'

'Why did the police have a problem with that?'

'They didn't believe me. They didn't believe anything I said. Why did I wait twelve hours before reporting Danny missing? I mean, is that so strange? He was a grown man, and that Buckley lunatic was murdering girls at the time. One had disappeared a few days earlier. I felt stupid complaining that a grown man had stayed out overnight. By four a.m. I was beside myself with worry, but even then I didn't think the police would take me seriously. I was sure they'd think he was having an affair. But that detective said my behaviour was "very unusual".' She sighed. 'I can't even remember half the questions they asked. I'm telling you, my brain is addled.'

Jack opened the office door and shouted, 'Guys!'

'Yeah?'

'Could someone bring me up a pot of tea, please.' He patted

Maura on the shoulder as he returned to his desk. 'Maura, you need to relax. I know this must have been very stressful, but the police can't connect you to a murder you didn't commit. Let them ask you all the questions they like. They'll soon learn they're barking up the wrong tree.'

'That's easy for you to say, Jack. Oh, that reminds me why I wanted to talk to you. The police claim Danny didn't go to work either Thursday or Friday. You met him most Fridays for lunch, didn't you? Did he say why he hadn't been at work?'

'We didn't meet that week. I had the flu. But I phoned on Thursday to cancel and he was definitely at his desk then.'

'Are you sure? You couldn't be mixing up the weeks?'

'I'm positive. I've often thought if only I'd met him that day, everything might have been different.'

'In what way?' Aoife asked.

'Well—' Jack scratched his head. 'You're right, of course. All this time I believed that if I hadn't cancelled our lunch, Danny might have told me why he felt the need to desert his family. But, of course, now we know he didn't desert them, so my cancelling our lunch didn't make any difference.'

There was a knock on the door and the young man wearing glasses brought in a tray with three mugs of tea to which milk had already been added. In the middle of the tray was a chipped sugar bowl. A wet spoon covered in sugar lay beside it. 'Thanks, Charlie.' Jack passed around the mugs. 'I had hoped for something more civilised, but we're a bit rough and ready around here. Now, why do the police think Danny wasn't at work on Thursday?'

'They said Stephen Mannion reported at the time that Danny had been acting strange the week before he disappeared and had called in sick on Thursday and Friday.'

'I am one hundred per cent certain he was at his desk on

Thursday. I phoned before lunch. Maybe he went home early and Stephen got mixed up. He must have been under a lot of pressure at the time.'

'No, that couldn't be it. I'd remember if Danny had come home earlier than usual that week.'

'What did Stephen Mannion say when you phoned him looking for Danny?' Aoife asked.

'He said he hadn't seen him, but he'd let me know if he heard anything.'

'Were things bad with his wife at the time?'

'I don't remember.' Maura shook her head. 'No, she must have been fairly stable because Steven phoned me later that evening to see if Danny had been in touch. I doubt he would have remembered if his wife had been bad.'

'Well, isn't it odd, then, that he never mentioned Danny not turning up for work the previous two days?'

'I don't know. Jack, do you think it's odd?'

Jack shrugged.

'How much contact did you have with Stephen Mannion after Danny's disappearance?'

'Not much, Aoife. We spoke on the phone a couple of times. A few weeks later he made an appointment to come to the house to go through the paperwork needed to take Danny off the payroll, but his wife was rushed to hospital, so somebody else came instead.'

Jack put down his mug. 'Maybe we're worrying about nothing. That young detective obviously wasn't around when Danny disappeared. He's probably interviewing everyone who ever knew Danny. I expect he'll interview me any day now. I'm sure we're just overreacting.'

Aoife frowned. 'We can't sit around hoping for the best,

Jack. This is Maura's life we're talking about. We have to do something.'

A flicker of impatience crossed Jack's face, then he smiled. 'Anything I can do to help, Aoife. Just let me know.'

∽

On Tuesday night, Aoife was going through her wardrobe looking for something appropriate to wear to the funeral. Her black skirt was too tight. She might get away with her black trousers if she remembered not to eat too much, but what would she wear with them? She was trying to decide between a grey jacket that was poor quality but in good condition and a black jacket that had frayed cuffs and a missing button when her phone rang.

'Hi, it's Barbara. I've spoken to Cian Mannion. He'll meet you at his house at nine a.m. tomorrow morning. I'll email you the address. It's not the nicest place to work, but I know you're desperate for money.'

'I—'

'Don't be late. I've recommended you, so I'm counting on you to be professional.'

'I—'

Aoife could hear children laughing in the background. 'Greta, you know very well the children are not allowed in this room. Take them back to the playroom immediately. Aoife, I have to go. Honestly, you have no idea how difficult it is to find good staff.'

Barbara was gone. It took Aoife a moment to process what she had said. She was a little stunned Barbara had remembered her promise. Aoife's heart started pounding. She had been recommended for a job. She actually had a good chance of getting this one. All she had to do was not screw up the interview.

TEN

CIAN MANNION WAS one of those nondescript men who would blend into any crowd. He was average height and average weight; his hair was neither wavy nor straight and somewhere between fair and brown. His house had the distinction of being old, but other than that it resembled its owner. The small room Aoife was shown into had dark, heavy furniture which swamped it. The carpet, although probably good quality, was brown with beige flecks. The wallpaper, also beige, had a faded brown pattern. A single painting hung above the fireplace. Its colour scheme so closely matched the wallpaper that it was difficult to tell them apart. Knick-knacks that appeared to belong to someone of a different generation covered every inch of the three side tables.

'Why did you leave your last job?'

'I worked for DCA. You may have read about it in the papers last year?'

'Yes, of course. Good heavens! That must have been an experience.'

'It was certainly different.'

'Right. Well, I'm looking for somebody to work part-time. I've been an art critic since I finished college, but I started an art blog last year and it's really taken off.'

'You're an art critic!'

'That surprises you?'

'No, of course not. I didn't mean—it's just that—' Aoife looked around the room desperately. 'There isn't any art here. Well, aside from that.' She pointed at the gloomy print of workers in a field.

Cian laughed. 'It's terrible, I know. This house has been in my family for generations. Everything in this room is either my mother's or my grandmother's. There may even be one or two things that belonged to my great-grandmother.'

'I'm sorry, I didn't mean to imply—'

'No, you're quite right. I suppose I should redecorate, but I rarely use this room. There's an extension out the back and I spend most of my time there.' He scanned her CV again. 'Anyway, to get back to the job, I travel most weeks and I write a lot of art reviews and blog posts. I'm looking for somebody to make my travel arrangements, research articles for my blog, manage my diary, type up the book I'm dictating and help with research. Do you know anything about provenance?'

'Something to do with proving that a painting isn't a forgery?'

'Yes. Ideally every piece of art should have a document listing the owner from the day it was painted. Then you could be reasonably certain it was the genuine article, but that's practically unheard of.' He began pacing the room. 'From time to time there are major legal cases disputing ownership of a painting. They generate huge interest in the art world. If I could be the first to break a story about a major work of art, it would be a great way of bringing my name to the attention of the people who matter.'

'What does tracing provenance involve?'

'Painstakingly poring over documents, some of which are

barely legible. I focus on the World War II era, so the documents are a little easier to read. Would that interest you?'

'I'm always anxious to learn new skills. What kind of book are you writing?'

'I'm only at the developmental stage at the moment. My dream is to make art accessible to everyone. Like the three tenors did to opera? The book is my first step. But I haven't even decided on its format yet. I have to figure out a way to make it engaging. Something that a person who knows nothing about art would find interesting.'

'Well, I may be able to help you there. I know very little about art, so I can be your target audience, and I trained as a journalist, so I might be able to help with the book.'

'Mmmm.' Cian put down her CV. 'Aoife, I'll be straight with you. I've been thinking for a while that I need a secretary, but this morning I had second thoughts.'

Aoife's heart sank. 'Why?'

'I started looking into the practicalities of hiring someone. I think I might have to form a company to pay you. Then I'll have to hire an accountant to do all the tax and regulatory stuff and get a lawyer to look at your contract. Even if I don't have to set up a company, I'll need someone to do your tax and salary.'

'I don't think my salary would be that much work. I'm sure I could learn to do it.'

'Maybe, but what if I accidentally do something I shouldn't? I've been reading up about employment law and it's terrifying. If someone comes into my house and sexually harasses you, I'm liable.'

'Not exactly. It would have to be repeated—'

'And what if you got pregnant? I'd have to go through the whole thing again with someone else while you're on maternity leave.'

'I'm not planning to get pregnant.'

'And even asking you that question is illegal. You see? It's all just too difficult.'

This was worse than screwing up an interview. For a moment there, she'd thought all her problems were sorted. Aoife picked up her bag. 'Well, thank you for seeing me anyway.'

Cian walked her to the door. He paused, one hand on the latch. 'There is one way out of it. How do you feel about being paid in cash?'

※

Aoife was so excited she had barely hit the sidewalk before she phoned Jason.

'I'll be working three days a week. He's going to give me thirty euros an hour and I'll be paid in cash every Friday. Isn't that amazing! I've never earned anything like that.'

'Is he a criminal?'

'Of course not. He doesn't want to be bothered with all the legal stuff, that's all. He's paying me extra because technically I'm unemployed so I won't have any pension contributions and I can't claim sick benefit or anything, but who cares about that.'

'It sounds very dodgy to me, Aoife. What if he doesn't pay you at all or he pays you for a while and then comes up with some excuse for weeks and pays you nothing in the end.'

'I'm getting cash every Friday. If he doesn't pay me, the most I've given him is three days' free work. It's worth the risk.'

'Hmm.'

'Jason, it's this or nothing, and I already agreed.'

'Well, I hope you're not making a mistake, that's all I'm saying.'

※

What was she thinking of, phoning Jason? There was no possibility he would ever see her working as a good thing. Never mind. Maura would be happy for her.

⁓

'Cian Mannion? Stephen Mannion's son?'

'You don't seem very pleased for me. It's really good pay, Maura. And Stephen's father worked with Danny. His dad must have mentioned the disappearance. In a small town like this, I'm sure everyone was gossiping about it. Cian might have information that would help us with the investigation.'

Maura shook her head. 'Cian was a teenager at the time. I doubt he was very interested. Why do you want to be a secretary, Aoife? What about your journalism career? You went through so much to get it started last year. Why abandon it now?'

'I'm not abandoning it. I'm determined to work in journalism eventually. It's even more important now that I'm a single mother. I submit stories to newspapers all the time, but I make very little money from it. I need a job that pays the bills.'

'Maybe you could write about Danny's murder once you find out who killed him.'

'I'd thought of that, but I didn't like to mention it.'

'Don't worry about upsetting me, Aoife. If anything good could come out of this mess, I'd be more than happy.'

ELEVEN

'AM I OVERDRESSED? I had no idea what to wear.'

Aoife looked at Orla's black designer suit. 'Maybe a little. Normally only the next of kin wear suits. Keep your coat on and nobody will know. Thanks so much for coming, Orla. I'm dreading this. Bridget and Maura aren't talking again, and Jason and his brothers are too upset to be sociable, so I'm going to have to be the go-between.'

'Shouldn't we be leaving?'

'Oh God, yes.' Aoife straightened her skirt. 'Do I look okay?'

'Here, wear my jacket.'

Orla's jacket transformed Aoife's drab outfit. Looking at it gave her confidence. She took a deep breath. 'Okay, let's go.'

⸙

Like most Irish funerals, particularly country funerals, the church was packed. Distant relatives, friends, neighbours and work colleagues all turned up in force.

Maura and her sons sat in the front pew on the right, the seats reserved for relatives of the deceased. Bridget refused to sit with them. She and her brood occupied the front pews to the left. Jack stood in the aisle between them. 'I think you should do the second reading, Jason,' he said as Aoife and Orla approached.

'I can't. Aoife will do it.'

'She's not family.' Bridget grabbed the arm of a middle-aged man and ushered him forward. 'Mike will do it.'

'Very well. Aoife, you sit—who's this?'

'This is my friend, Orla.'

Jack pointed halfway down the church. 'The next of kin take the front seats. Friends sit at the back.'

Orla gave him a smile guaranteed to stun almost anyone into submission.

'Of course. I'll move the minute the service starts. Right now I want to help Aoife get everyone settled.' She nodded at the pews opposite. 'Is that Jason's grandmother and her family?'

Her magic didn't appear to be working on Jack. 'Yes,' he said, turning to Maura.

Aoife counted six middle-aged men wearing what appeared to be brand-new black suits. Behind them sat several, mostly middle-aged, women and a smattering of teenagers.

'They look manageable,' Orla said. 'You take care of Maura and her family and I'll handle that lot.'

❧

The funeral went without any major hitches. Aoife had worried there might be a scene at the graveyard, but Bridget and Maura stood on opposite sides and were both too upset to pay the other any attention. The problems started when they reached the hotel.

Bridget and Maura had been delayed by people offering their condolences. Aoife arrived shortly before them. All the tables were now taken, but the mourners had left the two top tables vacant for the family. As Aoife watched, Bridget headed straight for the smaller table. Her family filled the seats beside her, then poured into the larger table, leaving just enough space for Maura and her sons to join them.

'Oh God! That woman! Why would she make Maura sit with her family? She's going out of her way to make the day as difficult as possible.'

'Don't worry, Aoife. I'll handle it.'

Orla strode over to one of the sons, touched his arm and whispered in his ear. The son spoke to his siblings and they all rose. Four of them surrounded Bridget and ushered her to the bigger table.

'Okay, that's sorted. Anything else I can do?'

'Oh my God, Orla, how did you manage that?'

'I told the son that his mother was sitting in a draught and she'd be more likely to catch a cold at such an upsetting time.'

'You're a genius.'

'I have my gifts. Oh, here's Maura. I'll go distract Bridget.'

'You can do that?'

'It's easy. All I have to do is sit close to one of the sons. Half the reason they got her to move was she was distracted watching me.' Orla smothered a laugh. 'I'm sure she sees me as the next generation of tart out to lead one of her little boys astray.'

Sure enough, when Maura entered, Bridget didn't even glance in her direction. Her gaze was focused on Orla, who was sitting between two of the middle-aged sons, nodding sympathetically. 'Mam's furious,' Aoife heard one of them mutter as she walked past. 'She wanted Danny laid out at home and the service in our local church.'

'Of course she did.' Orla patted his hand. 'But Danny's sons would have felt very out of place in a house they didn't know.

Maura wanted them to feel they were the chief mourners at the funeral. Wouldn't Danny have wanted that?'

'You're probably right,' the man said, nodding at Maura.

'And Maura did compromise. She agreed to have the meal here in Bridget's local hotel. Even though everyone had to trek halfway across…'

Aoife thanked God for Orla. She could charm any man with a pulse. Well, any man except Jack. After the first glance, Jack had completely ignored her. During the funeral service, he had been behind the altar, assisting the local parish priest. Now they were seated in the hotel dining room, he seemed unsure where he belonged. While everyone else ate, he darted from one table to another, never stopping anywhere for longer than a few minutes.

Jason had chosen to sit with his work colleagues and Evan was surrounded by his college friends. The other three boys flanked their mother, occasionally glaring at their grandmother. Aoife sat opposite, trying to distract them. The tables at the back were occupied by Maura and Bridget's neighbours.

Sitting in the corner nearest the door, Aoife was surprised to see Tadhg and a bunch of young lads, presumably from the halfway house. Why were they here?

The room was emptying and Orla came to sit with Aoife. 'The uncles are taking Bridget home. Don't worry, they promised they wouldn't let her anywhere near Maura.'

'Thanks so much, Orla. I don't know what I would have done without you.'

'It wasn't any problem. I was glad to help and they're quite a nice bunch, really. One or two of them even spoke to Maura when their mother was in the ladies'.'

Aoife laughed. 'Real heroes, aren't they?'

'Don't mock them. She's one scary woman, that Bridget. I wonder if she was always like that. Have you met Elaine?'

'The daughter? We spoke for a few minutes. She said she would be staying with Bridget for a few week—'

'Excuse me, are you finished with those?' Tadhg pointed at their glasses.

'You don't have to tidy up, Tadhg. The hotel will take care of it.'

'The hotel didn't want to give us this room today. There's a wedding here this evening. Jack promised them we'd clear the room and set it up for the wedding.' He brushed his hair out of his face. 'The clearing up is the easy bit. What do we know about setting up a room for a wedding? Kevin worked in a hotel, so he can tell us how to set the table, but there's a load of flowers none of us has any idea what we're supposed to do with.'

'We'll help. Orla's very artistic. She'll tell us how to make them look good, won't y—'

'The boys can manage on their own.'

None of them had heard Jack come up behind them.

'No, we can't, Jack. Do you want the poor bride to have a fit when she sees the state of the place?'

'Tadhg—'

'Jack! Are you coming home with us or do you intend to move in with the floozy?'

'Now, Bridget.'

'Don't "now Bridget" me. You've hardly spoken to me all day and don't think I didn't see you hanging around that tart. Whose side are you on, anyway?'

'There aren't any sides, Bridget. We're all one family. Come on, let me walk you to the car. Who's driving you home?'

❧

'Not very friendly, is he?' Orla said as they watched Jack leave the room, his arm around Bridget's shoulder.

'He doesn't like me either. Maura says he's uncomfortable around women, but he doesn't seem to have a problem with Bridget. Or with Maura either, for that matter.'

'Jack doesn't dislike either of you,' Tadhg said. 'He's worried about me and the lads. He doesn't want us to have anything to do with girls. We have to sign a contract promising not to bring any girls into the house.'

'What!' Orla laughed. 'Is he trying to turn you all into priests?'

Tadhg laughed and leaned across them to collect the empty glasses. His hair brushed against Orla's shoulders. They looked like a pair of movie stars, golden and shining.

'We have to leave the house when we're twenty-one. Jack says we need to concentrate on getting our lives together and we'll have plenty of time for girls later.'

'I feel like the town harlot,' Orla said. 'What is it about me? First Bridget thinks I want to lead her middle-aged sons astray and now Jack thinks I'm going to corrupt a teenager.'

Tadhg grinned. 'You can corrupt me any time you like.'

TWELVE

THE DAY AFTER the funeral Aoife checked in on Maura. She rang the doorbell and waited. After a few minutes she rang again. She heard footsteps in the hall and the door was opened by a small, slight middle-aged man with balding mousy-brown hair. He held an open newspaper in one hand.

'Can I help you?'

'Hi. Where's Maura?'

'She's not available right now. Are you a friend?'

'I'm Jason's wife.'

The man smiled. 'Aoife, I've heard so much about you. Come in. Maura's upstairs getting ready. We're going out for lunch.'

'I'm sorry, you are?'

'Brendan.' The man stuck the newspaper under his arm and held out his hand. 'I'm Maura's brother.'

'Oh, hi. Maura didn't mention you were coming.'

'I didn't tell her in case it didn't work out. I'd hoped to make it for the funeral, but I had business in the States and I couldn't get back in time. Maura tells me you organised everything.'

'Jack did most of it. I just tagged along.'

'She's lucky to have you and Jack to count—'

'Aoife! I wasn't expecting you today.'

'I should have called, Maura. I just wanted to check you were okay.'

'You never have to make an appointment to come to my house, Aoife. And if you hadn't come today, you might have missed Brendan. It's the first time I've seen him in twenty-five years, and would you believe I can't even talk him into staying longer than the weekend.'

'I wish I could stay longer, Maura, but you know I have to be in Belfast on Monday and then there's that conference in London.'

'What kind of work are you in?'

'Brendan owns his own computer company.'

Brendan grinned. 'She makes it sound so grand. I'm the only employee.'

'If you get that contract in Belfast, you'll be able to hire more staff and it will be easier for you to visit me.'

'Yeah, that would be good, but I have a sneaking suspicion those people are just stringing me along. They've insisted I go to Belfast three times in the last four months and they still won't discuss terms.'

'You were in Belfast?' Maura looked shocked. 'Why didn't you tell me? I'd have gone up to meet you.'

'They never give me more than a few hours' notice. I usually fly straight in and out. Actually, they made me go to Dublin a few weeks ago, but it was the same thing. I got no notice and had to spend the entire night in the hotel room preparing my presentation. The second it was over I got a taxi to the airport. There was no time for socialising.' He sighed. 'If I didn't need the money, I'd tell them what they could do with their contract.'

'Oh no, your business is in trouble again?'

'No more than anyone else in the current economic climate.

You don't have to worry about me, Maura.' He pulled her into a hug. 'These days I'm very sensible and boring. It's a wonder Cassie still puts up with me.'

Maura's face froze. She drew away. 'We'd better hurry or we'll be late. Aoife, will you join us? You're more than welcome.'

✺

'What's Cassie like?'

Jason waved the electricity bill. 'There has got to be something wrong with this. December and January I can understand but we have to be using less electricity now.' He slammed the bill down on the kitchen table. 'This is ridiculous.'

'Jason?'

'What?'

'Brendan's wife, Cassie. What's she like?'

'Never met her. Do we have any older bills?'

'I think they're online. I got the impression Maura doesn't like Cassie.'

Jason nodded. 'She hates her.'

'Why?'

Jason flicked through his phone. 'Cassie insists on a lifestyle they can't afford. Mum thinks that's what started Uncle Brendan's betting problem.'

'He's a gambler?'

'Used to be. He gave it up about ten years ago. Mum says he's still up to his eyeballs in debt, though, and if the photos he showed me are anything to go by, Cassie's spending habits haven't changed.'

'Cassie doesn't have a job?'

Jason looked up from his phone. 'She runs her parents'

company. It does quite well, I think, but you'd need ten companies to fund their lifestyle.'

'How do they live?'

'They own two houses, one in Edinburgh, one in the Highlands, and they used to have one in France, but they had to sell that. Their kids attend private schools, they go on four holidays every year and Cassie always travels in style. Your average five-star hotel is slumming it in her mind.'

'Brendan told you this?'

'No. I barely know him. I remember Mum and Dad arguing about it. Mum wanted to lend Uncle Brendan money. Dad agreed the first time, but he wouldn't do it again. He said they couldn't afford to subsidise Uncle Brendan's gambling problem or Cassie's compulsive spending. Mum was really upset. She said if they didn't lend him money, Uncle Brendan would lose everything.'

'You never mentioned your parents arguing before.'

'Uncle Brendan's the only thing they ever argued about. They had several shouting matches about him. Or rather, Mum shouted. I don't think I ever heard Dad raise his voice.'

'Were they still arguing about it when your dad was killed?'

'I think so. I know Dad hadn't given in yet. He probably would have lent Uncle Brendan the money eventually, but after he disappeared, Mum hadn't any money to lend.'

'How did they manage?'

'Some relative of Cassie's died and left them enough to muddle by until Uncle Brendan got help for his addiction.' Jason put down his phone. 'I'm going to check the electricity metre and I'm taking a reading every week from now on.'

Aoife smiled. She'd be starting her new job on Monday. She couldn't wait. Finally, the days of worrying about utility bills would be over.

THIRTEEN

CIAN MANNION OPENED the door and stepped aside to allow Aoife to enter. 'This is your office. Is something wrong?'

'No, of course not.' Aoife admired the large room with cream walls and the patio doors that led to an overly manicured garden. 'It's beautiful. I didn't expect the extension to be this large. It's all so bright and airy.'

'Well, this is where I live. I don't use the front of the house much. I've got you a laptop, a PC and an iPad, and there's a phone, mobile and a printer. I've never had a secretary before, so if there's anything I've forgotten, please tell me.'

Aoife fingered the gold handles on the light grey oak desk. 'This is perfect.' Two gold shelving units with black glass shelves lined one wall. 'Are these for filing?'

'Ridiculous, aren't they? We won't even see the glass shelves when they're full of files, but I couldn't resist.' Cian pointed at a wooden chest that was slightly lower than the desk and ran behind it. 'This will hold hanging files. If you need more filing space, see what you can find online and I'll order it, but please, none of that ugly metal furniture.'

⤚

Midway through the morning, Cian popped his head into Aoife's office. 'All okay? Is there anything you'd like to ask me?'

Aoife had been waiting for her chance. She went through a list of questions, then asked, 'Did you know my father-in-law?'

Cian looked alarmed.

'Who's your father-in-law?'

'He was Danny Walsh. He's in the papers at the moment. His body was found recently in the grounds of an abandoned building in the city centre. I thought Barbara would have mentioned it.'

'Oh, right. I knew about the body, but I didn't realise he was your father-in-law. How could I have known him? That was years ago, right? I was only a kid at the time.'

'Danny worked with your father in the bank.'

'Yes, but I was only ever in the bank once or twice. I didn't know any of the people who worked there.'

'Your father never mentioned that Danny had disappeared?'

'Hmm, I think I remember Dad saying something about it, but that was a very bad time for us. My mother was dying and then there was the robbery. We didn't have the energy to worry about anything else.'

'You were robbed?'

'Not us, the bank.'

'When was this?'

'A couple of months before my mother died. April, I think.'

'Did the police find the bank robber?'

'Somebody was arrested. I don't remember who. I was preoccupied with my own problems at the time. Are you alright?'

'Huh? Oh yeah, I'm fine. I think that's all my questions for now. I'll get on with this and I'll let you know if I need any help.'

Cian was barely out of her office when Aoife grabbed her

phone and did a quick internet search. A few minutes later, she phoned Maura.

'I know why the police are suspicious of you. They think Danny robbed a bank.'

FOURTEEN

'It makes sense, Maura. I checked online. The robbery was the same day Danny disappeared. The money was never recovered. I'll bet the police think you've been living off it all these years.'

'I'm sure they do.'

'Did you know about the robbery?'

'Of course. It was all over the papers. The police suspected Danny almost immediately.'

'What did they say when you told them about the money you received each month?'

'I never told them.'

'Huh? You told Detective Moloney that the police knew all about it.'

'Yes, I did.'

'Why?'

'The detective who handled the investigation into Danny's disappearance died five years ago. There were no computers when Danny disappeared, so there's no permanent record of the investigation. When I was a kid, one of the neighbours had his speeding charge dropped because his entire paper file disappeared. Who's to say a single report didn't fall out of Danny's file? Detective Moloney might not believe me, but there's nobody to testify against me now. He can't prove I'm lying.'

'But, Maura, why didn't you tell the police about the envelope? You thought it came from Danny. Surely it would have been the easiest way for the police to find him.'

'And then what? I thought Danny had deserted us. Why would I believe he was likely to come back? How would it help me if the police found him?'

'You didn't want to know why he left you?'

'Of course I did. It was all I could think about for weeks. Then I realised it was far more important to feed my kids and keep a roof over their heads.'

'You thought if you found Danny, he'd stop sending you money?'

'No. I thought if the police found Danny, he wouldn't be able to send me any money.'

'I don't understand.'

'What if the money he sent me was the proceeds of the bank robbery?'

∽

Cian came into Aoife's office and she quickly ended the call. She thought about Maura's revelation all day. Maura hadn't wanted the police to find her husband. She had deliberately misled them, and she had been willing to accept money she believed was stolen. Five years ago the detective who handled Danny's case had died. Five years ago Maura had started banking the money she received each month. That was unlikely to be a coincidence. Maura had been afraid to bank the money earlier in case it attracted the attention of the authorities and the police had reopened their investigation. With the detective dead, she was willing to take the chance. She had deliberately misled the police, and less than two weeks ago she had lied to Detective Moloney. Aoife tried to rationalise Maura's behaviour. Maybe anyone with five children and no income would be tempted to be an accomplice to bank robbery. But would they lie to the police? What bothered Aoife most was the growing realisation that she didn't know her mother-in-law at all.

Aoife spent her lunch hour googling everything she could find about the bank robbery. There wasn't much to read. The robbery was mentioned in all the papers, but not in any great detail. Their priority at that time was the recent disappearance of a college student. The day Maura was taken in for police questioning, she'd said something about a girl disappearing. What was it? Something about feeling stupid reporting a grown man missing when that Buckley lunatic was kidnapping young girls. Buckley was the only serial killer who had ever operated in Ireland in Aoife's lifetime, so she'd often heard his name mentioned. She'd only been a kid when he was arrested, though, so she didn't know much about him. Was it possible the police had been so caught up in searching for the missing girl that they hadn't enough resources to devote to Danny's disappearance? Her watch beeped to remind her she had to return to work in twenty minutes. She went back to her research. Several papers mentioned that a man called Martin Hanrahan had been arrested in connection with the bank robbery. He had been released without charge. Martin Hanrahan had several previous robbery convictions, but according to the papers he was a small-time criminal and would have been unlikely to undertake a bank robbery on his own. Was it possible Maura had been right about Danny being involved in the robbery? Could Danny have been Martin Hanrahan's accomplice? Was Martin Hanrahan a murderer?

FIFTEEN

At 5 p.m., Aoife phoned Maura. 'Do you know why Martin Hanrahan was questioned about the bank robbery?'

'He's local and everyone knows he's a criminal. Isn't that reason enough?'

'I don't know. I'd like to interview him. How could I get his phone number?'

'I'll ask Jack. He can contact the local parish priest. Someone in the community is bound to be able to get Hanrahan's number.'

It seemed unprofessional to leave work without saying goodbye, so Aoife went in search of Cian. He'd told her his office was at the opposite end of the corridor from hers. She knocked on the door and waited. When there was no reply, she looked inside. What an office! She'd been employed by companies that would have fit up to twenty people in that amount of space. Two walls of the room were lined with fitted bookshelves that ran from floor to ceiling. Ancient leather-bound books filled every shelf. The books were so dark they would have created a gloomy atmosphere had it not been for the three large windows overlooking a lush green lawn. From two of the windows there was a clear view of a small pond that held an elaborately sculpted fountain. From the third she glimpsed a multicoloured rose garden.

Aoife was half afraid to touch the books in case they were valuable, but when she reached out with one finger, she discovered they were fakes. What appeared to be bookshelves was actually a painting.

The fourth wall was covered in red flock wallpaper. The last time she'd seen something similar was on an episode of *Downton Abbey*. Aoife wondered if the wall covering was also fake. At least half the wallpaper was hidden by a large painting in pastel shades. It appeared to be an enactment of some complicated scene. She could make out half-naked figures, something that might have been angels and was that a serpent?

It might be best not to be caught here. She didn't want to appear nosy. Aoife closed the office door gently and called out: 'Cian! I'm leaving now.'

'I'm in the kitchen.'

Aoife followed his voice. It was a dull day, but she blinked as she entered the kitchen. The room was gigantic. It must run the whole length of the extension. The walls, units and even the floor tiles were sparkling white. One entire wall was made of glass. It was a little sterile but very impressive.

'You have a lovely kitchen.'

'Thanks. How was your first day?'

'It was great. I've made your travel arrangements to Milan. I paid for it on my own credit card. I hope you don't mind but that was a lot easier than trying to figure out a way to pay for it in cash. Have you already cancelled your credit card, or do you want me to do it for you?'

'I did it yesterday, thanks. The new card should be here the day before I leave. Actually, I meant to talk to you about the hotel. One of the main art critics is going to the exhibition. I've been wanting to meet up with him for a while and he's finally agreed to see me, but he can only fit me in the day before I'm scheduled to arrive. Can you change the flight?'

'Sure. Can it wait until tomorrow?'

'I'm afraid not, but take the laptop home and you can change it there. Oh, and can you text me when it's done. It's really important I meet with Giorgio and I want to be sure everything's arranged.'

'No problem. See you tomorrow.'

∽

'Jason!'

'Yeah.'

'Could you look after Amy for fifteen minutes? I need to book a flight for my boss.'

'You're working from home?'

'It won't take long.'

'He has no right to ask you to work outside your agreed hours.'

'I don't think fifteen minutes will kill me. Amy, put that down! Jason, please! Take her downstairs until I finish this.'

'Okay but you're setting a bad precedent. Most bosses will take advantage of you if you let them.' He paused. 'You're paying for it with your own credit card?'

'Cian lost his. He says he'll include the cash with my salary on Friday. I'll have time to pay it off long before the bill arrives.'

Jason threw his eyes up to heaven. 'I knew there was something dodgy about that guy. You're never going to see that money, Aoife. You're working for nothing and you're paying for that creep's holidays.'

'He's not a creep. He lost his credit card, that's all. And he didn't ask me to put his flight on my card. I chose to do that because it was more convenient for me.'

'He's a con man.'

'He isn't. And I'll prove it to you on Friday when I get paid.'

'Okay, I can see there's no point talking to you, but when you can't pay your credit card, I'll be the one out of pocket.' He held out his hand. 'Come on, Amy. Let's see if we can find some biccies. Not too many, though, they might be all we have to eat soon.'

⁂

Aoife had expected Jason to be in foul humour until she got paid, but he was a little more cheerful than usual. Aoife suspected he believed she would be unemployed by Friday and that, in Jason's mind, a plane ticket to Italy was a small price to pay for Aoife being at home all day. He didn't even object when Aoife told him she was having dinner with Elaine. Amy did enough objecting for both of them. It took a bowl of ice cream, a bar of chocolate and her favourite princess DVD to reconcile her to Aoife's absence.

Elaine had suggested they meet in Roly's. Aoife would rather not have to drive all the way to Ballsbridge, but she could hardly expect Elaine to travel to Kildare. Besides, she'd always loved Roly's. It was the first place she'd ever tasted pork with prune stuffing. It was a revelation and had led to a stage of experimental cookery which had almost driven Jason crazy. Of course, Amy had put an end to that. As yet, Amy's tastes were decidedly unadventurous. Unless chocolate was involved. Then she would try anything.

Aoife gave Elaine's name at the desk and was shown upstairs.

She was led to a booth where the table was set for four. Aoife hoped Elaine was coming alone. They needed to have a private conversation. Aoife worried Maura was keeping secrets from her. After all, Maura had never mentioned she suspected Danny had been involved in a bank robbery. Aoife needed a different perspective on Danny. She hoped Elaine could provide that.

꿍

'Hey, we got a booth.' Elaine threw her bag on the empty seat and sat opposite Aoife. A waiter arrived and removed two of the place settings. 'I reserved a table for four,' Elaine said when he left. 'They wouldn't give me a booth otherwise. I love Roly's, but there's barely room to move out there.' She nodded at the main seating area which was so packed the chairs were almost touching. 'Isn't the weather frightful? I tell you, I can't wait to get back to Florida. There's no place like home and all that, but really, are they trying to drown me?' She shook out her raincoat, ran her fingers through her short black curls and smiled at Aoife. 'Hi.'

'Hi, Elaine. Thanks for agreeing to meet me.'

'We're family. I'm thrilled to get the opportunity to know you. I was hoping you'd bring Amy. I'd love to meet Danny's granddaughter.'

'We wouldn't get much of a chance to speak if she were here, but you're always welcome to drop around to the house.'

'I'd like that.' Elaine nodded at the waiter, who handed her a menu. 'What did you want to talk about?'

'The police think Maura was involved in Danny's death. I'm trying to talk to everyone who knew him. See if I can come up with anything to prove Maura's innocent.'

'Are you sure she is?'

'Innocent? Of course! I know Bridget hates Maura, but do you really see her as a murderer?'

'I hope she's not. I don't want Danny's kids to find out their mother killed their father, but—'

'What?'

'There have always been rumours about Maura. She comes across as pleasant and ordinary, but there is nothing ordinary about Maura and she is very, very far from normal.'

SIXTEEN

'Not normal? How do you mean?'

'Well, have you ever noticed that Jason looks very different from his brothers?'

'I figured they took after their father. Jason has Maura's colouring and he's a smaller build than his brothers, but they all have the same nose. Ryan and Jason have the same chin.'

'I think Jason looks completely different. He bears no resemblance to Danny at all.'

'You think Jason isn't Danny's son?'

'He's darker and shorter. Danny was broad and Jason's slender.'

'Maura's slender.'

'She's thin. She doesn't have a small frame. Do you know anything about Maura's family?'

'I met Brendan. The others are dead, aren't they?'

Elaine snorted. 'It would take a lot to kill the Shaughnessys. Hard as nails, every one of them—well, except for Brendan. He was always on the delicate side. When I said Maura wasn't normal, I meant—' She paused.

'Yes?'

Elaine opened her mouth, closed it again, then burst out, 'I probably shouldn't tell you this, but there were rumours back then that Maura and Brendan were a bit too close, if you get my meaning.'

'What! You mean—? You can't be serious, Elaine. You think Maura got pregnant by her brother and passed off the child as Danny's? That's sick! And, anyway, Jason's perfectly healthy. Wouldn't a child of siblings have developmental problems?'

'Not necessarily. Brendan and Maura are only half-siblings. Maura's the product of their father's second marriage. I googled it when I first suspected Danny wasn't Jason's father. There is a greater risk of passing on inherited conditions, but it's also possible that the child would be completely normal.'

'The fact that Brendan is a half-brother doesn't make it any better. How could you even think Maura was capable of such a thing?'

'I'm not the only person who thought it. Maura's own family believed it. Not one of them has spoken to her since the day she moved out. And they threw Brendan out around the same time.'

'He went to Scotland.'

'I know. I heard he was in Kildare last weekend.'

'Yes. It was his first visit since he was teenager.'

'No, it wasn't. He was there the day Danny was murdered.'

'No, Elaine. Brendan goes to Belfast occasionally and he was in Dublin overnight a few weeks ago, but he hasn't been in Kildare since he was a kid.'

'Like I said, he was there the day my brother was murdered.'

'What makes you think that?'

'Well…' Elaine paused. 'I suppose I can't be certain he was in Kildare. He certainly made it as far as Dublin.'

'You must be mistaken, Elaine. Brendan might have intended to come to Dublin, but he must have cancelled. He definitely said he'd only been in Dublin once since he was a teenager and that was very recently.'

Elaine gave her order to the waiter. 'I'm not mistaken. He was here the day Danny died, and he met with Maura. I'm absolutely positive.'

'Why would Brendan lie?'

Elaine raised an eyebrow. 'Why do you think?'

'You're saying Brendan was involved in Danny's murder? Why would he want Danny dead?'

'Jealousy?'

'Oh, come on, Elaine! You can't really believe that. This whole brother and sister thing is ridiculous. You have brothers. Did you ever think of them sexually?'

Elaine laughed.

'See? People just don't do that.'

'That's not true, Aoife. There have been several cases of siblings having sexual relationships.'

'Not siblings who grew up together. It just doesn't happen. You said Maura's brother was a slight man. Obviously that's where Jason got his build.'

'My thoughts exactly.'

'I mean that Maura shares her brother's genes. It's not unusual for a child to resemble his uncle.'

'If you'd seen them together back then, Aoife, you'd understand. Brendan always had his arm around Maura. He never stopped touching her. It wasn't natural.'

'Plenty of brothers and sisters are affectionate.'

'Not like that, and we're talking twenty-six years ago. In those days the Irish weren't known for being tactile. The norm then was for adult siblings to have no physical contact whatsoever. Something was definitely wrong there. Everyone said so.'

❧

The waiter arrived with their starters. Neither spoke until he was out of earshot.

'What you're saying doesn't make any sense, Elaine. Even if you were right about them, Brendan and Maura hadn't seen each other in over ten years. Why suddenly decide to kill Danny?'

'That Saturday, the older kids were at a party and the younger ones were too young to know what was going on. Danny was at Mum's. What if Danny came home unexpectedly and caught Maura and Brendan together?'

Aoife raised an eyebrow. 'That's your theory? And then I suppose they stuffed Danny somewhere until his children were asleep, left the kids in the house alone and drove to Dublin to dump the dead body?'

'It's possible.'

'It's not likely. Why would they kill Danny in the first place?'

'I don't imagine Danny would have been very happy to find his wife and her brother having sex. He and Brendan probably got in a fight. Maybe Brendan's the murderer and Maura's covering for him.'

'How could Brendan be the murderer? You said Danny was bigger and stronger.'

'You don't have to be stronger to stab someone in the back. Maybe Maura and Danny were arguing and Brendan came up behind him and stabbed Danny. Or maybe it was the other way around and Maura was trying to defend Brendan. I'm not saying I think Maura's a cold-blooded murderer.'

'I don't believe it for a second.'

'Really? Then you tell me why Brendan stayed less than twenty-four hours on his first visit home in years.'

'There could be any number of reasons. Problems with his business, one of his kids was sick, his wife needed him. Anyway, I don't believe Brendan was in Ireland.'

'Brendan was seen in Dublin the night Danny was murdered.' Elaine leaned forward. 'In Dublin, Aoife. Where Danny's body was found. And Maura was with him. They were standing in a taxi queue. Brendan hugged Maura, then got into the taxi. That was around eleven p.m. They had plenty of time to murder Danny and bury his body.'

'Who saw them? The people who claimed they were lovers?'

'Somebody who had no reason to lie.'

'Who, Elaine?'

'A member of Danny's family.'

A waiter approached. He nodded at their untouched food and asked, 'Is everything okay?'

They both picked up their forks. 'Lovely, thank you.'

Aoife crammed three forkfuls into her mouth in quick succession. She didn't even taste them. 'Why won't you tell me who it was, Elaine?'

Elaine hesitated. 'My mother is convinced that Maura murdered Danny. Not all of us are certain she's right, but most of us agree that nothing can be achieved by having Maura convicted. We have a responsibility to her sons to ensure they don't lose both their parents. Whatever type of wife she might have been, Maura's always been a good mother. It would destroy those boys if they believed she murdered their father.'

Aoife nodded. 'I agree, but I don't understand your point.'

'Mam would have a stroke if she knew any of us had evidence that could convict Maura, and we refused to tell the police. None of us want to have to choose between her and Danny's kids. The person who saw Maura and Brendan doesn't want to have to lie to the police or to my mother.'

'It's you, Elaine. Isn't it?'

Elaine reached for her coat. 'I have to go now.'

SEVENTEEN

AOIFE BARELY SLEPT that night. She didn't believe for a second that Maura and her brother had been lovers. It was a ludicrous suggestion. Ordinary people didn't do things like that. But she was going to have to mention it to Maura. If Maura and Brendan's relationship had once been public gossip, it wouldn't be long before the police heard about it. Maura needed to be warned. But how the hell do you raise a subject like that?

She woke late and barely made it to work on time. Cian was standing at her desk waiting for her.

'You didn't change my hotel.'

'Yes, I did. Didn't you get my text? You're booked into the hotel a day earlier.'

'But it's the airport hotel. I told you Giorgio wanted us to stay in the same hotel so he could fit me in when he had a few minutes between appointments. It would take me an hour to get to him from the airport.'

'I'm sorry, Cian, but you never mentioned changing your hotel.'

'Yes, I did.'

'Well, it's not a problem. I'll book you into Giorgio's hotel now.'

'I already tried.' He held up a printed list. 'I phoned every hotel on that street. They don't have any vacancies.'

'Okay, well, there must be hotels nearby. Give me a minute and I'll look into it.'

Aoife's heart raced as she googled hotels in the area. Cian had never mentioned changing the hotel, she was sure of that. But he was convinced he had, and in his eyes, she had screwed up.

Most of the hotels in the area were booked out. Aoife had a provisional booking in a three-star hotel that was a fifteen-minute taxi drive from Giorgio's. Cian would hate it. On her second occasion phoning every hotel in the area, Aoife finally struck gold. A five-star hotel that was a two-minute walk from Giorgio's had just had a cancellation. Aoife was so relieved she couldn't stop thanking the receptionist.

She found Cian in the kitchen and told him of her achievement. 'I didn't want to risk losing the reservation, so I gave them my credit card number. Can you give me the number of your new card?'

'I don't give my credit card details to anyone. I'll pay the hotel in cash when I check in. Let me see that printout.'

Aoife handed him the hotel's details. 'It will have to do, I suppose,' he said and turned his back on her.

She returned to her desk, but she couldn't concentrate on her work. Cian obviously doubted her abilities as a secretary. But he definitely hadn't asked her to change his hotel. Had he? Could she have misunderstood?

❧

Aoife was so stressed by the mix-up over the hotels that she was still thinking about it as she drove home. While preparing dinner, she went over and over the conversation with Cian in her head. She was so distracted it was several minutes before she noticed that Amy had dragged a chair across the kitchen floor, climbed up on it to reach the treat jar and helped herself to a packet of chocolate stars.

In the midst of Amy's howls at being denied her chocolate, Aoife's phone rang. She glanced at the screen. Why would Jack ring her? She let the call go to voicemail. It was several hours before she remembered to listen to the message. Jack wanted to hire her.

As an experiment, Jack had asked Maura to help out in the halfway house last week. She had got on so well with the boys that he decided to offer her a job as his secretary. It was a four-day-a-week role, but for the first six months, Maura would work three days and Aoife would work one. At first they would work together while Aoife taught her how to run an office. After a few weeks, Maura would work alone and Aoife would come in on one of her days off to pick up the slack until Maura was fully up to speed. Aoife couldn't believe her ears. She replayed the message. Jack was definitely offering her work. Jack, who had always seemed to dislike her! Aoife would have to take the job, of course. As a single mother, she couldn't afford to turn down work. Jason would have a fit when he found out.

She couldn't accept the job without talking to Jason, so she phoned him at work. 'I know you don't want Amy in a crèche, Jason, but we don't have a choice. Your mother can't live on her savings forever. It was very good of Jack to give her a job.'

'He must be out of his mind. What does Mum know about

office work? It's unreasonable to expect someone her age to manage computers and stuff.'

'For heaven's sake, Jason. Maura's in her early forties. Of course she can learn. And even when I'm working at Cian's, she can call me if she has any questions.'

'So that's four days you're planning to leave Amy in a crèche?'

'Only temporarily.'

'I'm not having it.'

'Then you come up with another solution, because I can't think of one. And don't even suggest I give up work, because that is not an option.'

'Don't you want what's best for Amy? Didn't you watch that programme about the dreadful things that happen in crèches?'

'This crèche is different. It's much smaller and it's not a chain. The owner, Mrs Stafford, is a retired teacher. Alison was in her class and she says all her pupils loved her.'

'She must be ancient by now.'

'She doesn't look after the kids herself, but she's on the premises every day. She makes sure her staff give the kids the best possible care. Alison's daughters loved that crèche and so will Amy. It will be good for her to be around kids her own age.'

'This is not what I wanted for her, Aoife.'

'I know, but it will all work out. Trust me.'

∽

Once Jason had reluctantly agreed to accept reality, Aoife phoned Jack, thanked him and accepted the position. It must have been her imagination that Jack disliked her. He couldn't have been more pleasant on the phone. He'd even gone to the trouble of getting a phone number for Martin Hanrahan.

'The local parish priest got it for me. He said you'd better hurry if you need to speak to Martin urgently. He's going on holidays tomorrow.'

Aoife thanked him, gave a few minutes' thought to how she would handle the conversation, then phoned the number. She began by explaining that she was a freelance journalist. The words made her shiver. The last time she'd said that was when she'd worked in DCA, and look how that had turned out. Was she mad going down that path again? Was she mad speaking to a man who might be a murderer?

'Where did you get my name?' Hanrahan demanded.

'It's a matter of public record that you were brought in for questioning regarding the Kildare bank robbery in 19—'

'I don't want to talk to any reporters.'

'Of course, Mr Hanrahan, I understand. I thought you might have been a victim of police harassment, but if you feel the police were right in their assumption—'

'Hey, I had nothing to do with that robbery.'

'No, of course not. Sorry to bother you. Good—'

'You listen to me. I said I had nothing to do with that robbery. The police had no right pulling me in.'

'I'm glad to hear that, Mr Hanrahan, because I am only interested in talking to people who were treated unfair—'

'Those bastards had it in for me from the start.'

'Could we meet somewhere to discuss it, Mr Hanrahan? How about six-thirty at Starbucks?'

Aoife was pulling up in the car park when she got a text. 'I'm in the back corner, at the right.'

Hanrahan was a small, thin, wiry man in his mid-fifties. Aoife wondered if his build was due to a deprived childhood.

If so, the reasonably expensive brands he now wore suggested his criminal lifestyle was fairly prosperous.

'Mr Hanrahan?'

The man nodded.

Aoife took a seat.

The man glared at her. Aoife withdrew a notebook from her bag.

'You can quit the crap,' the man growled. 'I know who you are.'

EIGHTEEN

'I'M AOIFE WALSH, I told you that.'

'You told me you were a reporter. You're a secretary.'

'I told you I was a freelance journalist. I work as a secretary to pay the bills until my journalism career takes off.'

'You're Danny Walsh's daughter-in-law.'

'That's right.'

'So why are you lying to me? What do you want from me?'

'I want to know what happened the night of the bank robbery.'

'Are you wearing a wire?'

'No, of course not. Do people do that outside TV?'

'What's your game, then?'

'I don't have any game. I probably will do a story on police harassment someday. But my immediate interest is in researching everything leading up to my father-in-law's murder.'

'I had nothing to do with that.'

'I'm not suggesting you did. Mr Hanrahan, Danny disappeared the night of the robbery. He had a key to the bank. It seems odd that the police would decide you were the thief.'

'I didn't—'

'I understand, but why did the police arrest you?'

He leaned back in his seat. 'I had a record. It was harassment, pure and simple.'

'What excuse did they give?'

'They had CCTV coverage of me in the bank five times in the three weeks before the robbery.'

'Why were you there?'

'Some guy from the bank phoned me. Said a cheque I'd written had bounced and did I know that was a criminal offence. He said the bank manager wanted to meet with me. Well, in my line of business, you don't bring yourself to the attention of the guards.' He picked up his coffee and grimaced. 'Hate these places. What's wrong with Nescafe, for God's sake?'

'You went in?'

'Yeah, and I asked to speak to the Mannion guy. Some girl said he wasn't in the office that day. I went back three times before he was in. The fourth time they said he was at a meeting and couldn't be disturbed. The final time he told the cashier to deal with it. Said he was too busy.'

'So why do you think you were set up?'

'There was nothing wrong with the cheque. I went off my head when they told me. I said I'd spent half the last three weeks coming in and out of the bank. That idiot bank clerk said he had no idea what I was talking about and nobody from the bank had phoned me. At the time I thought it was just typical bloody banks screwing everything up as usual, but when I was picked up for questioning, I knew I'd been set up.'

'Set up how?'

'Someone wanted me on camera going in and out of the bank all the time. The guards didn't even bother looking for anyone else. They harassed me for years. They tore my house apart trying to find the stolen money. They followed me around so much it was years before I could do a proper job. I tell you, if

I ever find out who did that to me—' He leaned forward. 'Hey, I don't want the police hassling me all over again.'

'The police will never know we spoke. Do you know which bank teller you dealt with?'

'Different people. One of them was your father-in-law. I told the police at the time that he was obviously the bank robber. Why else would he have disappeared? But they didn't listen. Easier to blame it on me, wasn't it? Of course, I had no idea he was dead.' He paused. 'Look, I wasn't going to bother coming when I found out who you were. I changed my mind because I wanted to warn you.'

'Warn me about what?'

'You're a young girl with a baby. I don't want it on my conscience if anything happens to you.'

'Why would anything happen to me?'

'Stay out of this. Let the police deal with it.' He lowered his voice. 'I hear you and your husband split up a few months ago. Keep it that way. The less you have to do with that family, the better.'

'Why?'

'I've been in my line of work since I was in my teens. My father and grandfather were the same. I have a lot of contacts, and when I was arrested, I asked every single one of them about the bank robbery. No one knew anything about it.'

'What does that mean?'

'If anybody even vaguely connected to the criminal world was involved, I would have found out. It had to have been an inside job. Your father-in-law must have taken the money. I think his wife still has it.'

'Maura doesn't have any money.'

'Are you sure about that? I kept an eye on her over the years. She always had a nice car. The kids were well dressed. She didn't work. You don't live like that on social welfare. So where did all the money come from? It has to have been from the robbery.'

'Did you ever consider she might have another source of income?'

'Like what? Anyway, even if she did, it doesn't change anything. Criminals don't steal millions and bury it in the front garden. For one thing, they haven't got that kind of patience, and for another they can't risk being caught with stolen property. My contacts would have heard if anybody had tried to move large sums of money, and nobody did. But a single mother with five kids might stash the money somewhere and use small amounts over the years.'

'Maura didn't do that.'

'Hey, I've warned you now. That's my conscience clear.'

He stood up.

'You believe what you want. But remember one thing. The only way she could have got that money was by killing her husband. If she killed a member of her family once, what's to stop her from doing it again?'

NINETEEN

AOIFE AND JASON took Amy to the crèche the following morning. Aoife stayed with her for an hour. Jason insisted on staying until lunchtime. He would have stayed all day, but Mrs Weston convinced him he had to give Amy an opportunity to get used to being there on her own. Their agreed compromise was that Jason would return home at noon, but Mrs Weston would phone him if Amy showed any sign of anxiety. Aoife was rather touched by his concern. She ignored the little voice in her head that wondered if Jason was hoping Amy would be unhappy so he would have an excuse to remove her.

There were no seats on the train to Dublin, and Aoife had to stand the entire way. She'd forgotten how much she hated the rush-hour commute. It didn't help that she was dreading today. When she'd woken up this morning, she'd been excited about having a second job, even if it was only for six months. Then she'd remembered Elaine. The previous evening, Aoife had phoned Maura to tell her she'd accepted Jack's offer. She'd filled her in on the interview with Hanrahan, omitting all reference to his belief that Maura was a murderer and Aoife was likely to be her next victim, of course. But today she would have to mention Elaine's theory. She tried to think of a diplomatic way to raise the subject. 'Elaine thinks you had sex with your brother' did not seem very appropriate. When several people surged past her, jostling her to one side, Aoife realised the train had pulled into Heuston. She'd spent an entire hour worrying about what she would say to Maura, and she still hadn't come up with anything even vaguely appropriate.

⤜

Aoife looked around Maura's large, cold, shabby office with its high ceiling and ornate plasterwork.

'It must once have been so beautiful.'

'It will be fine once I bring in a few plants. Maybe I'll ask Ryan to paint it. A nice cheerful colour will do wonders.'

Aoife switched on the computer. 'How well do you type?'

'I used to plod away with two fingers, but I started doing an online typing course.' Maura sighed. 'I'm still very slow, but I'm getting there.'

'Is Jack in?'

'No. He was here earlier in the week, but I haven't seen him today. The computers and the office furniture only arrived this morning. I can't believe Jack offered me a job. I would have been happy just helping out with the boys.'

'What are they like?'

'Ah, they're great, Aoife. You'd feel so sorry for them. They've no family worth talking about. How is a young lad supposed to manage without anyone to turn to? And they're so grateful for everything. I've been baking every day and you should see their faces! Mine barely noticed when I baked for them. Actually, I think they preferred junk food.'

Aoife smiled. 'Jack made a good choice when he hired you, Maura. You'll end up being a second mother to them.'

'That reminds me, we'd better get down to work. I don't want Jack to suffer because I don't know what I'm doing. I got him to go through everything with me and I wrote it all down.' She took out a notebook. 'It doesn't look too complicated, but perhaps we could go through it together.'

They spent a few hours setting up the office and going through Maura's responsibilities. When they broke for lunch, Aoife decided this was as good a chance as any. To avoid eye contact with Maura, she pretended to be looking for something in her bag. 'Elaine and I had dinner last night. She mentioned your brothers. I thought Brendan was the only member of your family who's still alive.'

Maura put down her sandwich. She went over to the stationery cupboard and straightened an already tidy stack of envelopes. 'Why were you discussing my brothers?'

'I'm curious about anybody who might have a grudge against Danny or anyone he might have got into an argument with. It sounds like your brothers might be possible suspects.'

'My brothers haven't set eyes on Danny since we were teenagers.'

'There's obviously some sort of bad blood there. Danny's body was found in Dublin. Isn't that where your brothers live?'

'Them and about half a million other people.' Maura returned to her desk and picked up her lunch. 'Look, Aoife, I'm not saying I'd put it past them, but they had no reason to kill Danny. They got what they wanted years ago.'

'How do you mean?'

'My father married twice. My brothers are really half-brothers. Their mother died from complications after giving birth to Brendan. Mam raised Brendan as her own, but the others never accepted Mam or me. They didn't really accept Brendan either. In their minds he had sided with the enemy.'

'Why were you the enemy?'

'At first it was resentment at having a stranger foisted on them, but later they started worrying about their inheritance.'

'Your father was rich?'

'No, but families have fallen out over less. All my dad had was the house. And this was before the property boom. It couldn't have been worth more than eighty thousand. My brothers resented that I'd inherit part of it. I can still remember how happy Tom was when he found out I was pregnant. His entire face lit up. He thought Mam and Dad would disown me for sure.'

'They didn't mind?'

'Oh yes, they minded very much. They were angry, upset, disappointed. Mostly they were embarrassed. Remember, we're talking twenty-six years ago. Unmarried mothers weren't being locked up in the Magdalene Laundries any longer, but we were still a huge embarrassment. Especially to people of my father's generation. But they had no intention of disowning me. They said I would live with them and Mam would take care of the baby while I was in college.'

'They sound like decent people.'

'They tried to be.'

'What went wrong?'

'My brothers were horrified. Brendan and I were the only ones still living at home. Brendan would have moved out in a few years and I'd be left in what they saw as their house with a baby. When my father died, he wasn't likely to make me homeless. The way my brothers saw it, I was cheating them of their inheritance.'

'So you decided to move out?'

'No. I ignored them. It was the biggest mistake I ever made.'

~⚮~

The phone rang and Maura answered it. By the time she'd finished, Aoife had eaten her entire lunch.

'What happened then, Maura?'

'Tom and the others never accepted Brendan. He was small and quiet, totally unlike them. Even though he was their full sibling, they didn't want anything to do with him. Dad meant well, but he was old and tired by the time Brendan and I were born. Mum was rushed off her feet taking care of the house and looking after everyone. All Brendan and I really had was each other. We became very close. And Brendan was exceptionally tactile. He was always putting his arms around me and hugging me in public. That was pretty unusual back then.'

She munched on her sandwich and Aoife wondered if she intended to continue.

'People often commented on how close Brendan and I were, and Tom decided to take advantage of it. He started a rumour that Brendan and I were—' She looked away. 'That Brendan was the father of my child.'

When Aoife didn't say anything, Maura looked at her. 'You knew?'

Aoife nodded. 'I'm surprised your parents believed it.'

'They didn't at first. They were horrified, of course. They said Brendan and I shouldn't be seen in public together as it was only adding fuel to the rumours, but they never once considered that it might be true until—'

'What?'

'Until Tom told them he'd seen Brendan and me—together.'

'Oh my God! How could he do that?'

'Because he's a filthy, lousy piece of—anyway, the point is they did believe it. Tom pretended to be embarrassed. He said he was sorry he hadn't told them earlier, but he was afraid the shock would kill Dad.'

'He did that to his family for a few thousand pounds?'

'Unbelievable, isn't it! That bastard would put his own wife on the game if it would earn him a few extra quid.'

'Was that when your parents threw you out?'

Maura shook her head. 'I was pregnant and had nowhere to go. They sent Brendan to relatives in Scotland. I was to stay at home and when the baby was born, I would give it up for adoption. What I did after that was up to me.'

'So what happened?'

'I said I was keeping the baby. Even my mother was against it. They said they had obviously failed me and Brendan, but they wouldn't fail their grandchild and the least they could do was make sure that innocent baby never found out who his parents were.'

'You didn't tell them about Danny?'

'Of course I did, but I'd never mentioned him before. I was in my final year at school when we met, and Danny was in college. They'd never have allowed me to go out with him.'

'Didn't he phone the house looking for you?'

'No, we'd had a big fight. It's too long a story to get into now, but I knew there was no possibility of him phoning me after that. My parents thought I was making him up.'

Maura put the sandwich back in her lunch box and pushed it to one side. 'Anyway, Dad trusted Tom above everyone else. And Tom was so calm while I was hysterical. The scumbag even pretended to feel sorry for me. He said they shouldn't blame me for lying. That I was just a kid, that I'd probably rationalised my behaviour by saying Brendan was only my half-brother and that of course I was afraid to admit the truth.' The phone rang again. Maura hesitated, then pressed a button to divert the call to voice mail. 'My parents could barely look at me and I was so angry I spent most of my time in my room. A few weeks later I heard them discussing adoption agencies. They were wondering if they could find one that sent the children abroad. I had a fit. I screamed that they couldn't force me to sign adoption papers. My parents said either I signed the papers or they would forge my signature.'

'They couldn't get away with that.'

'Couldn't they? I don't know. You hear stories every day of Irish girls whose children were forcibly taken from them and nobody would help get the children back. There was a story in the paper recently of one woman who had proof her child's adoption papers were forged and it took her twenty years to get the court to agree.'

'I remember, but I think she'd been in one of the Magdalene Laundries. If the nuns forged her signature, the State would try to squash the case so they didn't have to pay compensation. They wouldn't care what happened to your parents.'

'Maybe not. I was a teenager. I didn't know my rights and there wasn't any Google back then. I knew babies were taken from unmarried mothers and I was terrified mine would be stolen as well.'

'What did you do?'

'It was a terrible time. I was practically a prisoner in the house. My parents took my keys and kept all the doors and windows locked. My mother didn't work and my father was retired, so they watched me all the time. At night the house alarm was on and they changed the code so I couldn't get out without waking them. There were no mobiles, of course, and they unplugged the phone every night and took it to their room.'

'That sounds dreadful.'

'It was. I thought I'd never escape. I watched my stomach

get bigger every week and I knew I was running out of time to save my baby. Then, when I was just over seven months pregnant, I got my chance. One Sunday my mother went to the shops and my father fell asleep reading the paper. I used the phone to ring Danny. They were such a large family I figured somebody would be in the house, but I was really lucky because Danny was there. It was only a few weeks before his exams and he was trying to do some last-minute cramming. I gave him a very short version of what was happening, and not long afterwards he and all his brothers turned up at my house. My father answered the door and they pushed their way in, pulled me out and that was it.'

'Your parents didn't come after you?'

'They couldn't find me. By then I was seventeen, so the police weren't interested. We stayed with Danny's aunt until Jason was born. After we were married and Danny was officially listed as Jason's father, there wasn't anything they could do. They were convinced I'd lied to Danny. They never even considered that Tom might be the liar. And, of course, I couldn't have convinced Danny he was the father unless we'd already had sex, so clearly I was a harlot who'd led Brendan astray. They were absolutely disgusted with me. And, just like Tom had planned, they didn't mention me in their wills. So you see, Aoife, my brothers had no reason at all to be angry with Danny.'

'But Danny had reason to be angry with them. Maybe he bumped into them and they had a fight.'

'I wasn't going to tell Danny those dreadful rumours. If my own parents believed it, how could I be sure he wouldn't? No, I told Danny they'd kept me imprisoned in the house, but he thought it was because they were horrified that I was an unmarried mother. He never knew about those disgusting rumours. Who told you about them?'

'Elaine.'

'I wonder who told her. I bet Bridget found out after Danny disappeared. If she'd known beforehand, she'd never have let me live it down. I suppose when she decided I was having an affair, she went looking for gossip to back up her belief.'

'You must really hate your brothers.'

Maura nodded. 'Apart from Brendan, of course. I'll never forgive them.' She grinned. 'Although, I did get a tiny bit of revenge.'

'How?'

'It was a couple of years later. Danny and I were walking back from the shops when Tom practically rolled out of the pub and nearly crashed into us.' Maura took a sip of tea and grimaced. 'Stone cold. I'll make more in a minute. Tom must have come to Kildare for the races, and he was obviously either celebrating or drowning his sorrows. For a few seconds all three of us just stood there, staring at each other. Then, calm as anything, I handed Jason to his father, picked up the bag containing two ceramic utensil holders I'd just bought, raised it in the air and bashed that bastard over the head again and again until I'd knocked him to the ground.'

'You didn't!'

'God, Aoife, you can't imagine how good it felt. I'd taken Tom completely by surprise, and once he was on the ground, he couldn't get away from me. Danny had to drag me off him. There was blood on the ground afterwards. Danny said it was pure luck I hadn't murdered him. Tom got to his feet and stumbled away. When he was at a safe distance, he screamed that I was a mad bitch who should be locked up. But I'm telling you, I'll never forget the look on his face.' She laughed. 'The big ugly bastard was terrified of me.'

TWENTY

'Was Brendan left out of your parents' will too?'

Maura nodded. 'Once my parents decided I was the one to blame, they tried to reconcile with Brendan, but he wanted nothing to do with them.'

'And he never saw your parents again?'

'No. He wouldn't even come to their funerals. Last weekend was the first time he'd set foot down south since he was a teenager. Well, apart from the night he was in Dublin recently.'

'That's a long time not to see your favourite brother.'

'It was hard, but we both had financial problems and kids. Travelling wasn't that easy.'

Aoife put her lunch away and picked up Maura's to-do list. Could Maura be telling her the truth? But she had been seen in Dublin with Brendan. Unless Elaine was lying? One of them was definitely a liar.

❦

Before Aoife could make up her mind what to do next, the door burst open and Tadhg rushed in. 'I need your help. What do you think of this for Jack's birthday?'

'It's Jack's birthday?' Maura said.

'You didn't know? It's next week. We don't usually do presents, but I convinced the guys we had to get him something. He's done so much for us all.' Tadhg held up a screenshot of a cigarette lighter. 'What do you think of this?'

'A hundred and sixty-nine dollars for a lighter! Tadhg! Are you out of your mind? You can buy lighters for a few quid.'

'I know, Maura, but you're not supposed to use those things for cigars.'

'I didn't know Jack smoked.'

'Like a chimney,' Maura said.

Tadhg shook his head. 'Only when he's stressed. When he's relaxing, he smokes cigars. That's why I think the lighter would be a good idea. It's something to be used on special occasions. It should last forever, and it will be a reminder of how grateful we are for everything.'

Maura's brow furrowed. 'Surely you could get something cheaper, Tadhg.'

'It wouldn't be as good. I researched it for ages. Cheap lighter fluid affects the taste of the cigar, and the weak flame means you can't light the cigar evenly. Cigar lighters should have a double or a triple flame. They say the flame in this one is as strong as a candle.'

'But a hundred and sixty-nine dollars! How much is that in euros?'

'About a hundred and fifty. It would be cheaper if I could buy it in Ireland and save on the shipping costs, but I can't find one as good as this. The guys are giving ten quid each.'

'That leaves you seventy dollars short.'

'I know, but I answered an ad for a maths tutor. I met the mother this morning. I played up the "one of the top six in the country" bit.'

'You came in the top six in Ireland in your Leaving Cert?' Maura said.

'You didn't know? That's how I got my scholarship to Trinity. It's usually the first thing Jack tells everyone about me. "This is Tadhg. He got top marks in all subjects in his exams."'

'That's impressive, Tadhg. No wonder you were hired as a tutor.'

'Would you believe the mother googled me? In the photo they printed in the newspaper, I'm looking down at my Cert. She kept twisting her phone around to see if it was really me.' He laughed. 'I pretended to be insulted, so she upped the price. She's paying me fifty euros per session and the first one's next week.'

'Okay, I'll chip in the extra twenty and I'll lend you the fifty until you get paid.'

Tadhg hugged her. 'You're the best, Maura. I don't know how we ever managed without you.'

TWENTY-ONE

IT WAS AOIFE's day off. Amy had been excited about her second day in the crèche and had run into the room without even a backward glance. Aoife had cried in the car on the way home. Her baby was growing away from her.

As she ironed an enormous pile of laundry which seemed to consist mostly of Jason's shirts, Aoife decided she needed a distraction. She also needed to talk to someone about Danny's murder. The investigation was branching off in all directions, but it wasn't actually getting anywhere. She needed advice. She couldn't discuss the investigation with Jason. For one thing, she never wanted him to hear some of the things said about his mother, and for another, Jason had absolutely no interest. 'I don't know why you're worrying about it, Aoife,' he said. 'Mum had nothing to do with Dad's death. Any idiot could see that, and eventually, even the police will work it out.' Aoife needed to talk to someone who would take her concerns seriously.

Aoife hadn't seen Orla since the funeral, and as Orla shuddered at the thought of visiting any other part of Ireland, Aoife would have to go to Dublin to meet her. She would be very frugal, she promised herself. She'd been stuck with the bill when Elaine had run out of Roly's. Fortunately payday was tomorrow, but until then she couldn't afford to waste a cent. She'd take the bus rather than the train, and for lunch she would limit herself to soup and a coffee. If Jason could buy expensive wine, she was entitled to one little extravagance, wasn't she?

⁓

The bus was late. While she waited, Aoife phoned Orla. There was no answer, but that was to be expected. Orla always put her phone on silent during lectures and tutorials. She'd go to Fallon & Byrne's and wait for her. Orla had never really accepted that she was now based on the north side. Most days she made the long trip to Exchequer Street to have lunch with her friends.

By noon Aoife was standing outside the restaurant. The large canopy sheltered her from the rain, but it wasn't much protection from the cold. She pulled her coat tighter and stamped her feet while she waited. Where the hell had the spring gone?

Fifteen minutes later, Orla and a gang of beautiful jeans-clad but exceptionally well-presented girls came running up the street. They ducked under the awning with shouts of 'Get me out of the rain, quick!', 'Oh my God, my hair is a mess!' 'These heels were never meant for running.'

'Aoife! What are you doing here?'

'I hoped we could have lunch.'

Orla smiled. 'Sure. Guys, I'll see you later. We're still on for tonight, right?'

As Orla's friends headed upstairs to the restaurant, she and Aoife went to the counter to choose their food. Orla chose soup, scallops and a cappuccino, so Aoife didn't feel too conspicuous with her meagre lunch. They took their food down to the basement. It was a little early for the lunch crowd, so they had one of the long wooden tables all to themselves.

'I just don't believe Maura murdered anyone,' Aoife said when she'd filled Orla in on the recent developments. 'And the idea that Maura might kill me is absolutely ludicrous.'

'I don't know, Aoife. I mean'—Orla counted off on her fingers—'Martin Hanrahan thinks she's a murderer, her finger-prints are on the envelope with the money, she didn't want the police to find her husband, she lied to the detective and she's obviously lying about Brendan being in Ireland.' She waved the five fingers in the air. 'That's a lot of evidence against her.'

'Maybe Elaine's the one who's lying.'

'Why would she? Elaine doesn't want to cause trouble for Maura or Brendan. She has nothing to gain by not telling the truth.'

'I've been thinking, Orla. Whatever Maura or the police might have believed, I don't see how Danny could have been involved in the robbery.'

'Why not?'

'How could he have broken into Stephen Mannion's house? Even if his face was covered, it was too risky. I think Stephen would have recognised him. And he wouldn't have been able to speak. That would definitely have given him away.'

'Maybe his accomplices handled that part of it.'

'But why break in at all? Danny had a key to the bank. He was the acting bank manager. What did he need Stephen for?'

'As a cover, of course, Aoife. Otherwise it would be obvious it was an inside job.'

Aoife stirred her soup. 'What if Brendan was involved?'

'As one of Danny's accomplices?'

'My idea was that Brendan might have done it without Danny's knowledge. It makes a lot more sense. Danny was a devoted family man with a good career. Why would he throw it all away? But everyone says Brendan was desperate for money at the time.'

'Didn't he inherit money from someone in his wife's family?'

'That was later, and Brendan could have made that up to explain his sudden wealth.'

'Robbing a bank is a bit extreme, Aoife. If Brendan had money problems, why didn't he just declare bankruptcy?'

'That might not have been an option. Banks don't generally lend to unsuccessful gamblers. He probably had to borrow from criminals. Brendan might have been desperate. Maybe the criminals were threatening to kill him or his family if they didn't get their money back. A relative who worked in a bank would be very tempting if you were under that kind of pressure.'

'So Brendan finds two other guys to help him? Do you think that Hanrahan guy was one of them?'

'I don't think so. How would Brendan even know Hanrahan?'

'True. But if Brendan was involved, he must have at least a third of the stolen money now. Why does he still have money problems, Aoife? They stole millions, didn't they?'

'A gambler could go through millions in a few years.'

'True. But if Danny wasn't involved in the burglary, who murdered him and why?'

A young couple sat down at the opposite end of the table. Aoife pushed her chair closer to Orla's. 'I don't know,' she said. 'That's where I get stuck.'

Orla popped one of the scallops into her mouth. 'Hmm, these are marvellous.' She pushed the plate towards Aoife. 'Have one.'

Aoife could have devoured them all in a few gulps, but she shook her head. 'I'm not hungry, thanks.'

'You sure? You're really missing out on something special.' She paused. 'How about this? Brendan and the other two guys, whoever they were, fall out over the money. One or both try to attack Brendan, maybe even murder him. Danny comes across the fight—maybe it's near his home—tries to help Brendan and gets killed.'

'But the papers said Stephen Mannion's house was broken into in the middle of the night. They'd have to wait a few hours in the bank for the time locks to take effect. The earliest they could have fought over the money was nine a.m. Where was Danny all that time?'

'Good point.' A lady pulled out one of the chairs in the middle of the table. She put her lunch tray down, settled herself comfortably and opened her book. Orla lowered her voice. 'Okay. Brendan wants to rob the bank. He knows Danny can get the money for him. He knows Danny isn't going to become a criminal just to help him. Brendan doesn't want Maura and her kids traumatised by a break-in. We can assume Maura will have mentioned that Danny visits his mother every Saturday. Brendan gets his accomplices to kidnap Danny and force him to open the bank. Danny puts up a fight. Things get out of hand. Danny is murdered. Then Brendan and his accomplices have to break into the house of the only other person who can get them into the bank, Stephen Mannion.'

'It's possible, I suppose. And it means Maura couldn't be involved. She'd hardly agree to her husband being kidnapped. And it would explain the money. Brendan felt so guilty about the murder, he sent Maura money every month.'

'Yeah. But the one thing it doesn't explain is why Maura lied about Brendan being in Kildare. She must be involved.'

'Why do you insist she's involved, Orla? Couldn't Maura have found out about Brendan's involvement months or even years later? Turning in her brother wouldn't bring her husband back, so she covers for him by saying Brendan was never in Ireland that weekend. It would explain why they hadn't seen each other in years. Maura might be prepared to cover for her brother, but maybe it took a long time before she could forgive him.'

Orla shook her head. 'What about the money Maura got each month?'

'Maybe at first Maura thought the money was from Danny. By the time she discovered Brendan's involvement, she was dependent on the money and continued to accept it. She couldn't tell the police the money came from her brother, so she said she had no idea who sent it.'

'How did Maura's fingerprint end up on the envelope?'

Aoife sat back in her chair. 'I give up. I have no idea.'

⇜

Aoife noticed that the lady sitting near them had abandoned her book. Was she listening to them? Aoife nudged Orla and nodded in the lady's direction. Orla threw her eyes up to heaven. 'Typical. People in this country are so nosy. I have an idea.' She spoke so softly Aoife could barely hear her. 'What if Maura helped Brendan plan the robbery? She knew Brendan needed money desperately. She might have believed that robbing the bank was literally the only way to save Brendan's life. Maura couldn't talk her husband into giving Brendan the money, so she suggested Brendan get his accomplices to kidnap Danny and force him to open the bank. If it had worked, it would have solved everyone's problems. Brendan would have the money and Danny would never know of her or Brendan's involvement.'

'How did Danny die?'

'He refused to have any part of it. Maybe he tried to escape. One of Brendan's accomplices might have killed him.'

Aoife raised an eyebrow. 'So Brendan's faced with the prospect of telling his sister that her husband is dead, and his first thought is "Who else can I force to break into the bank?"'

'Think how desperate Brendan must have been by then. His life and that of his family is still at risk, and now he's an accomplice to murder. What has he got left to lose?'

'So he decides to break into Stephen Mannion's house? How would he even know where the Mannions lived?'

Orla nodded. 'Maura must have told him.'

'But—'

'Let me finish, Aoife. Brendan and his accomplices dump Danny's body. Or maybe Brendan's accomplices took off once they got their share of the loot and Maura had to help Brendan with the body. It would explain why she was in Dublin that night. Maura knows she's equally to blame for her husband's death, so she accepts part of Brendan's share of the robbery. She's been living off it ever since. Once Danny's body was found, Maura knew the police would ask questions. She made up the story about the envelope of cash. She sent money to herself to make it seem more credible, but she accidentally got a thumbprint on the envelope.'

'Nonsense. Maura's not an idiot. If she sent herself money, she'd make sure her fingerprints weren't on the envelope.' All the tables were filling up now and there was so much chatter it was possible to speak at a normal level again. 'And Maura would never agree to Danny being kidnapped. Who would risk their husband's life like that?'

'Face it, Aoife. Maura has a reckless side. If Danny hadn't stopped her, she might have killed that other brother of hers.'

'Tom? She hit Tom. She wasn't trying to kill him. Wouldn't you want to hit him if you were her?'

'Sure, but I wouldn't have left him bleeding on the ground and I wouldn't have had to be pulled off him.'

'Maura wouldn't kill anyone.'

'You keep saying that, but would you have believed she'd accept stolen money? Would you have believed she would lie to the police?'

'Well, no, but—'

'Be honest, Aoife. Is Maura the person you thought she was a year ago?'

'No, I guess not.'

'So who's to say there isn't a lot more to her that we can't even guess at?'

TWENTY-TWO

AOIFE FROWNED AT her computer. She still felt guilty about splurging on lunch with Orla, but when she'd spent that money she had expected to be paid shortly. It was already noon on Friday and Cian hadn't mentioned anything about her salary. Each morning Aoife typed out a to-do list for Cian and put it on his desk. The first thing on today's list was 'Pay Aoife.' Cian had glanced at the list. Instead of going through it point by point as usual, Cian had suggested she read up on some well-known legal cases regarding provenance.

She was trying to concentrate on her research, but she kept picturing Jason's reaction when she came home without any money. Okay, she had to stop worrying. Maybe Cian didn't intend to pay her until the evening.

She would hate to lose this job. Not only was the pay brilliant, but at times it was fascinating work. At the moment she was reading about an elderly couple who were selling off their art collection to finance their flight from one European country to another in an effort to outrun the Nazis. It was the early days of the war and there was no way people their age could survive years in the camps. Aoife bit her lip as she scanned the long document, trying to figure out if they had survived.

Cian rushed into the room, his mobile clamped to his ear. 'I understand. Give me ten minutes to sort it out and I'll get back to you.' He disconnected the call. 'Aoife, I'm going upstairs to pack. Check when is the next plane to New York?'

He hurried out of the room and Aoife could hear him running up the stairs.

A quick online check later, she went looking for him.

'Cian!'

'Top of the stairs, first room on your right.'

It was more like an art gallery than a bedroom. The walls seemed to go on forever. You had to look closely to see that the walls were cream because there was barely any space between the paintings. Aoife had never seen so many primary colours in one place.

'It's my modern art space,' Cian said, noticing her stunned expression. 'When's the next flight?'

'Two hours from now, but the only remaining seats are first class. Are you willing to pay that much?'

'Of course.'

'I'm not sure you can make it in time. Even without checking your luggage, it takes at least two hours to get through customs these days.'

'There's got to be some way around it. Bribe somebody.'

'What?'

'Whatever it takes, Aoife. You have to be on that plane.'

'Me?'

'I can't go, I'm flying to Milan shortly.' He sat on a two-seater couch at the bottom of the gigantic bed and motioned for Aoife to join him. 'You have to understand, Aoife, this is vitally important. There's a woman called Danielle Stern who lives in Switzerland. She claims a painting that the Nazis stole from her grandparents is now owned by the Museum of Modern

Art. She's in New York today and has proof of ownership with her. She's agreed I can have the papers for one day, then she gives them to her lawyer. I need you to collect the documents, bring them to me in Milan, then return them to New York. It all has to be done overnight.'

'Cian, I have a child who expects me to collect her from the crèche this evening. I can't just take off, flying all over the world at a moment's notice.'

'I wouldn't ask if it wasn't important. Aoife. Once Danielle's solicitor files her claim in court, the entire world will know about this painting. This is my one chance to make a name for myself.'

'Let me rearrange your meeting with Giorgio.'

'No, Giorgio thinks he's being very generous agreeing to see me in the first place. He won't rearrange. If I don't meet him, he will never speak to me again. You can bring your child with you. I'll pay first class for her as well.'

'Oh, Cian, you can't just pick up a toddler and cross the world at the drop of a hat. By the time I'd got all her stuff together, the plane would be long gone. Look, you just need someone to act as a courier. It doesn't have to be me, does it?'

'I can't send a stranger. It has to be someone I can trust.'

'How about someone I trust? A friend of mine is a student. I'm pretty sure she could drop everything and leave right now, and she's in Dublin, so she has a shorter journey to the airport.'

'You're sure she's reliable?'

'We've been friends since we were four. And if anyone can charm their way to the top of the baggage queue, it's Orla.'

'Okay, you sort that out. I'll see to the flights.' He grabbed his bag. 'Tell your friend I'll meet her at the Aer Lingus departure desk in one hour.'

He ran out of the house. There was no mention of paying Aoife.

❧

'I told you. He's a crook.'

'He was in a hurry, Jason. He forgot. I'm sure he'll pay me on Monday when he gets back.'

'Oh yeah, of course he will. If you have a brain in your head, you'll cut your losses now. I'm surprised he didn't make you pay for Orla's flight too.'

'Well, he didn't. Isn't that proof he's not a crook? I had a good day today, Jason. Don't ruin it.'

'What was good about it? You didn't even get paid.'

'It was exciting. I'm not used to handling that kind of crisis. I was lucky Orla answered her phone and agreed to go. Although when Cian said he would cover her hotel costs if she spent the weekend in New York and buy her a flight to anywhere in Europe, I didn't think there was much chance she'd refuse.'

'Wait until she has to pay for the ticket herself.'

'Don't be so negative. Cian flies so much he could probably pay for it with his air miles.'

'But will he?' Jason's eyes narrowed. 'I haven't seen you this excited in a long time.'

'Cian phoned me from the airport. He said, "You're a treasure". I was beginning to think this job wasn't going to work out and, well…' She felt her cheeks redden. 'Nobody's ever called me a treasure before.'

'All you did was ask Orla to fly to New York.'

'Yeah, well, you weren't there. I sorted out his problem and he was grateful.'

'Not grateful enough to pay you. You need to give up that job today, Aoife, before he cons you out of all our money.'

'He'll pay me.'

'That's what you said last week.'

'Okay, I promise if Cian hasn't paid me by five p.m. on Monday, I'll leave and I won't go back.'

'Good.' Jason smiled. 'You're so gullible, Aoife. I knew he was a crook the second you mentioned him.'

Aoife glared at him and walked out of the room. It took every ounce of her strength not to bang the door.

≪

When Aoife arrived at work on Monday morning, there was an envelope of cash on her desk. The attached note said "Salary + flight + bonus for ingenuity." An extra hundred quid was included.

Aoife spent half the day smiling. When Amy was in bed, she spread all the money on the kitchen table and placed the note carefully in the middle. She went into the sitting room and switched on the TV.

Jason came home. As usual, he went into the kitchen to put his phone in the charger. She thought she could hear him counting the money, but that was probably her imagination. A few minutes later, he went upstairs. She didn't see him again that evening.

The following morning Aoife was making Amy's breakfast when she heard Jason coming into the kitchen. She didn't turn around. She would let him raise the subject.

'Mum just phoned,' he said. 'The police are going to do a re-enactment of the night Dad was murdered.'

TWENTY-THREE

THE FILMING WAS taking place on the Grange Road in Rathfarnham, the last place Danny had been seen alive. Somebody had provided them with folding chairs and they had settled down for the long wait. The buggy was packed with bottles of water, containers of chopped fruit and enough toys to keep Amy amused for a few hours.

During a break in filming, Jason had gone to speak to Ryan, who was playing the part of Danny. Amy had insisted on going with him. Aoife took the opportunity to lie back in the chair and close her eyes. She felt the sun beating down on her face and sighed with pleasure. Days like this were one in a million in Ireland, especially this early in the year. The sky was azure blue without a single cloud to be seen. She intended to enjoy every minute of it. Although she couldn't help wishing filming could have taken place on any other day. It would have been a perfect day to bring Amy to the seaside.

As she drifted off, Aoife remembered days on the beach with her own parents. She still had videos of some of those trips. In one she was about Amy's age. She had been scared of the waves, so her dad had walked into the water carrying her in his arms. She had squealed as her feet trailed in the ocean.

A car driving past brought her back to reality. The film crew were returning from their break, Jason, Amy and Ryan amongst them. Aoife watched as Amy tugged at her father's sleeve, trying to get his attention. Jason patted her head occasionally but continued talking to his brother.

'It always feels like these things are never going to end,' a voice behind her said.

'Detective Moloney. If you're looking for my mother-in-law, she isn't here.'

'I can see that.'

'She felt it would be too much for her. I came to let her know what happens.'

'You're very good to her.'

'No, I'm not. This is a difficult time for her. I don't want her to have to deal with it alone.'

'She has sons.'

'They're guys. They're not the best on emotional support. Maybe no guys are.'

'I don't know about—' His phone rang. He checked his caller ID. 'Excuse me,' he said and crossed the street.

⁂

'Ryan says he'd forgotten everyone he knows will see him on TV,' Jason said.

Aoife nodded. All Ryan had to do was walk down the street and into the shop, but he was so self-conscious he looked like an extremely large puppet.

'Any chance we could slip away?'

Aoife reached for Amy, who was desperate to join some older kids she could see playing at the end of the street.

'I promised Maura we'd stay. She doesn't want Ryan to have to go through this alone.'

'I'm starving. Do you want anything from the shop?'

'No, thanks. Take Amy with you. She needs something to distract her.'

❧

Aoife watched Jason and Amy coming out of the shop. Amy hugged a giant packet of crisps, something Aoife had refused to buy her since learning that they might be carcinogenic. She was hopping up and down with excitement.

Aoife's phone rang.

The voice on the other end was panicked. 'My meeting starts in five minutes and there's no sign of my presentation.'

'What? Cian?'

'My presentation, Aoife! You were supposed to put it on my laptop. It isn't here.'

'It was there yesterday, Cian. I checked. It's in "Presentations, Italy".'

There was silence as Cian checked his folders. 'Okay, I got it. I told you to put it on my desktop so I could find it easily, but at least I have it. Bye.'

He was gone. Aoife stared at the phone. Cian had never mentioned anything about putting the file on his desktop and she'd told him twice that she'd set up a new folder for him. She'd thought she and Cian had turned a corner. Obviously she'd been mistaken.

Her thoughts were interrupted by a screech of brakes. Aoife swung around. Somebody must be driving like a lunatic. She hoped the kids she'd seen earlier were okay. At the opposite side of the road, a bus was approaching. It almost blocked Aoife's view of the incident. She could see a large car, probably a BMW, skidding slightly as it tried to avoid a small obstacle in the middle of the street. The bus passed and Aoife gasped. The obstacle was Amy.

TWENTY-FOUR

Aoife heard Jason shout. They both raced up the street. Aoife screamed 'Amy!' and the child turned, her back to the car. Jason was a little ahead, but the car was only seconds from impact. Eyes glued on her daughter as if that could offer her some protection, Aoife tore down the street. It happened so quickly, Aoife barely registered it. A pair of hands seemed to come from nowhere, enveloped Amy and pulled her to safety. Jason groaned. He stopped, panting heavily, arms resting on his knees, trying to recover his breath. Aoife raced past him and almost grabbed Amy out of Detective Moloney's arms.

Amy patted the tears that ran down Aoife's face as she hugged and kissed her.

'Yucky!'

Aoife laughed and hugged her tighter.

'Thank you so much, Detective.'

Detective Moloney nodded and went to check on the driver, who was slumped in the seat, his head resting on the steering wheel.

Jason joined her and kissed Amy's head. His face was ashen. 'I left her with you, Aoife.'

'I was on the phone. I didn't know. Why didn't you tell me?'

'I did. You weren't listening. You were too busy talking to that Cian about your precious job.' His voice shook. 'Well, I hope your job will be some comfort to you when our child is dead.'

'Jason!'

But Jason had stormed off. She saw him get into the car and drive away. How were they supposed to get home?

Amy was wriggling to be let down. Aoife put her on the ground but kept a firm grip on her hand. She put her other hand out to stop Detective Moloney as he walked past.

'Detective, I'm so grateful. Thank you so much. If it wasn't for you—' Her eyes filled with tears.

'You're welcome.' He started to walk away, then turned back. 'Look, don't blame yourself. Everyone has near accidents with kids. It's a wonder half of them survive infancy.'

'Honestly, I don't know what happened. I was on the phone and I didn't hear Jason coming back. I'd never have let her out of my sight if I'd known—'

Aoife's legs felt shaky and she sat down. Amy tried to pull away, but Aoife wouldn't loosen her grip. Amy whinged, held her free arm out to the detective and cried, 'Moaney! Moaney! Up!'

The detective laughed. 'Do you mind?'

Aoife shook her head.

Detective Moloney lifted Amy on to his shoulders. He hopped up and down. Amy shouted 'More!' The detective ran down the street, Amy bouncing up and down on his shoulders. They disappeared out of sight and returned a few moments later. In the distance Aoife could hear Amy shout, 'Horsy, horsy, more, more.'

Aoife smiled. She'd have to go rescue him or Amy would treat him as her mode of transport for the rest of the day.

Ten minutes later she felt strong enough to stand. 'Amy,' she called, 'time to let the horsy rest. You don't want him to get too tired, do you?'

The detective grinned. 'Let her stay up there. I'm bored out of my mind. I always am at these things. It's nice to have a distraction. She's a great kid.'

'When she isn't trying to kill herself.'

'Don't worry. Every parent has at least one scare like that. I lost Blaine when he was seven.'

'Blaine's your son?'

'Yes.'

'How old is he?'

'He's fourteen now.'

Amy rested her head against the detective's. Aoife felt a pang she couldn't quite understand. 'I think she's ready for the buggy now.'

The detective lifted Amy down and helped Aoife strap her into the buggy.

'You must have been a very young father.'

'Eighteen.'

'That is young.'

'Yes, well, if I had my time over, I'd do it very differently.'

'Wouldn't we all.'

'You think you were too young when you had Amy?'

'No. I planned Amy and I'm glad I had her, but I didn't have a clue what I was getting into.'

'Does anyone?'

'I suppose not. What I mean is, maybe I should have given more thought to—' She shrugged. 'Don't mind me. I don't know what I'm talking about.'

One of Moaney's colleagues was speaking to the film crew. 'Conor,' he called, 'give us a hand here, will you?'

Moaney grinned. 'See. I'm indispensable.' He tickled Amy. 'See you later, munchkin.' Amy giggled. 'Can I give you a lift home?' he asked Aoife. 'I have to drop into the Kildare police station anyway.'

'Thank you. That would be great.'

❦

'I forgot Amy needs a car seat.'

'I think we'd better take the train, Detective.'

'Wait there, just one minute.' He walked over to his colleague and they both disappeared around the corner. Moaney returned a few minutes later carrying a car seat.

'Where did you get that?'

'I borrowed Joe's. He's a weekend father, so he won't need it today. I'll give it back to him tomorrow.'

When they'd eventually managed to get the seat installed, Aoife sat in the back with Amy. She felt obliged to continue their conversation, but it was difficult from that distance. She had run out of things to say when the detective's phone rang. He pressed the button on the steering wheel.

'Hi, Blaine. I'm driving. Can I phone you back? Great. Bye.'

'Blaine is an unusual name.'

'His mother's Australian.' He hesitated, then chuckled. 'I shouldn't tell you this, but his full name is Blaine Happiness Johnson Moloney.'

Aoife suppressed a smile. 'It's—unusual.'

'His mother's name is Johnson. She called him Happiness because she was so happy when she found out she was pregnant.'

'That's sweet. Especially as she was so young.'

'She was twenty when we met. I went on a two-week holiday with my friends to celebrate finishing my Leaving Cert.

Katie was on a mission to see the entire world before she reached twenty-one.' He smiled. 'Katie really should have been born in the sixties. I think a hippie commune would have suited her down to the ground.'

He pulled up outside Aoife's house. Aoife looked at Jason's car in the driveway and wished she could stay where she was, with a sleeping Amy in her arms and a kind, undemanding man to keep her company.

∽

'I shouldn't have said that, I'm sorry.'

'It was a terrible thing to say, Jason. Amy is and always has been my priority. I would never put her in front of my job.'

'I know. I should have made sure you knew I was leaving Amy with you. It was entirely my fault.'

'Yes, well—'

'How did you get home?'

'Detective Moloney gave us a lift.'

'The detective drove you the entire way to Kildare! He lives in Dublin, doesn't he?'

'Yes, but he had to call to the police station here.'

'Why?'

'I don't know.' She helped Amy remove her shoes. 'Why do you ask?'

Jason shrugged. 'It must have something to do with Mum, mustn't it? What else would he be doing in Kildare?'

'That's the only reason you're asking?'

'Who's the suspicious one now, Aoife? Of course I'm concerned when a detective drives all the way from Dublin to my mother's local police station.'

TWENTY-FIVE

SATURDAY MORNING AND Aoife was enjoying her solitary breakfast. She was reading a report in the local newspaper about Danny's disappearance. *Crimecall* had covered the case the previous evening, but the national newspapers hadn't thought it worth mentioning. The doorbell rang. Aoife ignored it. It was at least a year since she'd eaten breakfast alone and she had no intention of allowing anyone to interrupt her. The bell rang again, longer and more insistent. Aoife muttered to herself as she tramped into the hall. When she found Orla on her doorstep, she was momentarily stunned. Almost two weeks had passed since Orla had done her the favour of flying to New York with no notice. She'd texted Aoife the day she'd returned, letting her know everything had gone well. Since then she hadn't replied to Aoife's texts or answered her phone calls. Aoife figured she was busy and would get in touch eventually. Given Orla's attitude to Kildare and indeed all towns outside Dublin, Aoife was alarmed to find her outside her front door at 9 a.m. on a Saturday.

'What's wrong?'

'Nothing. Aren't you going to invite me in?' Aoife opened the door and Orla strode into the kitchen.

'There's no way you drove from Dublin at this hour on

a Saturday morning unless something major happened, Orla. What is it?'

'I stayed in Kildare last night. Can't I visit my best friend without getting the third degree? Where's everyone?'

Aoife explained that Jason had volunteered to do the weekly grocery shop and Amy had insisted on accompanying him. Seeing Orla was about to start another lecture on the dangers of allowing Jason to live in her home, Aoife quickly changed the subject to Orla's recent New York visit.

'You don't have to keep thanking me, Aoife,' Orla said as she sipped her coffee. 'It was fun. And I get a free first-class flight to New York again next week. What more could a girl ask for?'

'Cian said a free flight, Orla, and to Europe, not New York. He didn't say anything about first class.'

'Yeah.' Orla put down her mug. 'That's what I wanted to talk to you about. The thing is, Aoife, I'm going to New York with Cian. I hope you don't mind, but Cian and I are kind of a couple now.'

'You're a couple? How did that happen? I thought you'd only met for a few minutes in airports.'

'We did, but when we met in Italy, Cian told me about a man in New York who does copies of all the great paintings. Cian thinks he's going to be famous one day. He gave me four hundred dollars and asked me to pick up a painting he'd commissioned. When I was flying home, I sent Cian a text and he met me in Dublin Airport. We went to dinner that night and we've been out every evening since.'

'He never mentioned it.'

'I wanted to be the one to tell you. Do you mind?'

'I'm not sure, but I don't suppose it matters either way.

You're really interested in Cian? I can't imagine anyone who is less your type.'

'I was a bit surprised myself. At first, I wasn't remotely attracted to him. I wouldn't even have gone to dinner with him if I hadn't been starving, but you know, he's very interesting. Over dinner he told me the story of the painting that was stolen from Danielle's grandparents—I mean, the things they went through! It's hard to imagine. And then we talked some more and he told me about the break-in and his mother and everything. I felt so sorry for him.'

'The bank robbery break-in? What did he say about that?'

'You know his mother was dying at the time, right?'

'Yes, that's why his father never discussed Danny's disappearance.'

'Well, remember the papers said three men broke into Cian's house, the place you work now. They tied up Cian and forced his father to go to the bank and wait until the time locks on the safe opened. Cian was in the house all night on his own. He was only fifteen and he could hear his mother upstairs calling for him. She was in pain and couldn't move, but he wasn't able to get her the drugs she needed. He was almost in tears telling me about it.'

'Poor Cian. I wonder he didn't mention it when we were talking about the night Danny disappeared.'

'I don't think he finds it easy to speak about his mother or that night.'

'Did he say anything about the burglars? Any reason to believe one of them was Brendan?'

'I asked him what they looked like. He says he remembers being terrified by the balaclavas, but other than that, the only thing that really registered with him was his mother calling for help.'

ॐ

Orla hurried off to meet Cian. He was driving her to Dublin and they were having brunch at some fancy restaurant. Aoife was trying to decide how she felt about that when Jason and Amy returned. Amy was munching the remains of a packet of crisps.

'Jason, please don't keep buying her those. The papers say they cause cancer.'

Amy tightened her grip on the crisps and ran out of the room.

'Okay, no more crisps. I'm exhausted. I'm going to watch TV for a while.' He went into the sitting room.

'Amy,' Aoife called. 'Would you like to help me put away the shopping?'

Amy's "help" meant it took almost an hour to put everything away. Aoife looked at her pile of ironing. It would have to wait. She didn't get enough time with Amy these days. During one of her Mother & Toddler sessions, Olive had practically fainted when Aoife admitted Amy had never experienced finger-painting. The following week she'd arrived with a large sheet of very thick white paper. 'Of course you must take it,' she'd insisted. 'You're a single mother. We're all here to support you and help with Amy's development.'

Aoife moved the kitchen furniture to one side. She covered the wooden floor with an old sheet and placed the paper on the ground. A half hour later Amy was covered in paint. She was using her hands and her bare feet to smear different coloured paints across the paper. When the page was a mess of colours, Aoife covered her hand in paint and made palm prints on the sheet. Amy copied her but was more interested in painting her face. Eventually she put her tiny palm on the sheet, then put one foot into the paint container and made prints with her feet. They were both laughing when Jason came into the kitchen.

'God, what a mess.'

'Join us. We can have a family hand portrait.'

'No way. Look at the state of the place.'

'It will all wash off. Come on, Jason. It's fun.'

'Forget it. I'm meeting Ryan in twenty minutes. I don't have time to wash all that stuff off.'

'You're going out? I thought we'd do something as a family. We've barely seen Amy all week.'

'You're the one who insisted on working four days a week, Aoife. How did you expect to spend time with your child?' He checked his watch. 'I'm off. See you tonight.'

Aoife and Amy finished their painting. Aoife stuck it to the fridge. The two sets of palm prints seemed to be mocking her.

❧

The following morning, Aoife made another attempt at family time. She had just opened her mouth to suggest a trip to the zoo when her phone rang.

'Aoife, it's Detective Moloney.'

'Hi, Detective.'

'I'm going to see your mother-in-law shortly. I think you should be there.'

'What's wrong?'

'There's been a breakthrough. Somebody phoned the police station after the re-enactment was broadcast on TV. It's given us a whole new perspective on your father-in-law's disappearance.'

TWENTY-SIX

'I'M NOT SURE I understand, Detective. A woman says Danny gave her sister a lift a few weeks before he disappeared?'

'A few weeks before her sister disappeared, Mrs Walsh.'

'Both of them disappeared? The same day?'

'We're not exactly sure when the girl disappeared. She sometimes stayed overnight with friends, so her family didn't raise the alarm immediately, but we think she disappeared the day before your husband's murder.'

'I don't see the connection, Detective.'

Moaney looked uncomfortable. He glanced at Aoife, then turned his attention to Maura. 'There's no easy way to say this.'

'Say what?'

'The girl he gave a lift to was Triona Cashman.'

Maura turned to Aoife. 'Why do I know that name?'

Aoife shrugged.

'She was one of a group of six girls who went missing between fifteen and twenty years ago.'

'Oh, yes, of course. The Buckley murders. I remember now. And Danny knew her?'

'We think so, yes. He certainly gave her a lift on at least one occasion.'

'Okay, but how does that help?'

'You remember Buckley's last victim?'

'The one who got away? Sarah something? I remember vaguely, but I was still trying to adjust to Danny's disappearance at the time and I wasn't really paying much attention to the news.'

'Buckley, the guy we arrested, kidnapped Sarah and brought her up the Dublin mountains. Two men who happened to be walking in the mountains that day heard her scream. Buckley ran away, but the girl could identify him.'

'Detective, I really don't see—'

Detective Moloney swallowed.

'Girls had been disappearing for over six years. We suspect Buckley was responsible for all the abductions, but he's always denied it. Although we can't prove anything, there's good reason to believe he abducted the first girl, and the third girl was seen with someone who fits his description, but we never found any connection between him and the other three.'

'Okay.'

'The point I'm trying to make, Mrs Walsh, is that girls stopped disappearing after Buckley was arrested.'

'I know that, Detective. That's how everyone was sure Buckley was the murderer.'

'Exactly. But Buckley was arrested fifteen years ago.'

'Oh my God!' Aoife muttered.

Maura turned to her. 'What?'

But Aoife couldn't bring herself to say it.

'Mrs Walsh, Buckley was arrested three months after your husband disappeared.'

'I know that, Detective.'

'So Buckley isn't the only person who's been off the scene for the last fifteen years.' When Maura looked at him blankly, the detective added, 'So has your husband.'

TWENTY-SEVEN

'THAT IS THE most preposterous, insane, ridiculous thing I ever heard.'

When nobody answered her, Maura shouted, 'My husband! The father of my—' She pointed at Aoife. 'Your child's grandfather!'

'Maura, I—'

Maura held up her hand. 'Don't! Get out, both of you.'

'I can't leave you al—'

'I don't want you here, Aoife. Either of you.' Maura charged to the front door, opened it and waited until they left. She slammed the door behind them.

'She's not going to get into trouble for throwing you out, is she?'

The detective shook his head. 'I'll come back tomorrow when she's had time to get used to the idea.'

'Do you really think Danny murdered all those girls?'

'I don't know. He might have been Buckley's accomplice. All the girls lived within a ten-mile radius of Rathfarnham and your father-in-law was there regularly.'

'Maura says he almost always had the boys with him.'

'I know. I spoke to your mother-in-law's neighbour. She said the boys often played with her kids while Danny ran errands for his mother.'

'But how long could he have been gone? A half an hour? An hour at most, surely? That's hardly enough time to kidnap and murder a girl and dispose of the body.'

'No, but your father-in-law might have kidnapped Triona, stored her somewhere and murdered her later. Remember, he didn't go to work for two days before he disappeared.'

'Jack says he was definitely at work.'

'Fr Byrne is a seventy-four-year-old man trying to remember a seemingly insignificant phone call he made fifteen years ago. Stephen Byrne was in his fifties when he reported something that happened a few days earlier. Who do you think is the more reliable witness?'

'Did you talk to the other people who worked in the bank?'

'We did. One colleague says she thinks your father-in-law was at work all week. Another thinks he wasn't. It's too long ago for anybody to be certain.'

'Wouldn't the bank have Danny's holiday records?'

'We'll check, but I doubt it. As far as I remember, organisations are only required to keep holiday records for five years or so.'

'Please keep me informed of any developments, Detective. We really need to know what's going on.'

'As soon as there is any news I can share with you, I promise I'll phone you, Aoife.'

<hr>

Aoife got home to find Jason pacing the hall.

'Great! You're back. I have to go. I told Ryan I'd meet him half an hour ago.'

As he passed her, Aoife put a hand on his arm. 'I have to tell you something.'

∽

Jason was stunned by the implications. 'That's crazy. My dad wasn't a murderer.'

'I know. Your mum's really upset. Can you go over there now? I think you should spend the night.'

'Not now, Aoife. Ryan's waiting for me.'

'Tell him what happened. You can meet up at Maura's house.'

'That wouldn't work. We booked a tennis court and Ryan's going to help me with my serve. I need to get some exercise and tennis is the only game I ever liked.'

'Jason! Your mother needs you.'

'She'll be fine. I'll phone her straight away.' He dialled the number, picked up his keys and hurried out of the house.

∽

Aoife had hoped Jason would spend the night with Maura, but he was home by 9 p.m.

'How is she?'

'Who?'

'Your mother, of course.'

'Oh, I'm sure she's fine.'

'You didn't visit her?'

'No. Ryan and I went for something to eat after the game and then we went back to his place. I meant to tell him about Mum, but it slipped my mind.'

'What? You forgot!'

'It's okay, Aoife. I phoned Mum twice today. She said she didn't feel like talking but she wanted you to know that she's sorry she threw you out of the house and she knows none of this is your fault.'

'I'm glad, but that was hours ago. Why don't you pop over there now and stay the night.'

'God, no, I'm exhausted. I'll have a cup of tea and then I'll phone her again.'

'We can't leave her alone all night, Jason. You didn't see how upset she was.'

'Okay, okay! God, Aoife, will you stop nagging me? Can't I have five minutes' peace?'

'I—you—' Aoife's mouth opened several times before she managed to form a coherent sentence. 'Showing concern for your mother is nagging? And I'd like to know why you're so exhausted. I'm the one who spent the day cleaning the house, keeping your daughter entertained and worrying about your mother.'

Jason threw his eyes up to heaven. 'You're in a mood again, I see. Women! Right, I'll phone her.' He picked up his mobile and left the room. Less than five minutes later, he returned. 'Mum is fine, but she wants an early night and she doesn't want any visitors. Now, if you don't mind, Aoife, I'd like to get something to eat. It's been a long day.'

Aoife went upstairs before she could say something she would later regret.

TWENTY-EIGHT

THE FOLLOWING MORNING Aoife checked her phone every ten minutes, but there was no update from Moaney. She wasted so much time checking, she was late for work. She rushed into her office to find a grinning Orla sitting on her desk.

'Surprise! I'm going to be working here for a few months.'

'What?'

'Well, I'll only be here occasionally until after my exams, but I'm going to spend the summer redecorating the house. I'm helping Cian organise a dinner for all his art critic friends. He'll be thirty in August, so we're going to call it a birthday celebration.'

'He never mentioned anything to me.'

Orla laughed. 'I only talked him into it last night. It will be great for his career. This is a fabulous house—well, apart from the outside. Honestly, you'd think a pauper lived here. But he won't let me touch the front of it and I can see his point.' She giggled. 'Everyone gets such a shock when they see the extension. And Cian has the most amazing paintings. Who wouldn't be impressed?'

Aoife's heart sank. Orla was her best friend, but she didn't fancy her as a colleague or, worse still, a boss.

᪥

Four days later and still no news from Moaney. Aoife couldn't relax. Jason was acting like everything was fine, but she couldn't forget the way he'd spoken to her. She was struggling not to hold a grudge. Jason was under a lot of pressure. He was as upset as anyone about the allegations made against his father. It wasn't that he didn't care about Maura. He wasn't emotionally strong enough to cope with the situation, so he was pretending it didn't exist. Aoife sighed. Nobody cared whether she was capable of coping with everything. Why was it her responsibility to plug all the gaps? Wouldn't it be lovely if somebody would step in and take care of everything? *Okay, stop right there*, she told herself. *That's how you got yourself into this situation in the first place. The last thing you need is somebody controlling your life. Get a grip.*

Aoife looked around her once immaculate office. Now that Orla's dinner preparations were in full swing, there were constant deliveries. It was a daily struggle just to find her desk. Orla bustled in and out with an ever-growing list of demands. Aoife heard heels on the stairs and ran into the kitchen to avoid her. She was boiling the kettle when Cian wandered in.

'This is a disaster,' he said. 'I should never have listened to Orla. Everyone will hate the house. I'll be a laughingstock.'

'Why would anybody hate it?' Aoife checked her phone for the five-hundredth time that morning. Still nothing from Moaney. 'Your house is beautiful. Even I can tell that the artwork is spectacular.'

'It's all fake. Everything is fake.' Cian looked at Aoife with wide, terrified eyes. 'Don't you see? I'm a fake. I can't paint, so I do second-rate copies of famous works or I buy them from other people. My kitchen and dining room are straight out of a magazine and my office is like an advertisement for tack. Nobody will take me seriously after this. I'll ruin my career before it's even properly started.'

'I think the paintings you did yourself are pretty good. I bet your colleagues would admire them.'

'Aoife, please—'

'I'm not saying they'll think your art compares to the masters. I'm saying they'll admire you for your skill as an amateur. I bet they'd all love to be able to paint as well as you.'

'Of course they would,' Cian scoffed. 'I'm moving all of my own paintings into my bedroom and that's where they will stay until everybody who knows anything about art is safely out of this house.'

The doorbell rang. Cian went out to answer it, leaving the kitchen door open.

'Hi, I'm Tadhg.'

'Sorry?'

'I'm your new employee. Orla said you needed someone to do the heavy lifting to get the house ready for some party.'

Aoife came to the rescue. It was over a month since she'd seen Tadhg. Back then he'd worn oversized jumpers or jackets. Now he was wearing jeans and a tight sleeveless T-shirt. He'd outgrown the awkward teenage stage, Aoife noticed. That was the body of a man.

'Hi, Tadhg. Orla isn't here yet.'

'Orla hired you?' Cian looked at him suspiciously. 'Why would she do that without telling me?'

Tadhg shrugged.

'We could certainly use some extra help around here, Cian. He could move those boxes out of my office to start with.'

'I don't like strangers in my house. Not unless I am the one who invites them.'

'Well, Tadhg's here now and there's lots of things he could do for us. You don't want to send him away, do you?'

Cian frowned at Tadhg. 'Are you studying law with Orla?'

'No.'

'How do you know her?'

'We met at a funeral.'

'What?'

'Tadhg is a student at Trinity. He helped out at Danny's funeral service. Orla obviously thought of him when she realised we needed help.'

Cian pursed his lips. 'I see. Well, Aoife's office is at the end of the hall. Put all the boxes in the garage. We'll decide what to do with them later.' Aoife went to follow him, but Cian put a hand on her arm to delay her. When Tadhg was out of sight he said, 'I don't like the look of him.'

Aoife smiled. 'He's barely eighteen, Cian. You don't have anything to worry about. Orla isn't interested in young boys.'

'What? I have no idea what you're talking about. I meant I have a lot of expensive paintings in this house and I don't want people like him hanging around here.'

'I'll vouch for Tadhg. Maura knows him well. He won't steal from you, I promise.'

⁓

A few hours later Aoife was eating her lunch when Tadhg came into the kitchen. 'How's it going?' she asked.

Tadhg checked behind to make sure they were alone. 'He's a bit odd, that boss of yours, isn't he?'

'In what way?'

'I don't know. Jumpy. Not at all the kind of guy I'd expect Orla to fall for.'

'He's not her usual type, that's for sure. But, you know, they're close in age and Orla has always liked older guys.'

Tadhg grinned. 'You don't need to worry about me, Aoife. I know Orla would never go for someone like me. Not yet anyway. In a few years, who knows?' He frowned. 'For the life of me I can't figure out what she sees in that guy.'

'Cian's just worried about having so many important people to dinner. Orla talked him into it. He's not really the socialising type.'

'I don't think that's it. I spent a good part of my life in and out of foster homes. I learned to judge people very quickly, and I'm telling you, Aoife, something isn't quite right with that guy.'

❧

Summer made its second early appearance this year. Ireland was celebrating its fifth consecutive day of sunshine and blue skies. The sun seemed to be reflected in everyone's smiles. Even people who normally ignored strangers now stopped on the street to discuss the fabulous weather. Barbecues made a rare appearance and the shops were running out of ice cream.

Orla had a week off college. In celebration of the glorious weather, she set up her office in Cian's garden. She was having difficulty deciding where she wanted to sit. First she tried the patio, then she moved to sit near the fountain, later she decided she'd prefer the lawn and finally she settled in the rose garden. Each time Tadhg was summoned to move Orla's table and chair while Orla carried her laptop, textbooks and a bundle of interior design magazines. As they strolled through the garden, Tadhg's muscles were displayed to their full effect and he and Orla always seemed deep in conversation. On one occasion Aoife spotted Cian watching them from the kitchen window. She wondered if he was comparing his own rather unimpressive physique with Tadhg's. She wondered if Orla was comparing them also. When Orla had finally settled in the rose garden, Aoife went out to join her.

'You do know Tadhg's in love with you, right?'

Orla shrugged. 'He knows there can never be anything between us.'

'Are you sure?'

'When we started hanging out—'

'You've been hanging out?'

'Of course, why not? I like Tadhg. He's very bright and he has a great sense of humour. Don't look at me like that, Aoife. I made sure Tadhg understands that I would never go out with someone younger than me. He knows we can never be a couple.'

'I'd be prepared to bet that doesn't stop him from loving you.'

'It doesn't stop me from loving him either. But nothing can happen between us and that's all there is to it.'

TWENTY-NINE

THE FOLLOWING EVENING, Jason was watching TV while Aoife sat alone on the couch, flicking through a library book on modern art.

'Aoife, what do you want to do about Amy's college fund?'

'How do you mean?'

'Well, now I'm living here again, should we consider restarting it?'

Aoife put down her book. 'You're not living here, Jason. You said you wanted to stay here until you felt able to cope with your mother. I assumed you'd be going back to her house soon. Especially now she's so upset about the Buckley development.'

'Oh, she's over that already. I convinced her nothing's going to come of it.'

'I'm glad Maura's feeling better, but if the police had dropped that line of enquiry they would have told us. Maura's going to need your support. I think it's time you moved back in with her.'

'I could, I suppose, but is that really fair?'

'Why not?'

'I'm an adult, Aoife. I don't want to live with my mother.' He took a seat on the couch beside her. 'We're husband and wife. I know your parents' life insurance paid for this house, but legally we are joint owners.'

'What are you suggesting? Amy and I move out?'

'No, but why can't we all live here together? There's plenty of room.'

'It would be too awkward, Jason.'

'Why? Am I getting on your nerves?'

Aoife ignored the question. 'We can't live as if we're a couple when we're not. What message does it give to Amy?'

'Short of us being a couple, what could be better for her? She gets to live with both of her parents and see us each day. Maybe it's not ideal for the two of us, but in the present economy, we don't have a choice. We can't afford two houses.'

'You want to live here forever?'

'Wasn't that the idea when we got married? We might have a few problems to work through, but won't that be easier when we're both in the same house?'

'Maura says Evan is moving into a house near Belfield. Apparently the rent is pretty reasonable. Couldn't you stay with him for a while?'

'The rent is reasonable because there are six of them in the one house. They don't have space for me, and even if they did, I'm not a student any longer. I can't live a student lifestyle. They'd be up half the night. I have to get to work.'

'There must be some other solution.'

'Not with our debts. You've seen how much of my salary goes to paying off the credit card. Where would I get money for any type of rent, no matter how low it is?'

'When will we have the debts paid off?'

'I figure another two years should do it.'

'Two years!'

'Well, you know what it's like with credit cards. The interest rates are so high, it's almost impossible to pay anything off the capital. But I've been managing to clear a little each month. Another two years or so and we should have it all repaid. Can you put up with me until then?'

'Jason, I'm not sure this is—'

'And now you're earning good money, we could restart Amy's college fund.'

Aoife was about to say they should spend any spare cash on counselling sessions, but she stopped herself. She couldn't face counselling right now. 'I need to get Amy some new clothes. She grows out of everything so quickly.'

'That's a good idea. When that's done, how would you feel about putting the surplus into the education fund?'

'Okay, but I have to keep enough to pay for food and bills.'

'There's no need. I'll cover those.'

'No, Jason. While we're living separately, I want us to have separate accounts. You continue to pay me the amount we agreed when we separated plus extra to cover your keep. I know exactly what's going on bills, so it will be easy to work out how much extra we spend while you're living here.'

'You want me to pay for my keep? Like I'm a lodger?'

'Why not? We're not a couple, Jason. Our agreement was you would give me enough to cover the utility bills and to feed and clothe Amy. Now that you're living here, the utility bills have increased. All I'm asking is that you pay the balance.'

'But—'

'I think I'm being very generous. I clean, cook, take care of your child and do your laundry. I'm not charging you for any of that.'

'But that means it's costing me more to live with you. Mum wasn't charging me for my keep.'

'Maybe you should live with her, then?'

Jason frowned. 'That job is changing you, Aoife. You're becoming hard and bitter.'

'What changed me, Jason, was trying to live on practically nothing last year. I could only afford one meal a day.'

'That wasn't my fault. If you had asked me for money, I would have given it to you. You never told me you'd lost your job. How was I supposed to know you had no money?'

'Well, maybe it wasn't your fault, but I'm not going through that again. I'll put a hundred a month into the college fund but no more.'

Jason smiled. 'It's a start, Aoife. That's all I'm asking. I just want to make sure Amy has a chance at a good college education. That's what a responsible father does, isn't it?'

THIRTY

AOIFE ARRIVED AT work to total chaos. Whatever Cian might say about his dining room, Aoife doubted there was anybody who wouldn't be impressed by the long mahogany table and the gold chandelier. But that was all that was in the room. Cian hadn't built the extension until after his parents' death, and as he had no use for a formal dining room, it had eventually gone the way of most spare rooms—everything that wasn't in constant use ended up there. Orla enthusiastically embraced the challenge of preparing it for its debut performance. The first step was to get the room painted. Workmen dressed in overalls passed through the hall and odd items of furniture were stored in the hallway.

'Hey!' a muffled voice greeted her as she entered. Orla's curls could be seen peeking over the top of a large painting. 'What do you think of this?'

Aoife examined what appeared to be a black canvas. 'Am I supposed to see something?'

'Cian painted it. It was hanging in the dining room, but it's better suited to the hall. Cian says if you look at it closely there are actually several different shades of black.'

'Hmm. I suppose there are, but it's still a black canvas.'

Orla giggled. 'We're hopeless, aren't we? Poor Cian. I think Tadhg's the only one who appreciates his work.'

'Tadhg likes my paintings?' Neither of them had heard Cian enter.

'We all like your paintings, darling. We just don't appreciate them the way a real art lover can.'

'I didn't realise Tadhg was into art.'

'Oh yeah, that's part of the reason I asked him to help out with the party. I knew he'd love your house. He sketches a bit himself, but he adores all forms of art.'

'Really?' Cian sounded sceptical. 'Not that one, Orla. I don't want anything I painted myself on display. These people are professionals. They'd despise my amateurish attempts.'

'I don't think it's amateurish.' Tadhg joined them. He put down the box he was carrying, took the painting from Orla and held it to the light. 'It's quite amazing, actually. I didn't realise you were so talented.'

'I'm not at all talented, and this painting is staying in my bedroom until the party's over.' Cian took the painting from Tadhg and headed for the stairs. 'Orla, we need to leave in fifteen minutes if we're going to make our flight.'

'Oh hell, is that the time! I'm not even dressed!' She jumped down from the stepladder and could be heard taking the stairs two at a time.

Tadhg watched her leave, a thoughtful expression on his face. 'Off on another holiday? Where are they going this time?'

'Vienna. It's only for the weekend. Tadhg, do you think it's a good idea to spend so much time around Orla? Wouldn't it be better if—'

'I'm okay, Aoife. Orla deserves a good life. Cian can give it to her now, but someday—' He smiled. 'Someday I'll be a qualified doctor and I'll be able to give Orla everything she ever wanted.'

Aoife stopped herself from pointing out that Orla wouldn't wait that long. Tadhg was so intelligent, sometimes she forgot how young he was.

◈

Jason's insistence that the police were no longer following up on Danny's involvement in the Buckley murders worried Aoife. She didn't think it was fair to give Maura false hope. If the police had dropped that line of enquiry, she was certain Moaney would have told her. She was googling newspaper reports about Triona Cashman's disappearance when Tadhg came into her office.

'Any idea where—' He glanced at the screen. 'That's the girl your father-in-law gave a lift to, isn't it? Orla told me about it.' He moved closer to get a good look. 'She was very pretty. Hard to believe she died not long after this photo was taken. Is that a pentagram she's wearing around her neck?'

Aoife peered at the screen. Triona wore a silver pentagram on a thin chain. In the centre of the pentagram was a tiny design. When Aoife enlarged the photo, she could see tiny white stones spelled out "Triona".

'It looks expensive,' Tadhg said. 'Whoever killed Triona might have tried to sell it. It might be worth asking the police if she was wearing it the day she went missing. Have the police been in touch?'

Aoife shook her head. 'I'm worried sick. I don't want Amy going through life as the grandchild of a suspected serial killer.'

'Maura seems to think the police have decided Danny wasn't involved.'

'That worries me too. If that were true, I'm pretty sure the detective would have been in touch by now.'

Tadhg perched on her desk. 'So, ask him. What's the worst that can happen?'

'You're right.' She searched through her contacts and made the call. 'Hi, Detective. This is Aoife Walsh. I was wondering if you have any update on the investigation into my father-in-law's disappearance.'

'Aoife!' She could hear the smile in his voice. 'No, I'm afraid I don't have any news. I'll phone you the minute there's anything I can share.'

'Have you ruled out the possibility that Danny was involved in those girls' disappearance?'

'We are still pursuing several lines of enquiry.' He paused. 'Aoife, you have to understand that I can't discuss the details of my investigation with you.'

'Right. One other thing. I was looking at the photo of the girl Danny gave a lift to. She's wearing a silver chain with something that looks like a pentagram. Was Triona wearing that the night she was murdered?'

She could hear the detective rustling papers. 'Apparently Triona made her own jewellery. That chain was a favourite. It disappeared the same time Triona did, so we're assuming she was wearing it when she was abducted. As her body was never found, we can't be certain.'

'Did anybody ever try to trace it? It looks like it could be real silver. Her murderer might have tried to sell it.'

'We looked into that. It appears expensive from a distance. Up close, apparently, it's clearly worthless.'

'Maybe the murderer didn't know that and tried to sell it anyway.'

'The report says anybody who touched it would know it

had no value. But the original investigators did follow up on it. They put a photo of the chain on TV and asked if anybody had seen it. There were no useful leads. In my experience, the type of person who abducts young girls isn't interested in their jewellery. It's probably still on Triona's body. If we ever find her, it will help with the identification.'

'Could the murderer have taken the chain as a trophy?'

'Again, in my experience, that's highly unlikely. In the movies, serial killers are always keeping trophies. It gives the public the idea that this is the norm. In fact, it's very rare. I can't think of a single serial killer outside the US who was ever caught with trophies from their victims.'

Aoife paused. 'Detective, this is a very difficult time for my family. If we didn't have to worry that you were about to arrest Maura or that any minute the newspapers might announce that Danny was a serial killer, it would mean a great deal.'

'I wish I could help, Aoife. All I can say is that we haven't closed any of our lines of enquiry and that I will contact you personally the very minute I have any information that can be shared publicly.'

'So you still think Maura may be a murderer?'

'I have said all I can on the subject, Aoife. I really hope you can understand.'

'Of course, Detective. Sorry to bother you.'

∽

Tadhg had been listening to every word. 'I don't think it means anything, Aoife,' he said when she disconnected the call. 'If the police never discovered anything and the investigation stalled for years, they'd still say they were pursuing many different lines of enquiry and could neither confirm nor deny anything.'

'So we have to live with this hanging over our heads for the rest of our lives? It was fifteen years ago, Tadhg. The murderer could have emigrated. He might even be dead. The police will probably never solve the case.'

Tadhg shrugged. 'All the more reason not to worry about it. Danny couldn't have been a murderer because Maura loved him. Maura's one in a million, and I don't believe she could love somebody who was capable of killing in cold blood.'

'What if the police decide Maura murdered Danny?'

'Only an idiot could come to that conclusion. Do you think this detective of yours is an idiot?'

Aoife stared at him. 'This detective of mine?'

Tadhg laughed. He stood up. 'Gotta go. It's less than a week to Jack's birthday. Loads to do. Bye.'

THIRTY-ONE

AOIFE ARRIVED HOME to find Jason sprawled on the couch watching TV. He hit the mute button when she came into the room.

'Jason, what are you doing here? Why aren't you at work?'

He sneezed. 'I've got a cold. I'm not well. Can you hand me that box of tissues?'

The tissues were barely an arm's length away. Aoife handed them to him.

'Any chance you could make me a cup of tea?'

'I just popped in to get my phone. I forgot it this morning. Can you make yourself tea? I have to collect Amy from the crèche.'

Jason sighed. 'Okay, the tea can wait until you get back.'

✍

'Aoife!'

Aoife gritted her teeth. If he asked her for a drink one more time, she was going to pour it all over him. He had a cold for God's sake. People went to work with a cold. They got up, did housework and took care of their kids. Jason was perfectly capable of making himself a cup of tea. It wasn't like he had a terminal illness, or even a broken bone.

She opened the door. 'Yes.'

'My head is killing me. Could you take Amy out of the room? She's making far too much noise.'

Amy was sitting at Jason's feet, chatting quietly to her toy elephant.

'She's not making any noise, Jason.'

'It's too much for my head.'

'Amy's making far less noise than the TV and your head doesn't seem to have a problem with that.'

Jason sat up. 'I'm sorry, Aoife. Am I causing too much fuss? I'll go upstairs and lie down. Do you mind if I make myself a cup of tea first? I'll be very quick, and don't worry about lunch. I don't have much of an appetite.' He stood up, put his hand on his forehead and sat down again. 'I just got up too fast. I'm fine, really.'

Was she being unreasonable? Colds could develop into flu. Maybe Jason was sicker than she realised. She supposed Amy's chatter could get annoying if you were in pain. And, well, really, how many times had she watched TV herself when she wasn't feeling a hundred percent?

'I'm sorry, Jason. I'm just tired. Stay where you are and I'll bring you another cup of tea. Come on, Amy. Daddy needs to rest.'

Amy looked at her. She dropped her elephant and wrapped both arms around her father's leg. 'No!'

'Would you like to play bubbles, Amy? Let's turn on the bubble machine.'

'Bubble! Bubble!' Amy squealed. She grabbed her elephant and ran out of the room.

'Thanks, love,' Jason said and turned back to his TV programme.

❧

At 8:15 on Monday morning, Aoife pulled up outside Cian's house. She felt guilty dropping Amy at the crèche so early, but she had to get out of the house. An entire weekend of Jason lounging on the couch and calling her every thirty seconds was more than enough.

The kitchen table was covered in paintings. Cian had his back to her and didn't hear her entering. She watched him place one painting carefully into the frame and then cover it with another.

'Morning, Cian.'

Cian jumped. 'Aoife! You startled me.' He looked at his watch. 'You're very early.'

'I am a bit. What are you doing?'

'I've taken down all my own paintings and I'm going to hide them in my bedroom until the critics are safely out of the house. They won't all fit on the wall, so I have to put two paintings in some frames.'

'Couldn't you just lay the extra paintings against the floor? It would be less work.'

'I could, but these paintings mean a lot to me. They may not be appreciated by art critics, but they're my own work. I don't want them to get damaged.'

The doorbell rang and Aoife answered it. 'Tadhg! Everyone's getting an early start today.'

Tadhg followed her into the kitchen. 'I need to leave by three and Orla left me a list of things to do that's a mile long. I figured the sooner I started the better. I'm going to see Bridget this afternoon.' He grinned. 'I can't wait. Maura makes her sound like a bloodsucking vampire.'

Aoife laughed. 'Why are you visiting Bridget?'

'I need photos of Jack. Maura says Bridget is the most likely person to have them. I'm hoping for photos at every major stage in his life. I'll have them blown up and pin them up all over the room for Wednesday's party. Morning, Cian.'

Cian nodded. 'Can you take these upstairs, Tadhg? Leave them against the wall in my bedroom until I get there. I'll hang them myself.'

'Sure.' Cian grabbed three of the paintings.

'One at a time, please. I don't want them damaged.'

Tadhg looked at the mound of paintings. 'That will take a while. Ah well, "no rest for the wicked" as my grandmother would say.' He lifted one painting and carried it carefully out of the room. They heard him running up the stairs.

Cian frowned. 'What do you think of Tadhg?' he asked Aoife.

'He's fine. Seems like a nice kid. Why?'

'I don't know. Something about the way he looks at Orla bothers me.'

'Really? I hadn't noticed.' Aoife glanced at her watch. 'Look at the time! No point in arriving early if I'm going to hang around the kitchen all morning. I'll type up today's to-do list and I'll have it on your desk in fifteen minutes.' She hurried out of the room.

❦

That evening, Aoife let herself into the house quietly. She had twenty minutes before she had to collect Amy from the crèche. With any luck Jason would be so engrossed in the TV he wouldn't hear her come in and she could wash her hair and have a quick shower before leaving.

She was about to tiptoe up the stairs when the sitting room door opened and Jason came out.

'Hi, Aoife. I'm going to make some tea. Would you like some?'

'You're feeling better.'

'Yes, much better actually. I'll go back to work tomorrow.'

'Great. Well, I'll have a shower and then I'll get started on dinner. Can you collect Amy?'

'I don't think that would be a good idea. My dizziness isn't completely gone and if anyone from work saw me, they'd think I was just pretending to be sick.'

'Okay. I'll collect her, then. Can you start dinner?'

'You know I can't cook.'

'You don't have to prepare anything. Dinner's in the fridge. Just heat up the oven, peel potatoes, chop some broccoli and boil them.'

'I don't know, Aoife,' he said doubtfully.

'You can't go wrong. Put the potatoes on now. Stick a knife in them after twenty minutes. If the knife goes through, they're ready to eat. I'll make Amy's mash when I get home.' Aoife made a mental note that no child of hers would ever leave home unable to look after themselves.

She took a bag of potatoes from the fridge and left them on the draining board. Jason was still frowning at them when she left.

When she returned, the casserole was in the oven. One half-peeled potato sat on the draining board. Jason was in the sitting room watching TV.

'What happened?' she asked him.

Jason held up a hand covered in a large plaster. 'The dizziness mustn't be completely gone yet. I cut my hand with the knife. I thought it was better not to risk doing any more.' He looked at his watch. 'The casserole should be ready in fifteen minutes.'

Aoife opened her mouth, thought better of it and went out to the kitchen.

⁂

On Tuesday Jason went back to work. Aoife had his meal prepared and Amy in bed when he got home. She sat opposite him while he ate, too stressed to do more than pick at her food and nod occasionally as he explained some problem he had at work. The second he swallowed his last mouthful, she said, 'Jason, this isn't working out.'

'What isn't working out?'

'Us living together. The whole idea of you moving out was to give me time to think. How can I do that with you under my feet? I need you to move back to your mother's.'

Jason gave her a sympathetic smile. 'I drove you mad when I was sick, didn't I? Mum always said I was a dreadful patient.'

'It's not only when you were sick, Jason. You're here the whole time. You're always under my feet. I can't breathe.'

'It's okay, Aoife. I understand. I'm a dreadful patient, I know I've driven you mad the last few days. What you need is a break.'

'That's not what I need, Jason. I need—'

'I mean a break from me.'

Aoife felt the tension seep out of her muscles. 'You'll move back to your mother's?'

'I don't think that would be the best solution. It's better for Amy that I'm here for her. I'd hardly see her if I was living with Mum.'

'You don't pay any attention to her as it is.'

'Of course I do.'

'You don't, Jason. You watch TV or play with your phone. You never play with her. It's like you don't even see her most of the time.'

'Really? I had no idea. I suppose it's hard for me. I don't remember how my dad was when I was a kid and I'm not sure what to do with her. I mean, it's not like she's capable of conversation. But it's really important to me that Amy and I have a good relationship. I'll work on it. I promise.'

'Good.'

'In the meantime, if you can put up with me for a little while longer, Ryan and a group of his friends are renting a house in Galway at the end of the month. I'll take two weeks off work and go with them. I'll even take Amy with me if you like.'

Aoife smiled. 'A guys' weekend wouldn't be the best place for her. They'll probably spend the entire time boozing. She's better off here with me.'

'Two weeks without me under your feet and you'll feel differently, Aoife. You'll see.'

'It will help, Jason, but it's not a long-term solution.'

'You're right. And we haven't been working on our relationship, have we? What happened to our Friday date nights? We'll stick to them rigidly when I get back. Okay?'

'You don't have to be living here for us to have a date night, Jason. In fact, I think they'd work better if we had a little time apart.'

'Maybe, but what about my relationship with Amy? It will be a lot easier to work on that if we're in the same house. Give it a try, Aoife. How about three months? Isn't Amy worth putting up with me for another three months? If we break up eventually, it will be even more important that she and I have a strong foundation to work on.'

'Okay. But only three months. After that, if it's not working out, you go back to your mother's house. Agreed?'

Jason smiled. 'Agreed.' He kissed her briefly on the lips. 'But you're going to miss me so much when I'm away that you'll never want me to leave again. You'll see.'

✧

On Thursday morning, Aoife felt relaxed and happy as she let herself into the halfway house. It didn't register with her that the kitchen was deserted and the entire house abnormally silent. She was thinking about Jason going to Galway for two weeks. Two whole weeks without him under her feet. An entire fourteen days to get herself together. She felt like she could breathe properly again. Jason was right. All she needed was a break. Jason was a pain when he got a cold, but then so were a lot of men. They didn't call it the "man flu" for nothing. Since he'd moved back to the house, he'd irritated her in ways she couldn't even have imagined when they were a couple. But irritation was no reason to break up a family. When Jason got back from his holiday, she would put all her thoughts and efforts into resurrecting their marriage. She would start a diary, she decided. Every day she would write down all the nice things Jason said and did. That would help her to concentrate on the positive. Each night she would re-read the entries and remind herself that Jason was the father of her child. Amy deserved a happy home with two loving parents, and it was up to Aoife to make sure she got it.

Aoife remembered a photo of herself and her parents on her first holiday abroad when she was a little older than Amy. Her parents had their arms around each other, and each had one hand on their daughter's shoulder. All three were smiling up at the camera. That was the family Aoife wanted and she would make it happen.

'Hi, Maura,' she called, lost in her daydream. It took her a moment to notice that Maura hadn't answered. She was standing looking out the window, her back to Aoife. 'Maura? Are you okay?' Maura turned, red-eyed, her face wet with tears. Aoife dropped her bag and ran towards her. 'What is it? What's wrong?'

'It's Tadhg. He's dead.'

THIRTY-TWO

'DEAD? TADHG? How could he be dead? What happened?'

Maura shook her head. 'I was only talking to him last night. I knew something was wrong. I should have made him tell me, but with the party and everything it didn't seem the right time. I planned to talk to him this morning.' The tears flowed again. 'And now I can't.' She sniffed. 'That poor boy.'

Aoife put her arm around Maura's shoulder. 'Did he… did Tadhg kill himself?'

Maura pulled away and stared at her. 'Of course not. Tadhg would never do something like that. He was murdered.'

∽

The phone rang but they both ignored it.

'Tadhg was murdered? Who murdered him?'

'The police think it was some small-time drug dealer.'

'Tadhg was on drugs? I don't believe it.'

'I couldn't believe it either. But he was found in an alley in Dublin. The only people who go into that area at night are selling or buying dugs. And there were pills in Tadhg's pocket. The police think there was probably an argument with whoever he was trying to get the drugs from. Tadhg might have owed him money or something.' Tears welled in her eyes again. 'Whatever happened, he's gone.' She sniffed. 'That beautiful young boy is gone.'

'But why would Tadhg take drugs?'

'I don't know, but he'd be alive now if it wasn't for me.'

'How could it be your fault, Maura?'

'I knew something was very wrong the last time I saw Tadhg. I should have made him talk to me.'

'What do you mean?'

'It was at Jack's party. Tadhg had been so excited about it. I was helping him set up the room. We'd bought balloons. I know it was stupid, but Tadhg said Jack never had much of a childhood and he wanted him to have the whole kids' birthday party experience. He'd bought candles for the cake and we had paper chains and balloons. All that nonsense.' She reached for a tissue and blew her nose. 'Anyway, the lads helped blow up the balloons, but then they started using them as footballs. They were out in the corridor, kicking them around the place. There were bits of burst balloons everywhere. I told them to forget the balloons and go tidy the kitchen. Tadhg was a bit annoyed, but he was laughing too. I left him setting up the room and I hoovered the corridor and got rid of all the burst balloons. That's when it happened.'

'What happened?'

Maura shook her head. 'I—' She sniffed. 'I have no idea. Tadhg was in the room by himself. I was in the corridor. Nobody went near him. When I finished hoovering, I opened the door and said, "Are you finished?" At first I thought he was sick. His face was a weird green colour. When I asked him if he was okay, he nodded. Then the lads came in and said they were going to get Jack and the party started.' She sniffed again. 'I don't think

Tadhg said one word the entire night. He was supposed to make the presentation to Jack, but he told the lads to do it. After the party I pulled him to one side and asked him what was wrong. He said he wasn't feeling great and he was going to lie down. That was the last time I saw him.'

'What could have upset him?'

'It must have been a phone call. I wouldn't have heard his phone ring over the noise of the hoover, but anyone who went in or out of the room would have had to pass me. It can't have been anything else.'

'And whatever someone said to him on the phone made him go buy drugs?'

'It looks that way.'

Maura wiped her eyes. 'Better get back to work. It must be at least twenty minutes since I told Jack I'd bring him in a cup of tea.'

'I'll do it.'

≪

Jack was sitting at his desk, puffing on a cigarette. A cheap Bic cigarette lighter lay beside a pack of forty cigarettes. Aoife could barely see him through the haze of smoke. He must have gone through the entire packet. He held the cigarette he was smoking in one hand, Tadhg's lighter in the other.

'I checked the cost of these on the internet,' he said as Aoife put the mug of tea on the desk. 'Maura told me it was Tadhg who organised everything. God knows how he paid for it.'

'He wanted to show how grateful he was for your help.'

'What help? He's dead, Aoife.'

'You helped him while he was alive. You gave him a place to live and a future to look forward to.'

Jack fiddled with Tadhg's lighter. 'Did you know both his parents were drug addicts?'

Aoife shook her head.

'I never thought he'd go down that road. He always swore he wouldn't.'

'You did your best for him, Jack. That's all anyone can do.'

'Maybe.' He picked up his mug. 'I try not to get too close to any of the boys. It's not fair on them. They're only here a few years. It's not right to let them think they can rely on me. But Tadhg—I thought he was going to be our success story.'

'How do you mean?'

'A lot of the kids who come in here, they don't have much chance in life. By the time they hit eighteen, they've experienced more abuse, neglect and tragedy than most of us could imagine. It doesn't make them good students. The best I can hope for is they live a normal life without ending up on drugs or in prison.' He smiled. 'Tadhg was so bright. If he'd grown up in a normal environment, he'd have been one of those child geniuses. And he was luckier than most of my boys. His parents were a liability, but his grandmother loved him and she kept him with her whenever she wasn't in hospital. That's how he ended up with me. If he'd spent more time in foster care, he'd have been entitled to a State allowance and he wouldn't have needed me. I used to joke that when Tadhg finished college and became a famous doctor, I wanted his face plastered all over my fundraising material.' He cleared his throat, stuck the lighter in his pocket and stubbed out the cigarette. 'Well, that's over. No point in crying over spilled milk, as they say. Thanks for the tea, Aoife. Tell Maura I don't feel like working today, so if she'd like to go home, I'll see her tomorrow.'

THIRTY-THREE

MAURA WENT TO the inquest alone. She phoned Aoife with the verdict.

'Of course we knew Tadhg had been stabbed, but nobody mentioned that he didn't die in that alley. There were signs that his body had been moved after death.'

'You mean he might not have been killed by a drug dealer after all?'

'I don't know, Aoife. I'm sure drug dealers move around the city. Maybe one of them killed Tadhg but dumped the body in the alley because he knew it was an area that would most likely be deserted at night.'

'When's the funeral?'

'I wish I knew. I've offered to arrange it, but Jack says he'll handle it. He hasn't done the first thing about it, though.'

'That's weird. Jack must be used to organising funerals.'

'I think once Tadhg is buried, Jack's going to have to face the fact that Tadhg's actually dead. Right now, he's refusing to face reality.'

He wasn't the only one.

⁊

'I'm not going.'

'Orla, you have to go. Tadhg was your friend.'

'Well, Tadhg isn't going to be there, is he? I don't want to remember him in a coffin. He was such a beautiful guy. And he had so much life in him.' Her eyes filled with tears. 'He was only eighteen, Aoife.'

Aoife put her arms around her.

'I know. But his grandmother is dead and he has no contact with his parents. If his friends don't go to his funeral, who will? Do you want him shoved in the ground without anyone around who even cares? He deserved better than that.'

Orla stood up and wiped her eyes. 'You're right. I'm going to give him the best f—' Her eyes filled with tears again and she brushed them away with her fist. 'I am going to give Tadhg the biggest, best funeral anybody around here has ever seen.' She pulled out her mobile and googled florists for several minutes before bursting into loud sobs.

∽

Orla had certainly done her best. There were so many flowers in the church, you'd have been forgiven for thinking you were attending a wedding. Once Orla had decided to take over organising the funeral, it was full steam ahead. The following morning she'd arrived at Jack's office, notepad in hand. She'd left an hour later with the address of all the different places Tadhg had lived and phone numbers for every choir in the locality. She'd contacted everybody Tadhg had ever known, right down to the foster parents who had looked after him for two months when he was four. She'd made sure everyone was aware of the funeral arrangements. The guys in the halfway house all had new suits which Orla, or rather her parents, had paid for.

Orla spent three days writing Tadhg's eulogy. It took twenty-four minutes to read, but it was the last sentence that caught everyone's attention.

'I only knew Tadhg for a short time, but we became very close. He told me everything. He told me he was terrified he had a genetic weakness towards substance abuse. That's why he wouldn't touch cigarettes or alcohol. It's the reason I didn't need an inquest to tell me that Tadhg hadn't been murdered in that alley. And it's how I know Tadhg wasn't killed by any drug dealer. Tadhg never touched drugs in his life. He wouldn't even go near areas where drugs were sold. I don't know who murdered Tadhg. I don't know why he was murdered. But if it's the last thing I ever do, I'm going to find out who killed him and I'm going to see that bastard's life destroyed the way he destroyed Tadhg.'

THIRTY-FOUR

'Okay, Orla, maybe a drug dealer didn't kill Tadhg. It could have been a robbery gone wrong. But I don't see how you can possibly hope to find the murderer.'

'Why not? You're looking for Danny's murderer.'

'That's different. I have a list of suspects. I have reasons why people might want to kill Danny. You don't have anywhere to start.'

'Yes, I do. I'm going to start with the phone call Tadhg received the night of Jack's party. Maura said he'd been perfectly fine before he got that call, so whoever phoned him knows the whole story.'

'How are you going to find out who called him? The police kept Tadhg's phone as part of the murder investigation.'

'I know. That's why I need your help.'

'What do you want me to do?'

'Call that detective of yours. Ask him to get a list of all the phone calls Tadhg made and received over the last week.'

'I'm sure they're not allowed give out that information, and what do you mean "my detective"? He's not "my" detective.'

'Aoife! For God's sake! I'm trying to find out who murdered Tadhg. I don't care about you and the detective.'

'There is no "me and the detective".'

Orla glared at her. 'Just ring him. Get a list of the numbers and give them to me. If that's not too much trouble. Thank you.' She stormed out of the room.

᠃

'I understand your friend is upset, Aoife, but we don't just hand out that kind of information. Orla isn't even the next of kin.'

'Orla, Jack and Maura were the closest thing Tadhg had to family.'

'Well, I certainly wouldn't give out information like that but, look, it's not my decision. I'll find out who's in charge of the investigation, ask him to phone Orla and what happens after that is up to them.'

'Thank you, Detective.'

'Conor.'

Aoife hesitated. 'Thank you, Conor.'

'You're welcome. How is a list of Tadhg's phone calls going to help your friend?'

'Tadhg was very upset the night he died. We think it was because of a phone call he received. Orla wants to contact everyone he spoke to recently. If she can't discover who made the actual call, she might find someone who knows what happened that night.'

'I don't think the phone numbers will help her much. The investigator will have already checked them. Drug dealers use pay-as-you-go phones that can't be traced back to them. And if a drug dealer was involved in a murder, the first thing he'd do is destroy his phone's SIM card.'

'I have a pay-as-you-go phone. The shop asked me for my name and address when I bought it.'

'They didn't ask for proof of identity, though, did they? Criminals always give false names and addresses.'

'Orla doesn't believe Tadhg was killed by a drug dealer. She says he would never have touched drugs.'

'It's not unusual for people to hide their drug use. Does your friend have reason to think somebody else was the murderer?'

'Not really. But she's convinced it couldn't have been a drug dealer.'

'I can understand she doesn't want to believe it. It's the most likely scenario, though. I know young lads get in fights occasionally, but Tadhg was stabbed in the back. Your normal everyday youngster doesn't carry around a knife with him. Tadhg was in Trinity, wasn't he?'

'Yes.'

'Almost all college kids drink and no doubt a lot of them take drugs, but I never heard of any Irish college kid, let alone a Trinity student, being murdered. And I don't imagine drug pushers hang around the Trinity campus either. Can you imagine the fuss if some of the wealthiest and most powerful people in the country found out that Trinity was allowing their kids to consort with criminals?'

'I know you're right, but Orla isn't ready to accept that.'

'Well, as I said, I'll pass on her number. That's all I can do.'

Aoife thanked him. If the detective in charge of Tadhg's case was male, she wouldn't have to bother Moaney again. Orla would have the list within hours.

᷍

Aoife was right.

Two days later she was at her desk when she heard Orla talking in the corridor. Assuming she was with Cian, Aoife followed them into the kitchen. A heavyset middle-aged man looked up when she entered.

'Aoife, this is Detective Tony Brennan. Tony's in charge of the investigation into Tadhg's murder.'

The detective nodded, but his gaze quickly returned to Orla. Aoife doubted Tadhg's investigation was the reason for the home visit.

'Have you found out anything about Tadhg's murder?' she asked.

'We've spoken to a number of people known to hang around the area where the body was found. Nobody reported seeing anything.'

'So what is the next step in the investigation?'

'I can't discuss that with members of the public.'

'You can discuss it with me, Tony, can't you?'

The detective smiled at Orla. 'I consider you to be Tadhg's next of kin. As such I am authorised to keep you fully informed on the progress of the investigation.'

Orla patted his arm and gave him her trademark smile. 'Thank you, Tony. I'm so glad you were chosen to head up the investigation. You'll do a brilliant job and I'll do everything I can to help. What do you plan to do next?'

'Next? Well, ahmm, I don't have the file with me, but there are standard procedures we follow in cases like this.'

᪇

Aoife went back to her desk. Over an hour later, she heard the detective leave. The door closed and Orla ran down the corridor. 'I've got it,' she said, holding up two pages of typed numbers. She handed one page to Aoife. 'We need to start checking these numbers right now.'

'Orla, I can't. I'm working. I'll phone them tonight.'

'We've wasted enough time already. It can't wait until tonight. Cian will understand.'

'No, he won't. He said he needs this report by four p.m. and I've only just started it.'

'Oh, for God's sake! Cian!' When there was no reply, Orla screamed, 'Cian!'

Footsteps hurried down the corridor. 'What's wrong?'

'Aoife's worried you'll be annoyed if you have to wait another day for your report. You don't mind waiting, do you?'

'Why? Do you have to go home, Aoife?'

'No. I—'

'She's helping me contact all the people Tadhg phoned or received calls from the week he died.'

'Isn't that a job for the police?'

Orla snorted. 'I just met the detective handling the investigation into Tadhg's death. He did not fill me with confidence. Aoife's a brilliant investigator. She was the one who uncovered the DCA murderer.'

'You did? You said you worked in DCA, Aoife. You didn't say anything about uncovering murderers.'

'I—'

'That's not important right now, Cian. What matters is Aoife needs to spend today phoning everyone Tadhg was in contact with the week he died. Your report can wait until tomorrow, can't it?'

'No, Orla. It can't wait. I need that report today and I don't want Aoife conducting investigations during her working hours.'

'Cian! Finding Tadhg's murderer is far more important than some stupid report.'

'Finding Tadhg's murderer is a job for the police. I don't

want Aoife getting involved in it during office hours, and I don't want you involved at all. It's dangerous.'

'How could checking phone numbers be dangerous? Cian, I'm serious about this. Either you tell Aoife she can make those calls or I am walking out of this house right now and I won't come back.'

Cian looked at her. Without breaking eye contact with Orla, he said, 'Make the calls, Aoife.'

Orla pecked him on the cheek. 'Thanks, darling.'

Without responding, Cian walked out of the room.

≪

After wasting hours on the phone, Aoife had learned nothing of consequence. She ticked the last name on her list. About half Tadhg's calls were to Orla. She and Tadhg spoke every morning and two or three times during the day, probably when they both had breaks in their college courses. They spoke for about an hour each evening, presumably on their way home from college. On average they had two or three conversations a week that started around 10 p.m. and ended around midnight. Aoife guessed these were the nights Cian didn't stay over. She'd known Orla and Tadhg were close, but she had no idea they'd been so involved in each other's lives. There were numerous calls to shops and businesses in connection with Jack's party. A few calls were to the guys in the halfway house, one to Bridget and two to Maura. Almost all his texts were to college friends, who were anxious to discuss Tadhg at length. But they all said they didn't know he was taking drugs and couldn't believe anyone would murder him.

Now the weather had cooled again, Orla had commandeered Cian's office. It was empty when Aoife entered, so she left the ticked list on the desk. "Contacted everyone on list," she scribbled at the bottom of the page. "No information."

✧

On her way back to her office, Aoife stopped off in the kitchen to refill her water jug.

Cian was sitting there working on his laptop. 'Orla threw me out.'

Aoife nodded and offered to make him a cup of tea. Cian declined. He worked in silence for a few minutes, then stopped and indicated that he wanted Aoife to sit beside him.

'Can I trust you to tell me the truth, Aoife?'

'Of course. What do you want to know?'

Cian leaned forward and stared at Aoife intently as if determined to read the truth in her expression.

'Were Tadhg and Orla an item?'

This was what happened when your friend was in a relationship with your boss. 'No.'

'You're certain?'

'Yes.'

Cian leaned back in his chair. 'She's taking his death harder than I would have expected.'

'She is.'

'And you're sure that's not because she loved him?'

Aoife hesitated. 'Tadhg loved Orla. It was written all over him. I mentioned it to Orla. She said she had explained to Tadhg that she could never go out with somebody younger than her.'

Cian nodded. 'You think she feels guilty because he loved her and she was the one who stopped them from being a couple?'

'Maybe.'

'Okay. Thanks, Aoife. That's put my mind at ease. Now I want to talk to you about the investigation. You're not—'

Orla burst into the kitchen.

'Cian, why did Tadhg phone you the night he was murdered?'

THIRTY-FIVE

CIAN FROWNED. 'TADHG didn't phone me.'

Orla held up the phone list. 'Yes, he did. He phoned this landline around eight p.m. The call lasted ten seconds. What did he want?'

Cian looked at her blankly. 'I don't know. There's absolutely no reason Tadhg would phone m—' He paused. 'Oh yeah, I remember now. He did ring. He was looking for you. He said you weren't answering your mobile.'

Orla leaned against the kitchen table. 'Oh, please God, no!' She hurried out of the room. She returned with a copy of the list of calls Aoife had checked.

'Mine is the very first number on your sheet, Aoife. It's my fault Tadhg died. Whatever was wrong, he wanted to tell me and I didn't take the call.' The colour had drained from her face and she sank down onto one of the kitchen chairs. 'It's my fault he's dead.'

Cian knelt down on the ground beside her. He put his arms around her. 'Darling, it's not your fault. Tadhg was in the wrong place at the wrong time. Nothing you or anybody else did or didn't do could have changed that.'

Orla pushed her chair away and stood up. 'Haven't you

been listening? Tadhg wasn't murdered in that alley. He wasn't killed by any drug dealer. Somebody deliberately murdered him, and Aoife and I seem to be the only people who care.'

'Of course I care, darling.' Cian tried to pull her into an embrace, but Orla stepped out of his reach. 'Leave me alone, Cian. There's no point talking to you. You don't understand.'

✧

As soon as Orla had left, Cian rounded on Aoife.

'This is your fault. You should never have agreed to help her. You're not a detective, Aoife. Can't you see you're making everything worse? Do you want Orla to get sick?'

'How is any of this my fault?'

'Oh, for heaven's sake. Aren't either of you capable of a sensible conversation?'

He stormed out of the room, banging the door behind him.

✧

It took Aoife ages to get to sleep. It felt like a mere fifteen minutes had passed before she was woken by Amy crying. She went into Amy's room to find the child covered in sweat and complaining that she was thirsty. When Aoife had taken her temperature, changed her clothes, given her medicine, got her to take as much liquid as possible and settled her back in bed, she checked her watch. It was 5 a.m. Jason had been talking all week about the important meeting he had this morning, so she couldn't suggest he take the day off. Maura was working. The crèche wouldn't accept sick kids and it would be unfair to ask Alison to take a sick child into her home. She was going to have to tell Cian she couldn't come to work today. The mood he was in, that wasn't going to go down well.

She took her laptop downstairs and checked her work diary. The only urgent thing was Cian's report, but there were hours of research involved and she had barely started. She'd begin working on it now. At 8:30 she phoned him.

'I'm really sorry, Cian, but I don't have anybody to take care of her.'

'What about my report? I checked and you've barely started it. I told you I needed it yesterday, but you were too busy playing detective.'

'I can do the report from home. I'll email it to you by ten a.m.'

'It can't be any later, Aoife.'

'Ten a.m., Cian. I guarantee if you check your email, it will be there.'

She felt safe making the promise because the report was almost complete, but ten minutes later Amy began crying again. There was fifteen minutes to spare when she got back to her laptop. The stupid password wouldn't work. Why the hell did she have a password on her home computer? 'Okay, stop panicking,' she muttered. 'You know your own password. Concentrate.' There was five minutes to spare when she eventually got in. She worked like a maniac and e-mailed the report at 10:07. At 10:10 her phone rang. It was Cian. Before she could answer, he hung up. Her email must have arrived in his inbox while he was phoning her. There were beads of sweat running down her back and she wondered for a minute if she might have caught Amy's illness. It was several hours later before she realised that, as far as Cian knew, she had completed a half day's work in one hour. He obviously thought that was a realistic expectation and that Aoife's achievement didn't even deserve a 'thank you'.

≼

Aoife was due to work in the halfway house the following day. That evening, she phoned Jack to say she wouldn't be able to make it. She was quite touched by his reaction. 'That's fine, Aoife. Of course you must take care of your daughter. I remember my own mother getting into a state any time I was ill. Her employers weren't very nice. By the time I was old enough to understand, I used to insist I was well no matter how bad I felt. You take all the time you need.'

Aoife had already booked the Friday off as annual leave. She had intended to do something special with Amy, but although Amy now seemed fully recovered, it was better not to take her outside, especially as it had been raining for the last few days. She would leave her with Alison, go to the halfway house and make up for the day she'd missed. When she arrived at the halfway house, she found Maura had everything under control. There had to be something she could do.

'Maura, do you think we should clear out Tadhg's room? I'd like to do something to thank Jack for being so understanding, and I'm sure it's a job he's dreading.'

'You're probably right. Can you remember where we put the skeleton key?'

Aoife stood up. 'It's in the petty cash box. I'll get it. Come on. We might as well get it over with.'

﷼

Twenty minutes later they had all Tadhg's worldly possessions piled into two boxes.

Maura wiped her eyes. 'So little. That's all his possessions in the entire world.'

Aoife nodded. She felt like crying herself. 'What are we going to do with them?'

'Better let Jack make the decision. I suppose Tadhg's personal belongings will be divided between the lads, and Jack probably knows somebody who could use the textbooks. I'll keep the art books in the office. Maybe someday some other young lad will read them.'

Aoife fingered the sketches they had found in Tadhg's desk. Not surprisingly, most of them were of Orla. 'Ask Jack if we can give the sketches to Orla. They'd mean a lot to her.'

～

Orla made a small choking sound when she saw the sketches. She reached out and touched one with her index finger, then pulled it away. 'I don't want them. Get rid of them.'

'Tadhg drew them. He'd want you to have them.'

Orla glared at her. 'What do you know about what Tadhg wanted? What do any of you know? You didn't care about him. Not really. And as for Cian, I wouldn't be surprised if he was secretly delighted Tadhg's out of the picture.' She looked at the sketch pads and her voice wavered. 'Take those away. It hurts just to look at them.'

'Oh, Orla!'

'What do you mean "Oh, Orla!" Get away from me. Go back to your work.'

～

Aoife put the sketch pads on her desk. Cian rushed in, face pale. 'What now? I heard Orla shouting.'

'I found some of Tadhg's sketch pads. I thought Orla would like them, but she got a bit upset.'

'These are Tadhg's?' Cian flicked through them. 'They're

good. He really captured Orla's essence, didn't he? Can I keep them?'

'If Orla doesn't want them, I'd rather keep them myself.'

'Could I have just one?'

Aoife shook her head. 'I can't part with them. Sorry.'

'You surprise me, Aoife. I know you liked Tadhg, but it was obvious you weren't close. Why are you so determined to hang on to all his sketches?'

'I think they're very good.'

'No, you don't. You always said you had no appreciation of art. Are you planning to sell them? I'd gladly pay you. I've been wanting to get Orla's portrait done, but she says she won't have time to sit for it until the summer holidays.'

'They're not for sale, Cian. Not now, not ever.'

❧

That evening Aoife examined the sketches. Orla from every angle imaginable. In a few she was smiling, but in most she looked wistful, almost hungry. Towards the back of one of the sketch pads were seven drawings of a rectangular box, shaded in with a dark pencil. Aoife shivered. They reminded her of Tadhg's coffin. She put the sketch pads in a plastic bag, got a stepladder and put them on top of the kitchen cabinets, where Amy would never find them. She didn't know enough about art to judge how good they were, but she didn't believe Cian thought they captured Orla's "essence", whatever that meant. If Aoife had given the sketches to Cian, most likely they would have ended up in the bin. She was pretty sure Cian's only concern was making certain Orla never laid eyes on the sketches again.

THIRTY-SIX

IT HAD BEEN a tough few weeks. Cian made several attempts to talk Orla into dropping the investigation. They did not go well. Then he made the mistake of asking Orla about the arrangements for his dinner party. Orla screamed so loudly, Aoife heard every word from her office at the opposite end of the corridor. 'Tadhg's dead! We don't even know who murdered him and you're worrying about dinner parties?'

Before Tadhg's death, Orla had never screamed at anyone. She never needed to. By the age of twelve, Orla had figured out that a display of charm could almost always be guaranteed to get her everything she wanted. Tadhg's death had affected her more than Aoife would have believed possible. But something changed after that last fight with Cian. All Orla's aggression seemed to have drained away. Now she spoke only when spoken to. Sometimes not even then. In an effort to get the old Orla back, Cian asked Aoife to organise a two-week holiday in Italy. Orla didn't even reply when he told her about it.

The tense atmosphere was getting to Aoife. She was so exhausted each evening, she barely had the energy to play with Amy. Jason had headed off to Galway full of holiday spirit, assuring Aoife this break was what they needed to repair their relationship. Aoife was so stressed, she barely noticed his absence. She was quite shocked when Jason phoned to say he was on his way home and would see her that afternoon.

She was thinking about Jason's return as she reached the crèche. One of the crèche mothers, whose name Aoife couldn't remember, waved as she closed the passenger door and ran around to the driver's side. 'Sorry. Can't stop. I'm running way behind.'

Aoife returned the wave and only barely managed to side-step a red-headed kid who appeared determined to crash his tricycle into everyone who crossed his path. 'Hi,' she said to a young girl she hadn't seen before. 'I'm Amy's mother.'

'Who?'

'Amy Walsh.'

'Oh! She's gone. Her dad collected her.'

'Her dad? He's in Galway. You're new, aren't you? You must be mixing her up with someone else.'

'No, I know all the kids and there's only one Amy. Her dad collected her around twelve-thirty.'

'He phoned me from Galway at noon.'

'Are you sur—I mean—God!—I'll get Mrs Weston.'

THIRTY-SEVEN

'DID YOU CHECK his ID?'

'Yes, Mrs Weston. He showed me a photo with "Jason Walsh" written on it.'

'Was it a driver's licence?'

'I don't know. Robbie had just driven his tricycle through a group of kids, and they were crying and one of them was bleeding.' The young girl bit a trembling lip. 'I remember he was holding a balloon and Amy ran to him.'

'What did he look like?'

The girl sniffed. 'I only checked his name. When the kids started screaming, I got distracted.'

'You're certain the name on the ID was Jason Walsh?'

The girl nodded several times. 'I read it carefully. It definitely said "Jason Walsh". I'm positive.'

'Aoife, is it possible you misunderstood your husband? Are you certain he said he was in Galway?'

'Yes, of course I'm certain. Who was this man? Why would he take my daughter?'

'Okay, there's probably a simple explanation for all this.'

'A simple—what are you talking about? My daughter is missing!' She pointed at the young girl, who was now crying openly. 'That girl let a strange man walk out of this building with my baby. What kind of an explan—'

'Aoife, this isn't helping. I'm going to call the police and then I'm going to make you a cup of tea. We'll—'

'Tea! Are you out of your mind? I'm going home. Tell the police where I am.'

Aoife raced outside and ran the entire way home. The house was empty. She phoned Jason, but again, there was no answer. She ran next door to Alison.

'Have you seen Amy or Jason?' she panted.

'No. Why?'

Aoife had to grab on to the wall to steady herself.

'Oh my God!' Alison helped her to a nearby chair. 'What's wrong, Aoife? Are you sick? Should I call a doct—'

'Amy's missing. Someone took her from the crèche. A man.' Aoife put a hand on her chest. She tried to take deep breaths. 'A man—his ID—his ID said he was Jason Wal—oh, Alison, I don't know what to do. I was hoping—hoping Jason would be here, but I know he—he's in Galway.'

'Dear Lord! Have you called the police?'

'The crèche phoned them.' Aoife jumped up. 'Moaney! I'd forgotten about Detective Moloney.' She grabbed her mobile and searched her incoming calls until she found his number. The phone rang and a few seconds later a deep voice said, 'Detective Moloney.'

'Thank God! Amy's missing. I'm sorry, this is—'

'Amy's missing? How long?'

'About a half hour. A man took her from the crèche.'

'Are you at home?'

'Yes.'

'I'm on my way to Cork. I'm almost in Naas. Text me the

address of the crèche and I'll call in there. Try not to panic, Aoife. We'll find Amy.'

⊷

Two policemen and a woman in plain clothes were in her kitchen. Alison had insisted on phoning Orla and they were both making sandwiches and tea for everyone. Aoife did a circle from the kitchen to the sitting room, into the hall and back to the kitchen again. Every couple of minutes she phoned Jason. Why hadn't they ever got Bluetooth? What a stupid thing to economise on! Jason would never hear the phone over the noise of the car engine. He probably had music blaring as well. She checked her watch. They'd spoken at noon. If he'd left Galway at 12:30, he should be home in about twenty minutes. Twenty minutes? Amy had been missing for almost two hours. Two hours! She felt a hand on her shoulder and shrugged it off. Everyone kept trying to get her to sit down. She didn't want to sit down. She wanted to be left alone. No, she wanted Amy. That was the only thing she wanted. The police could set up a permanent headquarters in her kitchen for all she cared once they'd found Amy. Why were they all hanging around her house? Why weren't they looking for her baby? Aoife passed through the hall again and into the kitchen. She stopped. Amy's painting was lying on the floor. It was the last straw. Aoife picked up the painting. She touched Amy's little palm print, then clutched the painting tightly against her chest. Raising her voice to be heard over the chatter, she said, 'Everyone, get out of my house.'

All talk stopped.

'What are you doing here? Why aren't you looking for my daughter? Put down your tea and go out there and search for her.'

'Mrs Walsh, we are looking for Amy. Right now there are police—'

'Right now there are police in my kitchen, eating my food and drinking my tea. If Amy walked by the front gate you wouldn't be any the wiser. She's not in my kitchen, is she? So what are you all doing here? Go look for her. Now!'

'Mrs Walsh, our role is to help you—'

'Help me? I'm an adult. I'm standing in the middle of my own kitchen. I'm not lost, am I? The only help I need is for someone to find my daughter.' Aoife marched to the front door and held it open. 'Go find her now.'

⌘

The police had hung around outside the house for a little while, but when Aoife opened the front door, they got into their cars and disappeared. Alison had gone to collect her daughter from school. Aoife and Orla were alone.

Orla cleared the table, leaving a plate of sandwiches and two mugs. She filled the mugs from a large teapot Aoife had never seen before. 'I know you don't want to eat, Aoife, but making yourself sick isn't going to help Amy.' She put a hand on Aoife's shoulder and guided her to the table. 'Sit down. Try to eat something. Even one bite.'

Aoife sat down on the chair. She looked at the sandwiches and her stomach churned. 'Who would take her, Orla? Why would some stranger want my baby? What is he planning to do to her? What if he's hurting her right now? What if she's crying out for me and—'

'Stop it, Aoife.' Orla knelt on the floor beside her. 'I've been thinking. The man who took Amy had ID with Jason's name. How do you know it wasn't Jason?'

꿇

The landline rang and Aoife made a dash for it. 'Yes.' She listened for a few seconds and hung up.

'Who was it?'

'I don't know. Someone trying to sell something.'

'Okay, I want to talk to you about Jason. What if Jason was the person who took Amy from the crèche?'

'Jason's on his way back from Galway.'

'How do you know he was ever in Galway? Because he told you?'

'What? You're saying he's having an affair? Orla, I don't care where he was or what he was doing. All I care about is finding Amy.'

'What I'm saying is maybe Jason told you he was in Galway but really he was planning to kidnap Amy.'

'Kidnap? What are you talking about?'

'You told Jason you wanted him to move out of the house. Then Amy disappears. Isn't that a little coincidental?'

'I told him that weeks ago, and we agreed we'd stay together for another three months. It was Jason's idea. He wouldn't steal Amy. What would be the point? Where would he take her? To Maura's? I'd go around and take her back straight away. He knows that.'

'What if he's taken her abroad? He might have suggested the three-month trial period to give him time to arrange his escape. Or maybe he had second thoughts. He realised you and he would never be a couple again, so he took his daughter and disappeared. Men have done it before when they realised their relationships were finished.'

'What men?'

'Well, there was the father of two in the paper last year

whose marriage broke up. When the mother was at work, he picked the kids up from school without telling her.'

'Orla! He murdered them! Are you saying Jason would—'

'Of course not.'

'But it's happened before, hasn't it? How many times have you seen women on TV saying their husbands loved their kids and would never harm them and then—' She jumped up.

'Where are you going?'

'Jason's a planner. If he took Amy, he'll have booked flights and hotels. They're might be bills, credit card receipts, online bookings. Come on.' She ran up the stairs and Orla followed. 'You search the drawers, the wardrobe, look for any bills or receipts or notes about hotel or flight reservations. I'll try to get into his computer.'

A half hour later, Aoife had to admit defeat. Whatever Jason was using as a password, she was never going to guess it. She joined Orla in tearing Jason's room apart. When they didn't find anything, they started emptying the drawers and the wardrobe. The floor was littered with paper and the bed piled high with clothes when Aoife's phone rang.

'Yes?'

'It's Conor?'

'Who?'

'Detective Moloney.'

Aoife grabbed Orla's shoulder. 'Have—have you found—'

'Are you sitting down?' he asked.

THIRTY-EIGHT

Aoife couldn't answer. She gave a faint groan.

'Aoife, everything is okay. Amy's with me. We're in the children's playground in the park near the crèche. Amy's just fine. She's—'

Aoife dropped the phone and raced out of the house.

⸎

She was running down the street when Orla pulled up beside her. 'Get in.'

Panting, Aoife jumped in. Orla held out her mobile.

'Moaney told me what happened. We'll be there in a few minutes.'

⸎

Three police cars were parked at the entrance to the park. Several policemen stood outside. Two were talking into their radios. Aoife ran past them. It took her a few minutes to reach the children's play area. At first all she could see was police. Then she saw a hand waving.

Amy was perched on top of Moaney's shoulders. Aoife's

world narrowed to that one tiny bundle. She didn't notice the police. She didn't hear Orla speaking to her. She had been crying since she'd got the phone call from Moaney, but now she choked back her sobs.

'Amy!'

Moaney put Amy on the ground and she ran to Aoife. 'Mama! Mama!'

Amy held her so tight the child started squirming. Aoife loosened her grip. 'Baby, are you okay? Where have you been?'

'No baby!'

'No, of course you're not a baby. Silly Mama.' Aoife put her on the ground and crouched down beside her.

'Ow!' Amy pointed at her knee.

'Did you hurt your knee? Mama will kiss it better.'

Aoife realised Moaney was standing beside her. His smile was so wide his muscles must be aching. She looked up at him and raised her eyebrows.

'Amy spent the morning in the park, didn't you, Amy?'

'And.'

'Yes, she played in the sandpit.'

'Bold boy!'

Aoife froze.

'A big boy pushed her. Well, he was about four. Amy fell down and hurt her knee. That's when the other mothers noticed she was alone. They called the police. I had been to the crèche and checked out their CCTV. I could see Amy and a man disappearing around the corner, so I drove in this direction. I was almost at the park when I got the call, so I came straight here.'

'I cream.'

Aoife laughed. 'Yes, I can see you had ice cream.' She got out a tissue and wiped Amy's mouth. 'Who bought you ice cream, sweetie?'

'Man.'

Aoife looked at Moaney. He shook his head. 'We don't know. His face was hidden by the balloon he was carrying. Now that Amy is safe, we'll examine the tape closely. We'll be able to see his height, probably guess his age. It's not much, but it's a start.'

⤚

They were home. Aoife couldn't get warm. Could it be shock? She kept turning up the heating. She hadn't realised how hot the room was until Amy started pulling off her clothes. Aoife turned off the heating, put on a heavy jumper and gave Amy an ice cream. Amy was now sitting on the floor playing with her toy elephant. Every couple of seconds Aoife looked at her. A few hours ago she had thought her life was over. Now she was in her own kitchen and Amy was beside her. She could hardly believe it.

Her phone rang.

'Aoife, are you okay? I've only just seen all your calls. What's wrong?'

'It's nothing, Jason. False alarm. I'll tell you all about it when I see you.'

'Okay. We stopped at Nigel's and had a few drinks, so we won't be able to drive any more today. I'll see you first thing tomorrow morning.'

'See you then.'

⤚

Aoife was plugging her phone into the charger when Amy gave a loud wail. 'Hands! Hands gone!' She was pointing at the fridge, where the painting had been hanging for weeks.

'It's around somewhere. Can you help me find it?'

Amy found it in one of the kitchen cabinets. Aoife couldn't even imagine how it had ended up there. She stuck it back up on the fridge. 'Let's get you washed up for dinner.'

'No!'

'We can watch your princess movie afterwards.'

'TV?'

The doorbell rang. Amy raced into the corridor. Aoife ran after her and picked her up. She opened the door.

'Moaney! I mean Conor.'

Amy held out her arms to the detective and Aoife handed her over.

'I thought I'd check on you before I went home.'

∽

Amy demanded Moaney play with her. He and Aoife were on all fours, pretending to be horses. Amy sat on Moaney's back, shouting 'Horsy! Horsy! More! More!' After the fifth race, Aoife put a stop to it. Amy was now sitting on the floor eating a biscuit and playing with her elephant.

'I can't believe she's alright.' Aoife stood on tiptoes and kissed Moaney on the cheek. 'You'll never know how grateful I am.'

The detective's grin stretched wider than Aoife would have believed physically possible. 'I have some idea. Remember I told you I lost my young lad? He was only gone for about ten minutes, but I swear I aged ten years during that time.'

'I know what you mean. I'm surprised my hair hasn't turned grey already.' She pulled it towards her. 'At least, I hope it hasn't.'

Moaney moved closer. She'd thought Jason was tall, but the detective was at least four inches taller. Using two fingers, he gently parted her hair. 'Nope, not a grey hair in sight.' He was standing so close, Aoife could feel his breath on her face.

Amy pulled on her sleeve. 'Biccie!'

Glad of the distraction, Aoife turned to her. 'No more biccies.' Had the poor child eaten any real food today? What kind of a mother was she? She really needed to get a grip. Amy was home now. It was time they returned to normal. 'Let's get you washed up for dinner. Mo—Conor, you must be starving. Will you stay for dinner?'

'I'm fine, thanks.'

'Please, we'd like you to. Wouldn't we, Amy?'

'I cream.'

'After your dinner, Amy. Come on.' They went upstairs. Aoife had been so distracted by the day's events, she hadn't noticed how dirty Amy's clothes were. There was no point in putting her into clean clothes now. She gave Amy's face a quick wash and changed her into her pyjamas. She picked up the dirty clothes from the floor. Out of habit she checked the pockets before throwing Amy's jeans in the clothes basket. That's when she found the note: "MIND YOUR OWN BUSINESS OR THE NEXT TIME YOU WON'T GET HER BACK".

THIRTY-NINE

AOIFE'S MIND RACED as she stared at the note. Amy ran into the corridor and was halfway down the stairs when Aoife caught her. Putting one finger on Amy's lips, she carried the child back to her bedroom and put her sitting on the bed. 'Now, we're going to play a very special game, okay?'

Amy grinned and hopped up and down on the bed. 'Pay!'

'Yes, we'll play. You're going to sit here as quietly as you can. You can play with your dolls and look at your book, but if you don't move or speak until I count to twenty, you win.'

Amy looked doubtful.

'And do you know what the prize is?'

Amy shook her head.

'A big lollipop.'

'Pop!'

'Only if you can stay quiet and don't get off the bed until I count to twenty.'

She hurried out of the room. Amy had no idea how to count and she wouldn't sit still for longer than a few minutes. There was no time to waste.

'Moan—I mean Conor, I'm so sorry. Amy's fallen asleep. It was a long day for her.' She gave a fake yawn. 'To be honest,

I'm exhausted myself. I suppose it's the stress. Would you mind terribly if we left dinner to another day?'

She had barely closed the front door when Amy came running into the hall. Aoife let her watch TV while she made dinner. She didn't eat herself. She sat on the couch, staring at a kids' DVD, her arms wrapped tightly around Amy until the child fell asleep. Then she phoned Orla.

෧

Orla had driven them home from the park, made sure they were settled, then hurried off to the airport, where Cian was waiting to take her on their Italian vacation. Their plane was now boarding, and Aoife had to shout to be heard above the noise.

'Oh my God, Aoife! Who could have taken her?'

'I can't imagine.'

'Did you tell Moaney?'

'No. He'd start an investigation. Half the country would know about it in no time. I can't risk that.'

'What are we going to do?'

'The only thing I can do is stay out of the investigation. Let the police figure out who took Amy and stop trying to find Danny's murderer.'

෧

Aoife woke at six the next morning. Careful not to disturb Amy, she slipped out of bed, went downstairs and made herself some coffee. She didn't feel like eating. She didn't feel like doing much of anything. She was sitting, staring into her mug when she remembered the mess she and Orla had made of Jason's room. It was bad enough she'd have to tell her husband she thought he had stolen their daughter; the least she could do was put his room back together again.

Half an hour later, all the clothes were back in the drawers and wardrobe. Aoife sat on the floor to sort out the mess of papers and bills strewn everywhere. She dreaded to think how Jason would react to this invasion of his privacy. He'd certainly have ammunition the next time she complained he was spying on her. She pushed a credit card statement into its envelope, wincing when she glimpsed the balance—€22,914. They'd be paying that back for the rest of their lives. She blinked and pulled the statement closer. She wasn't imagining it. There in bold black ink, were the two letters that ended her marriage.

FORTY

AOIFE WAS STANDING with the credit card statement in her hand when her phone rang.

'Hi, Aoife, how are things?'

This was all she needed.

'Everything's fine, thank you, Detective.'

Moaney hesitated. 'Are you okay?'

'Fine, thank you.'

'Right.' His tone became a little more businesslike. 'I've been searching the internet, and it seems the youngest person ever to give evidence to a court was a two-year-old in England. Mind you, at that age they're only capable of answering very basic questions like who, when, etc., and we'd need a very specialised interviewer, but it's worth a shot, isn't it?'

'No.'

'What?'

'I don't want anyone asking Amy questions. She's back and she's unhurt. If nobody ever mentions yesterday, she'll forget all about it.'

'But we have to find out who took her. What if whoever it was takes another child?'

'That's not going to happen.'

'How do you know?'

'Because—because who would take a child and leave her in a park? It doesn't make any sense. It must have been somebody who was out of his mind. Maybe he'd lost his own child. It's over now and he won't do anything like that again.'

'Aoife, that's ridic—wait a minute. You know who took Amy, don't you?'

'Of course I don't.'

'What did Amy tell you?'

'You spent half yesterday with her. You know the only thing she talks about is ice cream and a big boy knocking her down.'

'Something happened after I left. Are you scared, Aoife? Has someone threatened to hurt Amy?'

'I don't know what you're talking about, Detective. If you don't mind, I've got to go. I've a lot to do today.'

'You can trust me, Aoife. Whatever you're scared of, I'll help you. I won't let anyone hurt Amy.'

For a moment Aoife was tempted to tell him everything. No, it was too risky. 'Detective Moloney, I'm more grateful than I can say for everything you've done, but as you saw for yourself, Amy is fine and we won't be needing your help any longer. Goodbye.'

After disconnecting the call, Aoife checked on Amy. Still asleep. She hoped Amy wouldn't wake up before Jason arrived back. Theirs would be a conversation she didn't want her daughter to overhear.

⁕

'CR, Jason. It says CR.'

'You went through my stuff?'

'CR! You're twenty-two thousand, nine hundred and

fourteen euros in credit. In credit! We couldn't afford to go to marriage counselling, I've been scrimping and saving on everything I could think of and you were twenty-two thousand, nine hundred and fourteen euros in credit.'

'Aoife, I—'

'All this time, you've been lying to me. You told me the direct debit to your credit card was part of a repayment plan agreed with the credit card company and the entire time you were saving the money for yourself. Do you have any idea how worried I've been about finances?'

'I wasn't keeping it for myself. I was saving it for us.'

'Liar!' Aoife remembered Amy. She took deep breaths, trying to control her anger. *Speak calmly and rationally*, she told herself. Lowering her voice, she said, 'If you were saving the money, Jason, you would have put it in a bank account. You were hiding it away because as long as I believed we had no money, I was tied to the house. You could say you needed the car at any time. I couldn't afford a social life. You had me exactly where you wanted me. Best of all, you could convince me you weren't able to afford your own place, so there you were, right under my nose, where you could monitor everything I did.'

'I only did it because I love you. I can't bear the thought of losing you.'

'Yeah? Well, you'd better get used to it.'

'You're angry now, but in time you'll see that everything I did was to keep our family together. To give Amy a home with two parents and—'

'That's not going to work anymore, Jason. You can't guilt me into living with you. I'm going to a lawyer first thing tomorrow. The sooner we're divorced the better.'

'Aoife, you don't mean that. You—'

'Get out.'

'What?'

'I want you out of this house. Now. Don't pack your things. I'll send them on.'

'Where will I go?'

'I don't give a damn. Use your twenty-two thousand, nine hundred and fourteen euros to rent a hotel room. Go on a world cruise for all I care, just get out of my sight right now.'

๛

The locksmith was pulling out of the driveway when Maura arrived.

'I wondered how long it would be before you turned up. He went running back to Mummy, did he?'

'You changed the locks?'

'Yes.' She stopped herself from saying, "And you're not going to be my emergency keyholder any longer either."

'Can I come in, Aoife? Just for a minute? I don't blame you for being angry. I'm furious myself. I've been giving Jason money, you know. And it's not like I can afford it.'

Aoife felt her rage lessen.

'I'm sorry, Maura. I didn't mean to take it out on you. Of course you can come in. How much money did you give him?'

'Five hundred euros a month since you separated. He said he'll pay it back. Claims he never wanted it in the first place and that it was I who insisted on giving it to him.'

'Did you?'

'Yes, but only because he told me all his money went to you and the credit card company. He even had the cheek to tell me he hadn't lied to me because most of his money actually was going to the credit card company. I had to get out of the house before I strangled him.' She perched on a kitchen stool. 'How are you doing?'

'You mean am I having second thoughts? No, Maura. I'm not. I let you talk me into giving our marriage a second chance last year. I won't make that mistake again. Our relationship is over. I gave him every chance. Now I'm done with him. End of.'

'Well, I had to try. He's still my son.'

'And he's still Amy's father. You're still her grandmother. I want her to have a good relationship with both of you. I just can't see him for a while.'

'We'll sort something out, Aoife. You're not the first couple to split up. Everything will work out in the end.'

∽

Much as she had wanted Jason to move out, the house felt weird without him. She couldn't phone Orla again. Orla needed to get away from everything. She'd put her own grief aside when Aoife needed her, but it would be a long time before she got over Tadhg's death. If she and Cian were going to last, they needed time together without Aoife bothering them with her problems. The good thing about them being abroad was Aoife could now work from home. It meant she didn't have to find childcare for Amy. It also meant she hadn't spoken to another adult in the four days since Maura's visit. Or left the house.

She looked out at Amy, who was running up and down the back garden, chasing a butterfly. It wasn't fair to keep her cooped up. A trip to the playground ought to be safe enough. Maybe Alison would come too. She could do with some adult company.

∽

Alison hadn't been home and she wasn't answering her phone,

so Aoife stood in the almost-deserted playground and pushed Amy on the baby swing. She was going to have to buy a swing set. Another thing she'd been putting off because she'd thought they had no money. Her blood pressure started to rise, and she took deep breaths to calm herself.

She eventually coaxed Amy off the swing, and they were walking home when a car pulled up beside them.

'Can I give you a lift?'

'No, thank you, Detective.'

'Moaney!' Amy cried, struggling to get out of the stroller.

'Hi, Amy.' Moaney parked the car and joined them. 'Okay if I walk with you?'

'It's a public road, Detective. You can walk wherever you like.'

'Have I done something to annoy you, Aoife? I thought we were becoming friends.'

'You haven't annoyed me, and I don't mean to be unfriendly, but I have to think of Amy's best interests and I won't allow anyone to question her.'

'I heard about a woman who's very experienced in interviewing young children. Amy wouldn't be upset. I wouldn't even suggest this if I thought there was the slightest chance that could happen.'

Talking over Amy's loud protests at being confined to the stroller, Aoife said, 'Detective, I've made up my mind and you can't talk me out of it.'

'I think you're making a mistake.'

Aoife didn't reply. She walked a little faster but Moaney easily kept pace. Amy was now bawling. Aoife lifted her from the stroller. Amy held her hands out to Moaney.

Moaney tickled her under the chin, which made Amy more determined to get to him. Her entire body arched away from

Aoife. Aoife tried to put her back in the stroller, but Amy locked all her muscles. 'Amy, stop it!'

'Let me help.'

'No. We'd be fine if you'd just leave us alone.'

'Aoife, please.'

He leaned towards Amy, whose screeches were now so loud they were attracting the attention of passers-by. Aoife stepped away to allow him to pick her up.

'Horsy, horsy!' a delighted Amy demanded.

Damn it. She should have known that was what Amy wanted. Moaney put Amy on his shoulders and ran a few steps down the road. He came back immediately.

'More! More!'

Moaney ran down the street again, taking small hops into the air every few minutes. He looked ridiculous. Aoife couldn't help smiling. He kept it up the entire way to their front door, running slightly ahead, then running back, never getting more than a few feet ahead of her.

'Horsy is tired now,' Aoife said when they reached the front door. Moaney put Amy on the ground and she raced into the house. 'Thank you,' Aoife said. 'Amy enjoyed that.'

'I think she might turn out to be a showjumper.'

'I hope not. That's a really expensive hobby.' Aoife stood, waiting for him to leave.

Amy came running out to the hall with her sippy cup. 'Drink!' Moaney grinned and bent down to take the cup from her. He took a sip.

'More!'

'I think this particular horsy would prefer coffee.' Aoife took the cup from the detective. 'Will you help me make some coffee, Amy?'

'Yeah.'

Amy ran ahead into the kitchen and Moaney and Aoife followed.

Amy handed the coffee to Aoife. Aoife turned on the percolator, then went into the sitting room and switched on the TV. For good measure, she handed Amy a packet of chocolate stars and left her sitting in front of her favourite movie. Leaving the interconnecting door open, Aoife re-joined Moaney in the kitchen.

'She's soon going to associate you with TV and sweeties. She'll insist you come home with us every time she sees you.'

'I can think of worse things to do with my time.'

'You're great with kids. Your son is very lucky.'

'I doubt he'd agree with you. He's at the "my dad is an idiot" stage.'

'I suppose they all go through that. Is it just you, or is he the same with his mother?'

'He has a better relationship with Katie. It helps that she's a lot more easy-going.'

'In what way?'

'Well, take our latest problem. I want Blaine to choose sensible subjects for his O levels. Katie says let him do whatever interests him.'

'Why is he doing O levels? Doesn't he live in Ireland?'

'No, he and Katie live in England.'

'I didn't realise you were divorced.'

'We're not. We never married. It's an odd situation. I worry what effect it's having on Blaine, but he seems to be handling it okay.'

'I worry about Amy too. When Jason and I split up, I thought—'

'You split up from your husband? When?'

'Last year.'

'He doesn't live here?'

'No. He moved out when we split up, but then he moved into the spare room for economic reasons. He moved out again yesterday. I have an appointment with a lawyer next week to get the divorce started.'

'I'm sorry. That must be difficult.'

'It was very hard when we first split up, but this sharing a house wasn't working. A divorce is best for everyone. It's like they say: "Marry in haste, repent in leisure".'

'Is that what your parents said when you told them you were getting married?'

'No. My parents died in a car crash when I was eighteen. I don't think Jason and I would ever have got together if they'd lived. I felt so alone after their death and Jason was the only person who seemed to understand.' She gave an embarrassed smile. 'Sorry. I didn't mean to bore you with my life story. How did your parents react to the news that you were going to be a teenage parent?'

'They didn't know. I didn't know myself until Blaine was seven. When my holiday was over I had to go home. Katie continued her world tour. We stayed in touch for a few weeks, but when she found out she was pregnant, she cut off all contact and went back to Australia. I doubt she would have told me at all if it wasn't for her husband. When she got pregnant with their child, he insisted she tell me about Blaine.'

'That must have been a shock.'

'Completely changed my life. I wasn't long out of college, drifting around without any real plans, and suddenly I'm the father of a seven-year-old. I joined the police force a few months later.'

'Were you angry she hadn't told you?'

'Not at first. I was just shocked. Later, as I got to know Blaine, I really resented that I'd missed seven years of his life.'

'Why did she keep it a secret?'

'She said I was only a teenager and I lived in Ireland. When she married an English guy, she and Blaine moved countries. It made custody less problematic. She'd been afraid of ending up in a custody battle with someone living in a different continent.'

'Well, I can see that would be a problem. Still—'

'Yeah, well, it's done now. Holding a grudge won't change anything.' He paused. They sat in what Aoife thought was a companionable silence until the detective said, 'Aoife, why won't you allow Amy to be interviewed?'

Aoife stiffened. 'I already explained my decision.'

'There's something you're not telling me.'

The doorbell rang and Aoife jumped up. 'That's probably Alison.'

⁓

Alison explained that she'd been in town when Aoife had phoned, and they agreed to talk later. After closing the door, Aoife leaned her back against it, trying to think of a plausible explanation that would satisfy Moaney. She could hear him in the sitting room chatting with Amy.

'Amy, I have a really nice friend who wants to meet you. Would you like that?'

'Yeah.'

Amy felt her blood boil. How dare he!

She threw open the sitting room door.

'Detective, could I speak to you for a moment, please?'

He joined her in the corridor. 'Aoife, I only asked—'

Aoife opened the front door.

'Leave now, please.'

'What? All I said was—'

'Detective Moloney, if you want to enter my house again, you will need a search warrant. If you want to speak to me, you will need to place me under arrest. Unless you're prepared to do either or both of those things right now, leave my house this instant.'

The detective took one step outside the door. He turned to face her. 'Aoife—'

She shut the door in his face.

FORTY-ONE

Mrs Weston visited Aoife a few days after Amy's return. She took full responsibility for the incident, explained the procedures she had implemented to ensure nothing like that could ever happen again and offered Aoife six months' free childcare. She didn't seem surprised when Aoife refused.

Aoife tried to settle into a post-crèche routine. She had hoped Cian would allow her to bring Amy to work. He didn't. 'I'm sorry, Aoife but this house isn't set up for a child. I have to take down paintings from time to time. I can't be worrying a kid will get her hands on them. And you can see for yourself all the expensive furniture.' He pointed at a corner of his office. 'That lamp alone cost more than your yearly salary. It just wouldn't work.'

As a compromise, Cian agreed Aoife could work from home one day a week, which effectively meant she worked from Amy's bedtime until 2 a.m., but it was better than nothing. Alison agreed to take payment for one day's childcare and Maura took Amy on her day off. Alison didn't know about the threat Aoife had received, but she knew the man who had stolen Amy hadn't yet been apprehended. She kept a very close eye on both Amy and her own kids and never allowed any of them out of her sight. Aoife told Maura that Amy was going through a stage of running away and was getting good at opening doors. Maura immediately had bolts put on all her doors and promised she would watch Amy carefully.

Aoife was able to return to her job at the halfway house. She felt guilty about the way she'd been treating Jack. She hadn't been able to go to work the previous week because she still hadn't sorted out her childcare arrangements. Jack would have understood if she'd told him about Amy's disappearance, but she couldn't do that. She didn't want Maura to know. Maura would insist on telling Jason, and Jason would find some way of using it against her. For the first time ever, she'd lied to an employer and said she was sick. The guilt was eating away at her. It seemed a particularly dreadful thing to do when he'd been so understanding about Amy's illness and while he was still struggling with his grief.

Jack rarely came to the halfway house anymore. On the two occasions she'd seen him since Tadhg's death, he'd been very subdued. Maura said he'd lost all interest in the charity and that on the odd day he came into the office, he spent his time staring into space. There was a growing pile of papers on his desk marked "Urgent" which he completely ignored.

Aoife was halfway through her day when she took some papers into Jack's office. She jumped. 'God, Jack, you frightened me. I didn't hear you come in.'

'I've been here since seven a.m.' He pointed at the pile of papers he was working his way through. 'I'm a little behind.'

He seemed almost like his old self. The strain was gone from his face. He appeared rested. There was no sign of the cigarettes he puffed constantly when he was under stress. Most surprisingly of all, he was smiling at her.

'It's good to see you looking so much better, Jack.'

Jack's phone rang and he glanced at it. 'That's Orla. She came here yesterday and insisted I go to lunch with her. When I refused, she sat in that chair and said she wasn't leaving without me.'

'Oh no! Do you want me to have a word with her?'

Jack shrugged. 'I don't think you could keep her away. She's decided Tadhg would have wanted her to take care of me. I have a feeling once Orla makes up her mind, it's not easily changed.'

'I could try.'

'There's no need. I finally gave in and I quite enjoyed our lunch. I've decided Orla will be the exception to my "no women" policy. I like having her around. She reminds me a little of Tadhg—quite unique. It's no wonder she turned Tadhg's head. If Orla had been around when I was eighteen, she'd have turned my head as well. I might never have become a priest.'

'Really?'

He laughed 'No, I'm joking. The decision to become a priest was made for me when I was nine. I was barely aware women existed.'

'Nine! That's crazy.'

'It wasn't unusual in my day. Those of us who didn't come from money had very few choices. Free education ended at fourteen. If you were any way bright, you were shoved into the priesthood.'

'Because the priests paid for your education?'

'Partly, but also because it was considered a huge honour. Hard though it is to believe now, I was considered one of the lucky ones.'

'Did your mother agree?'

'To my mother, and indeed to most people back then, priests were like gods. She'd had a terrible few years, and in her mind, this was God's way of making everything okay.'

'It must have been hard on her when your father died so young.'

'It was, but things got a lot worse when my father's family threw us off the farm.'

'They left you homeless?'

Jack nodded.

'I cannot believe the things people will do for money. You were their flesh and blood.'

'Those few worthless acres in the middle of nowhere meant far more to them. Their family had farmed the land since at least the 1700s, probably a lot earlier. They'd managed to hang in there during the famine, bought it from the landlord when the Land Acts were introduced, survived the Great Depression and all the depressions since. They had no intention of letting it fall into the hands of someone like my mother.'

'Why didn't they like her?'

'Have you ever heard the saying "she came with both arms swinging"?'

Aoife shook her head.

'It's what farmers used to say about people like my mother who brought nothing to the marriage. No land, no money. In other words, completely worthless. The family couldn't wait to get rid of her.'

'And there was nothing your mum could do?'

'Nothing at all. It was quite common before the law was changed to allow women an automatic right to a portion of their dead husbands' property. Nobody cared about people like us. That's partly the reason I set up this charity. For all its faults, the Church ensured I didn't starve. Nobody else cares if these guys end up on the street or die in an alley like Tadhg.'

'Tadhg often said what a great person you were.'

Jack grunted. 'For all the good I did him.'

'You tried and he appreciated it.'

'Clearly I didn't try hard enough. I'm delaying you, Aoife. I'm sorry. I'm sure you have a lot of work.'

He turned his back on her and walked to the window. Aoife saw him raise his hand to his eyes. She was pretty sure he was wiping away tears.

FORTY-TWO

THE FOLLOWING MORNING Aoife got a text from Detective Moloney. 'I promised to keep you informed on the investigation, so I'm letting you know that I will be visiting your mother-in-law this morning.'

What should she do? When she thought of that scumbag sitting in her kitchen, pretending to be friendly, when all the time he'd just wanted to question Amy, it made her want to smash something. But who knew what disaster he was about to spring on Maura now? She couldn't let Maura face him alone.

Maura answered the door.

Aoife was sitting at the kitchen table waiting for them. The detective nodded at her. Aoife looked away.

When Maura was seated the detective said, 'The re-enactment of your husband's disappearance was replayed on TV on Monday night. Shortly afterwards a message was left on our Confidential Line. A man claimed he saw your husband talking to Eimear O'Leary.'

'Oh no!' Maura covered her mouth with her hand.

Aoife was determined to avoid any interaction with the detective. She turned to Maura. 'Who?'

'Another of the missing girls we assumed Buckley murdered,' Moaney answered.

Aoife glared at him, but he didn't appear to notice.

'Mrs Walsh, I must stress that this information came from an anonymous caller. We can't corroborate anything, but for the moment, we're working on the assumption that the information is correct.'

Aoife expected another explosion, but all Maura said was 'Why?'

'The caller gave a lot of details. He described how both parties were dressed—'

'He could have got that from TV.'

'Correct. He said they registered with him because they seemed so mismatched. Your husband wore a business suit. The girl was very casually dressed and the ends of her hair were dyed pink. At one stage your husband put his arm around Eimear. The caller said he wondered about their relationship as your husband seemed too old to be Eimear's boyfriend but too young to be her father. When news of Eimear's disappearance made the papers, he recognised her immediately.'

Aoife couldn't help herself. 'Why did he wait until now to say anything?'

The detective's expression, when he turned to her, was unreadable. 'The caller said he phoned the police. Someone took a message but nobody followed up on it. When he read in the newspaper that Eimear had been seen several times later that day, he assumed the police believed the incident he witnessed was unimportant.'

Maura stood. 'Thank you for telling me, Detective. I agree with the first investigation team. If the anonymous caller is telling the truth, which I doubt, then the missing girl was seen several times after she spoke to my husband. Clearly my husband had no involvement in her disappearance.'

Detective Moloney followed her to the door. 'One thing I should remind you is that we never found any connection between Eimear and Buckley. Now we have a link between your husband and a second of the missing girls.'

'Excuse me, Detective, you have no such thing. An anonymous phone call is not evidence.'

'You are correct, but I didn't say evidence, Mrs Walsh, I said we had a link. Your husband has been linked to a second of the missing girls by a member of the public. Unless you or a member of your family have been telling people that we are concerned there may be a connection between the cases, the odds of a stranger linking them must be astronomical.'

Maura showed Moaney to the door. When she came back to the kitchen, she looked at Aoife. Neither said anything. Maura sat down and buried her head in her hands.

'Whoever the anonymous caller is, he's lying,' Aoife said.

'The detective is right. How could a stranger know the police had connected Danny and Buckley?'

'He wouldn't have to know. He's just some lunatic causing trouble. He's seen Danny's name in the paper. He knows Eimear went missing around that time. If he was telling the truth, why didn't he leave his contact details? Or even give his name?'

'Maybe he can't afford to get involved with the police. He might be a criminal.'

'Then why did he contact the police fifteen years ago? Forget about him, Maura. He's a crank. Nothing more.'

FORTY-THREE

'I TELL YOU, Orla. I've had my fill of detectives. They are the most unscrupulous, self-satisfied, obnoxious, two-faced scum I've ever come across.'

Orla perched on the edge of Aoife's desk.

'Don't I know. Remember the guy who's investigating Tadhg's murder? He's practically stalking me. Four times yesterday he phoned me and he didn't have a single piece of relevant information.'

'Well, I could see that coming.'

'Me too, but I hoped he'd find Tadhg's murderer first. I don't think he's even trying.'

'What are you going to do?'

'Cian came up with a great idea. He said someone must have seen Tadhg's body being dumped in that alley. The only people who hang around there at night are drug addicts, and it's hardly surprising they didn't admit seeing anything. But what's the most important thing to addicts?'

'Drugs?'

'Money. Cian's going to offer a one-thousand-euro award for information leading to the arrest of Tadhg's murderer. That will be far more effective than anything that useless detective could do.'

᷼

Two days later Aoife was woken at 7 a.m. by a text from Maura. *That detective phoned. He says he wants to speak to me again today. Can you come around?*

Twice in one week! Surely that had to be police harassment? At the very least it was bullying. Aoife was quite looking forward to seeing Detective Moloney again. It was time somebody stood up to him for a change.

᷼

Detective Moloney got straight to the point.

'What is your connection to Angela Power?'

Maura shook her head. 'I don't know anybody by that name.'

The detective produced a photo of a girl in her twenties wearing a light pink suit with enormous shoulder pads.

Maura examined it carefully. 'When was this photo taken, Detective?'

'Twenty-five years ago.'

'It doesn't ring any bells. I know she's not one of the missing girls because I've been reading up on them. Who is she?'

'We believe she's the person who posted you the envelope of cash.'

'Really? Why would she send me money?'

'We haven't been able to interview her. She's on holiday in Australia. Apparently, her son lives there and he organised a family reunion. They're all touring the country and aren't expected back for another five weeks.'

'How do you know she was the person who sent the money?'

'The English authorities managed to trace the post office from which the envelope was posted. We know the date it was sent, so we went through the CCTV footage for the entire day. All the evidence points to Angela Power being the person we're looking for.'

Maura examined the photo again. 'I don't know her. Is she Irish?'

'She was born in Ireland. She emigrated to England in her twenties. Are you sure you've never seen her before? Did you know her before she emigrated?'

'I certainly didn't know her well, and I don't remember the face. Did she live locally?'

'Tell me, Mrs Walsh, how would you describe your relationship with your mother-in-law?'

Maura blinked. 'My mother-in-law? We've had practically no contact since my husband disappeared. She believed Danny walked out because I cheated on him. I didn't, of course,' she added hastily, 'but Bridget believed that was the only possible explanation for Danny deserting his family.'

'How did she react to your wedding? You were pregnant at the time, isn't that correct?'

Maura stiffened. 'That is correct, Detective.'

'And, as I understand it, unmarried mothers weren't too popular back then. Families frowned on that kind of thing, correct?'

Maura nodded.

'Did your own family come to your wedding?'

'No, they did not. What has this to do with anything?'

The detective continued as if she hadn't spoken. 'Did your husband's family attend the wedding?'

'Yes.'

'Was it a large wedding?'

Maura sighed. 'No.'

'So it's safe to say the only people who attended were close family and friends. There were no distant relatives or people you barely knew.'

'No.'

The detective withdrew another photo from the folder. 'Do you recognise this photo?'

Maura gasped. Aoife leaned over her shoulder to get a good look. The first photo had been cropped. In this photo, Angela was part of a small group. There were six people in total, all in their teens and twenties. In the centre were Maura and Danny. It was their wedding photo.

FORTY-FOUR

MAURA'S VOICE SHOOK as she stared at the photo. 'She wasn't a friend of mine.'

'Was she a friend of your husband?'

'I don't know. I don't remember ever meeting her.'

'But she was at your wedding, and you just said only close family and friends attended your wedding.'

'Where did you get this photo?'

'Your mother-in-law gave it to us.'

Maura held the photo to the light. 'Is it genuine? Could Angela Power have been Photoshopped into the picture?'

The detective raised his eyebrows. 'It's genuine. We had it checked. Let me ask you again, Mrs Walsh. What is your connection to Angela Power?'

'I don't know her. I don't ever remember seeing her before.'

'We've already agreed that only close friends and family were at your wedding. Was Angela Power a close friend of your husband?'

'Maybe she was and I don't remember. Maybe she's a distant relative or a friend of my mother-in-law.'

'But you just said your mother-in-law didn't invite people to your wedding. She wasn't of the generation that would want her family and friends witnessing her visibly pregnant daughter-in-law getting married.'

Aoife stood up. She folded her arms and glared at the detective. Who the hell did he think he was? She made a conscious effort to keep her tone as frosty as possible. 'What exactly are you implying, Detective?'

Again, she was unable to read his expression.

'I'm not implying anything. I am saying that we believe this woman, Angela Power, posted your mother-in-law an envelope full of cash. I am asking your mother-in-law what her connection is with this woman.'

'And she has told you there is none.'

'Correct. And I asked why a woman your mother-in-law has never seen would attend a small family wedding.'

As Aoife moved closer, the detective rose to his feet. Damn him! He was trying to intimidate her. 'And my mother-in-law has told you she doesn't know that either.'

'Correct.' He turned to Maura. 'Perhaps you would like to give a little thought to your relationship with Angela Power. When you remember the connection, Mrs Walsh, you can contact me at the station.'

≪

'Don't you remember her at all, Maura?'

Maura shook her head. 'I suppose someone must have introduced us if she was in the wedding picture. It was twenty-five years ago, Aoife. And let me tell you, that was not the most relaxing day of my life. What with Bridget glaring at me and pulling the younger kids away if they even tried to talk to me. I swear, she all but hung a "Whore of Babylon" sign on my back.' Maura picked up the picture the detective had left behind and examined it for the hundredth time. 'One thing I'm certain of. Angela Power was never a friend of mine.'

'Bridget will know who she is.'

Maura groaned. 'Oh hell! Did she specifically pick out that photo to give to the detective or was she asked to provide family photos and that just happened to be one of them? Either way, the police have obviously spoken to her. There isn't anything that woman wouldn't say to get me charged with murdering her Danny.'

'She might hate you, Maura, but she wouldn't lie to the police.'

Maura snorted. 'You don't even know her. You have no idea what she's capable of.'

'Do you really believe she would frame you?'

Maura stood up. 'Maybe not, but she'd definitely put the most unpleasant slant on everything. I need to lie down, Aoife. Can you let yourself out?'

<hr>

Aoife's heart thumped as she knocked on Bridget's door. She really didn't want to do this. What if Bridget refused to speak to her? Aoife felt her resolve strengthen. She would not stand by while Amy's grandmother was arrested. If Bridget wouldn't let her inside, they'd have their conversation on the doorstep. If necessary, she'd shout through the letter box. Bridget struck her as the kind of person who wouldn't want the neighbours knowing her business. Aoife was about to knock a second time when she heard feet shuffling down the corridor. Bridget peeked through the spyhole, then opened the door.

'Mrs Walsh, hi, do you remember me?'

'My brain still functions, thank you.'

'I'm sorry, I didn't mean to insult you. Can we speak?'

The old woman held open the door and led the way to the sitting room. She sat down in her armchair, pointed to the couch and sat in stony silence.

'I'm sorry to bother you,' Aoife began. 'I need your help.'

'You mean "that one" needs my help.'

'Bridget, I know you don't like Maura. I know you think she had something to do with Danny's death. But what harm can come of investigating Danny's murder properly? If Maura's guilty, the police will handle it.'

Bridget snorted.

'But if she's not guilty, do you really want the police arresting her? Think what that would do to Danny's sons. Would Danny have wanted you to help the police convict Maura of a crime she had no involvement in?'

This time Bridget's snort held less conviction. 'What do you want from me?'

Aoife withdrew the wedding photo from her bag. 'Do you know this woman?'

Bridget frowned. 'Why is everyone so interested in Angela Power all of a sudden?'

'How do you know her?'

'I don't.'

'You knew her name.'

'The police told me. They wanted to know why she was at Danny's wedding.'

'What did you tell them?'

'I've always tried to forget that dreadful day. But when Danny disappeared, I went looking for every photo of him that I could find. These were in an envelope at the back of a desk.' She pointed at the group photo. 'My husband must have taken that one. I was very careful not to take any showing 'that one's' big stomach.'

'How did Angela Power end up in the photo?'

'The detective asked me the same question. You tell me the truth, girl. Why is everyone asking me that?'

'The police think Angela Power sent Maura some money.'

'When?'

'Maybe every month since Danny died. The police are convinced she sent the final envelope at least. Angela's touring Australia at the moment, so they haven't been able to interview her. They want to know why someone Maura doesn't remember would send her money.'

Bridget smiled. 'So now it's all coming out.' She eased herself from the armchair and left the room without a word. Aoife could hear her in the kitchen. A few minutes later she returned with a tray and two cups of tea. 'Help yourself to milk and sugar.' She sipped her own tea, then put down the mug. 'That slut turned up here not long after Danny left. She waved an envelope of cash in my face. She said Danny had sent her money, that all this time she'd been worried sick about him and obviously he was perfectly fine. She insisted he must be in contact with me and demanded I tell her where he was.' Bridget nodded grimly. 'I knew immediately the money wasn't from my Danny. The police might have believed he was involved in the bank robbery, but I knew that was nonsense. I didn't raise any thieves. Now the thing we need to find out is why Angela Power sent money to that slut. Once we know that, we'll have the full story.'

'Could one of your kids have invited Angela?'

'When the detective asked me, I phoned the boys but they all said they had no idea who she was.'

'Did you check with Elaine?'

'Elaine was nine at the time. She wasn't issuing wedding invitations to anyone.'

'Maybe Jack invited her?'

'Jack was working in Africa back then. I put off telling him about the wedding as long as possible. The less people who knew about our disgrace the better. Jack didn't find out about it until he came home on holidays.' She pointed a finger at Aoife. 'I'll tell you the same thing I told that detective. The only person who could have invited Angela Power was the slut.'

'Bridget, I really wish you wouldn't speak about Maura like that. She was just a kid when she got pregnant. That doesn't make her evil.'

'Oh, she's pulled the wool over your eyes alright. She was always good at that. She's done the same to Jack. You're both too innocent to see what she's really like.'

Aoife smiled. 'I doubt Jack's innocent.'

'He knows the world, there's no doubting that. He spent his life amongst the desperately poor and needy, but he's not clever about people. If he was, he'd know "that one" was no good. I knew it the minute I met her.' She sniffed. 'I didn't even have to meet her. I knew it when Danny told me about their fight. Did "that one" tell you about their fight?'

'Maura said she and Danny weren't speaking by the time she discovered she was pregnant. She didn't say why.'

'She wouldn't, would she? Well, I'll tell you why. She saw Danny with another girl. They were only talking, but "that one" had a fit. She told my Danny that if he ever contacted her again, she'd have him arrested for statutory rape. Statutory rape! She was three weeks short of her sixteenth birthday when they—were intimate, and there was only eighteen months between them. Statutory rape is meant to protect girls from adults, not other kids.' She shook her head. 'I knew then what kind of a slut she was. Of course Danny was beside himself, but I was glad. After a threat like that I knew. Danny would never contact the whore again. If only she hadn't got pregnant, she'd have been out of our lives forever.'

The old woman threw a shovelful of coal on the fire. Aoife removed her cardigan. It was the middle of the summer, for God's sake. The room was like a furnace.

'If the slut had been sending money to Angela Power, I could have understood it,' Bridget said. 'She might have seen something and was bribing the whore.' She took another sip of her tea. 'But at least the police are still investigating "that one." I thought they'd given up on her.'

'I think we all assumed they were concentrating on the Buckley angle.'

'What Buckley angle?'

'The guy who was arrested for murdering all those girls who disappeared years ago.'

'I know who Buckley is. What have those girls got to do with your mother-in-law?'

'Nothing. I'm sure they've nothing to do with Danny either. But the link made the police wonder if there was some connection.'

Bridget put her hand to her head. 'What are you talking about?'

'Didn't you see the re-enactment on TV?'

'Danny's disappearance? Of course I did. What has that to do with Buckley and missing girls?'

'Nobody told you?'

Bridget raised her voice. 'Told me what? For heaven's sake! What are you talking about? What has my Danny got to do with Buckley and missing girls?'

Oh my God! It had never even occurred to her that Bridget wasn't being kept fully informed on the investigation.

'The police think Buckley and Danny might have been partners.'

The cup slid from Bridget's hands and tea seeped into the red carpet. Bridget didn't notice. Aoife grabbed a bunch of tissues and tried to clean up the mess. Bridget's hand clamped down on her arm. Her voice shook. 'People are saying that Danny, my Danny, was a murderer? That he murdered young girls? They're saying my boy was a monster?'

'The police know Buckley murdered some of the girls, but they can't link him to all of them. Two girls they can't connect him to are Triona and Eimear. Witnesses have come forward to say both girls were seen with Danny shortly before they disappeared. The only reason everyone believed Buckley murdered all the girls was because no girls went missing after his arrest. But Danny disappeared around the same time.'

The older woman's face turned purple. 'Jack knows this, doesn't he?'

Aoife nodded.

'You wait until I see him. How dare he keep this from me! How dare people even suggest my Danny would do such a terrible thing!' She continued in that vein for almost ten minutes. 'And I bet "that one" was delighted. Anything to put the police off her track.'

'Maura was furious when the police told her. She threw the detective out of her house.'

'Mmm.' The old woman almost smiled. 'Well, anybody who knew Danny must know it's nonsense.' She took another sip of tea. 'Still, I'll admit it, that's more than I expected from her.' She paused. 'Unless it's all an act, of course.'

FORTY-FIVE

AOIFE DIDN'T HAVE time for this. She withdrew a wedding album from her bag.

'This is Maura's wedding album. The photo with Angela Power isn't in it. Do you have other photos that aren't here?'

Maura left the room and returned with a photo album more than twice the size of Maura's. The earlier ones were of a baby and a young boy. As Aoife flicked through them, she realised the entire album was devoted to Danny. When she reached the wedding photos, Aoife examined each one carefully. There were only ten. Maura wasn't in six of them. In the four photos that included Maura, only her back was visible. One photo showed the couple standing at the altar. Only the priest faced the camera. He had his hand raised in a blessing and was smiling down at the young couple. *A priest smiling at a 'fallen woman'?*

'Who's the priest?'

'That's Brian Connolly. He lived locally and he was in the seminary with Jack. When I heard Brian was home for the holidays, I asked him if he'd perform the ceremony. The less people who saw "that one" with her huge stomach, the better.' She shuddered. 'When I think of the looks the neighbours gave us when a grandchild suddenly appeared. The disgrace "that one" brought on this family. I'm telling you, "that one" is no good. I don't know where Angela Power fits into it, but your mother-in-law killed my boy. I'm as certain of that as I am of my own name.'

FORTY-SIX

SATURDAY MORNING AOIFE woke early. She spent an hour googling Angela Power before Amy woke. She guessed Angela would be about fifty now. She'd heard fifty-year-olds were the Facebook crowd, so she logged in and flicked through 'Angela Power' profiles. It was a waste of time. There were too many possibilities. Why couldn't Angela's mother have given her a more distinctive name? She felt a stab of guilt when she remembered her own daughter's name was hardly unique. This was a waste of a Saturday. She'd never find Angela. All she knew about her was that she lived in England. She had no idea what Angela even looked like now.

The good weather was long gone, but at least it wasn't raining. Aoife decided to take Amy to the park. They no longer went near the park close to the crèche. Aoife couldn't bear the sight of it. But there was a small park in the centre of the town where Amy could play on the swings.

Aoife was pushing the stroller through the town when Cian and Orla rounded the corner, hand in hand.

'Aoife!' Orla bent down to hug Amy. 'Hey, Amy.'

'Whing!'

'What?'

'Amy's going to play on the swings,' Aoife explained.

'You're on your way to the park? That's nice. Cian and I are going to have a pub lunch.' She turned to Aoife. 'Can you believe that? I'm actually going to have my lunch in a pub.'

Aoife grinned. 'Oh, how the mighty have fallen.'

Cian laughed. He put his arm around Orla. 'We'd better hurry or there won't be any seats left.'

Amy held out her arms. 'I cream.'

Orla laughed. 'I don't have any ice cream with me.'

'I cream!'

'No ice cream,' Aoife said. 'We're going to the park, remember? You're going to have a great time on the swings.'

'Whing! Whing!'

'That's right.' She turned on a kids' app on her phone and handed it to Amy, who grabbed it eagerly. 'You look different, Orla. Did you cut your hair?'

'Four whole inches. I needed a new look. It's time I got my life sorted, and my hair was the first step.'

'It's good to see you looking happier. You must call to the house someday. Give us a chance to talk properly.'

'I'll try, but it's getting close to my exams and it's hard to fit in college and Cian, especially when he lives all the way out here in the sticks. You really have to help me talk him into moving to Dublin.'

Cian pulled Orla closer and kissed her briefly on the lips. 'You know I'd do almost anything for you, Orla. But I was born in that house and that house is where I will die. You take me on, you take my house too.'

'See what I mean, Aoife? I'm doomed to spending the rest of my life commuting.'

Cian looked pleased but shocked. Aoife was a little shocked

too. Orla saw Cian as a lifetime commitment? She would never have believed it.

'I cream! I cream!' Amy demanded.

'We'd better go before she screams the place down. Give me a call, Orla.'

'Sure.' Orla put her arm around Cian's waist and they turned into Flanagan's pub. A few minutes later, Aoife's phone pinged with a message from Orla. *Link to apartment overlooking Stephen's Green. Going to talk Cian into buying it. Wish me luck.*

Was Orla serious about settling down with Cian, or was she pretending to stronger feelings than she felt so he'd buy an apartment in the city?

❧

When Aoife arrived at work on Monday morning, she knew immediately that Orla's plan hadn't worked. There was no sign of Orla, and Cian was in a foul mood. He'd complained about the time she arrived—she was eight minutes late—and was now insisting she'd lost an email he sent her.

'You didn't email it to me, Cian. I'm certain of it.'

'Yes, I did, Aoife. It took me ages to put all the information together. I remember it was the weekend we went to Cannes. I typed it in the business lounge in the airport.'

'Well, it never came to me. Check your sent emails. Is it there?'

Aoife waited while Cian scanned his sent box.

'I know it's here somewhere,' he muttered.

'Try your drafts box.'

She was looking over his shoulder and spotted the email before he did.

'There it is! I knew I'd typed it. I'll send it to you now, Aoife.

I know you're taking a half day, but I need you to do this before you leave. It should have been sorted weeks ago.'

Aoife traipsed back to her office, muttering to herself. Sometimes she really disliked Cian. The least he could have done was apologise. And there was a definite edge to his voice when he said it should have been sorted out weeks ago. Like she was somehow derelict in her duties by not knowing he forgot to hit "send" on an email she didn't even know existed!

The other thing that had her in a bad mood was Jason. He had phoned this morning to say he couldn't take Amy on Saturday afternoon as planned, and could he take her this afternoon instead? Aoife had agreed because she was determined to do everything in her power to strengthen Amy's bond with her father, but it meant Maura had taken a half day. They were both struggling to cope with the workload now Jack had decided to tackle his backlog. He had made no objections to Maura's unexpected holiday, but Aoife felt obliged to cover the gap. Jack had been so good to her, she didn't want him to have to manage alone when he was so busy. She would rather not have to drive all the way to Dublin, but there were long gaps in the train schedule in the afternoon. There was no other way. It was the very least she owed Jack. The very least she could do for her one decent boss.

Aoife left the office without saying goodbye to Cian. She went home, had a sandwich and spent an hour driving to Dublin. Damn Jason for not sticking to the schedule. Damn Cian for being such a prat.

As Aoife shoved open the door of Maura's office, she caught a glimpse of herself in the glass. She put a hand on her forehead to straighten out the frown lines. If she didn't calm down, she'd look like a pensioner before she hit thirty. Jason was Jason. She would never change him. It was time she accepted that. And maybe she was being unreasonable about Cian. He probably didn't really blame her. Lots of people hated admitting they were wrong, and anybody could accidentally forget to hit "send" on an email.

That's when it hit her. She'd never thought to check Tadhg's draft emails.

⤚

Aoife took the key from the petty cash box and unlocked Tadhg's room. It was still unoccupied. Jack said he didn't want anybody new coming into the house until the lads had recovered from the shock of Tadhg's death.

Tadhg's laptop lay on the desk by the window. Aoife had no difficulty accessing his files. There were only three laptops in the halfway house, and they all had the same password. The lads had been managing with two since Tadhg died. Nobody wanted to ask Jack if they could remove the third one from Tadhg's room. She guessed his e-mail password included "Orla". Her first guess was wrong. On her second attempt she tried "MyOrla123". She was in.

There were quite a few draft emails on Tadhg's computer, but there was no missing the top one: *Maybe we should call the whole thing off. You know how I feel about you, Orla, and the very thought of you going near that poison terrifies me. I'd do almost anything for you, but I can't*— That was it. Tadhg must have been trying to figure out how to let Orla down, but he couldn't find the right words. So he'd gone looking for the drugs she needed?

FORTY-SEVEN

AOIFE HAD BEEN staring at the computer for ten minutes and she still couldn't figure it out. Orla and drugs! No. Orla didn't even smoke. She wouldn't touch anything that could damage her looks. What did she need drugs for anyway? Before Tadhg had died, her life had been almost perfect. Could the drugs be for Cian? It might explain the mood swings. But why would Orla get drugs for Cian? She was a law student. A conviction for drugs would end her career before it even started. Then again, Orla wasn't doing anything illegal. Tadhg was the one taking the risks. Aoife switched off the computer. Something didn't add up here. She didn't believe Orla would endanger Tadhg like that. She was certain Tadhg meant far more to Orla than Cian ever could. But Cian had the money. If getting him drugs was the price for a relationship with Cian, would Orla risk everything to protect the life she'd come to love? 'No, no, no!' Aoife muttered. Orla was thoughtless and a little selfish sometimes, but she was a good person and a loyal friend. She wouldn't help Cian get drugs and she certainly would never endanger Tadhg. There was a logical explanation for this.

She phoned Orla. There was no answer. She checked her watch. Orla had probably forgotten to switch the sound on after lectures. She should be at lunch with her gang by now. If Aoife hurried, she might catch them.

✍

Aoife was lucky enough to get a bus almost immediately. In the upstairs restaurant of Fallon & Byrne, she recognised several of Orla's friends.

'Hi, I'm looking for Orla. Will she be joining you?'

They all shook their heads. 'We haven't seen her today,' a dark-haired girl said. 'We were supposed to meet in the pub last night, but she didn't turn up and she isn't answering any texts.'

'Well, if you hear from her, could you please ask her to phone Aoife urgently.'

'No problem, but she's probably with that new man of hers. She's practically a stranger to us these days. She seems to spend most of her time in Kildare.' The girl gave an elegant shrug. 'Each to his own, I suppose.'

✍

Leaving the girls laughing, Aoife hurried out of the restaurant. Orla certainly hadn't spent last night at Cian's. They'd probably argued about the apartment in Stephen's Green. Maybe Orla had been too upset to go to college. She might have had a sleepless night, drifted off in the early hours of the morning and woken up around the time Aoife was driving to Dublin. If she regretted her argument with Cian, she might have gone to Kildare to make it up with him. But why wasn't she answering her mobile?

✍

Aoife hurried back to the office. Her mouth was dry and she

had a fit of coughing as she entered the building. She went into the kitchen to get a glass of water.

Kevin looked up as she entered. 'Not another one!'

Aoife sipped her drink.

'Another what?'

'Another one down with a bug. Charlie's only just recovered, Jack went home sick yesterday and now you?'

'Jack isn't here?'

Kevin shook his head.

'I wouldn't have come in if I'd known. I'll see you next week, Kevin.'

∽

The long drive to Orla's apartment in Dun Laoghaire was a waste of time. There was no answer. Orla's parking space was empty. She'd try Cian's. She took the Newbridge exit off the motorway. It was raining so heavily it took her a few minutes to recognise Jason's car. He was turning into the road which led to her house. She jammed on the brake, causing the driver behind to blow his horn furiously.

Aoife parked on the side of the road as Jason was getting out of his car. 'What happened?' she called as she ran towards him.

'We need to talk.'

'Is Amy alright?'

Jason looked puzzled. 'She's fine. Mum's looking after her.'

'It's supposed to be your afternoon with her, Jason. That's why we swapped, remember? What are you doing here?'

'I need to talk to you. It's urgent.'

∽

'It's not a good time, Jason. Call me tomorrow.'

'Aoife, please. Just listen to me for two minutes.'

Aoife checked her watch. 'Okay, but you have to be quick.'

'Can we go inside?'

'Jason!'

'We can't talk properly in the driveway. Please, Aoife. It's important.'

Aoife sighed. She opened the door and stood in the hallway. 'Let's go into the kitchen.'

'I haven't time. If you can't say whatever it is you have to say in the hall, it will have to wait.'

A shadow crossed Jason's face, then he smiled. 'That's okay. This won't take long.' He sat down on the bottom step of the stairs. Aoife stood with her back against the door, arms folded.

'Go on, then,' she said.

'You're right to be angry at me.'

'Thank you.'

'I mean it, Aoife. I shouldn't have hidden the money from you. But I never planned to keep the money for myself. I was only—'

'Doing it because you loved me. You've told me that over and over, Jason. Is that it?'

'I did it because—because if you thought we had no money you wouldn't insist we went to counselling. I didn't want to go.'

This was new. 'Why not?'

He fiddled with his watch. 'A counsellor would tell you to leave me. I couldn't bear that.'

'Jason, that doesn't make any sense. You must have been saving that money for years, and we were already separated when we went for counselling.'

He looked at her. 'I know, but I thought I could talk you into coming back to me. I was afraid a counsellor would tell you I was no good for you.'

'Doesn't that tell you something? You aren't any good for me, Jason, and I'm the wrong person for you too.'

'But that's just it, Aoife. When we broke up, you said I never knew the real you.'

'You didn't. I wasn't myself after my parents died.'

'But I wasn't myself either.'

'What?'

'It's true, Aoife. From the minute I met you, I knew you were the only woman I could ever love. When your parents died, you needed someone to take care of you, so that was the person I became.'

'Are you saying you controlled me because that's what I wanted you to do?'

Jason stood up. He put one arm out to touch Aoife, saw her expression and drew it away. 'I became the person you needed, Aoife. Ask Mum or any of my brothers—I was never one to take control. I always let others sort things out. But you needed someone to do everything for you, so that's the person I became.'

'Right, Jason. So everything that went wrong with our relationship was my fault. Is that it?'

'No, Aoife. That's not it at all. What I'm saying is I became the person I thought you wanted me to be. Now you need me to be somebody else, I can become that person too.'

'Oh, Jason! It doesn't work like that. You can only be yourself. I don't want you to pretend to be someone else.' She checked her watch. 'Look, I really can't do this now. We'll talk tomorrow, okay?'

He hesitated. 'Okay, Aoife, but all I'm saying is I don't adapt to change easily. I stupidly tried to keep our relationship the way it used to be because I thought that was the only way it would work. Now I see that it can't work that way, I'll change.'

Aoife patted his shoulder. 'Tomorrow, okay? We'll talk through the whole thing tomorrow.'

&

As she ran upstairs to the bathroom, Aoife tried Orla's phone again. Still no answer. She was washing her hands when she heard the front door close. Jason was back? Hadn't she shut the door properly? Had he somehow managed to get a copy of the new key? She ran downstairs and checked the front door. It was fully shut. 'Jason!' No answer. Aoife opened the door and looked out. The road was empty. As she was closing the door, Aoife noticed a receipt on the ground. Lunch for two. Jason must have dropped it. Who was he taking to lunch? When she examined the receipt carefully it was for Flanagan's pub in Kildare. On the back of the receipt was an address in Stephen's Green. The apartment Orla was trying to talk Cian into buying. The writing was Cian's.

&

That was odd. She must have picked up Cian's receipt by mistake and it had fallen out of her pocket while she was talking to Jason. But that didn't explain the door closing. 'Jason!' Aoife checked the downstairs rooms. There was nobody in the house. She shrugged and was about to leave when she noticed one of the kitchen chairs standing in the centre of the room. Aoife certainly hadn't left it there. She stared at the chair, hands covering her mouth. Had she and Jason disturbed a burglar? Was it the burglar she'd heard leaving when she was in the bathroom?

&

Aoife keyed 999 into her phone. One finger on the dial button, she checked every room in the house. They were all empty. Every window was shut. She returned to the kitchen and checked the back door. It was locked. Was she imagining she'd heard the door shut? Maybe she'd moved the chair and forgotten about it. No. She would never leave the chair where Amy could fall over it. It looked like somebody had used the chair to reach something and not had time to put it back with the others. Aoife opened the kitchen cupboards. She kept loose change in a box on the top shelf, but that was undisturbed. Anyway, if she could reach it without a chair, so could any other adult. The only thing she'd put where it couldn't easily be reached was Tadhg's sketches. She got the stepladder and climbed up. Tadhg's sketch pads were gone.

FORTY-EIGHT

CIAN HAD WANTED Tadhg's sketches. Surely he wouldn't break into her house to get them? But all the doors and windows were locked. Whoever had come into Aoife's house had used a key.

Aoife sunk into the kitchen chair. She was always leaving her bag lying around the office. Cian could have copied her key. Actually, he wouldn't have needed to do that. When Aoife had changed the locks, she'd given the emergency key to Orla. Cian was in Orla's apartment all the time. He could easily have taken the key without Orla missing it.

She had told Cian she would be working in Dublin that afternoon. Had he borrowed Orla's key, let himself into Aoife's house and stolen Tadhg's sketch pads? Why would he do that? Had he been in the house when Aoife had come home? She shivered. Why did Cian want Tadhg's sketches so badly? Whatever the reason, how dare he break into her house? She grabbed her keys. Cian might be her boss and her best friend's partner, but that didn't give him the right to steal from her. He would return Tadhg's sketches right now or she was calling the police.

᷍

As she parked beside Cian's car, Aoife had second thoughts. Was she mad confronting Cian like this? No normal person broke into somebody's house. Maybe she was wrong. What if she accused Cian and he was innocent? Maybe Jason had somehow got a key to her house and let himself in. Was it possible Jason let himself in regularly? Why had he come to the house looking for her today? She hadn't told Maura she planned to go to Dublin. Shouldn't Jason have assumed she was at work? Had he made up that whole speech because Aoife had come back unexpectedly? It would be just like him to search the place for proof Aoife was cheating on him. She wouldn't put it past him to take Tadhg's sketches either, simply because they were drawn by another man.

Aoife let herself into Cian's house. She would play it by ear. If Cian appeared guilty, she'd mention that Tadhg's sketches had gone missing and see how he reacted. If she got the impression Cian didn't know what she was talking about, Aoife would say she came here to see Orla.

She opened the kitchen door. Cian was sitting at the table, the sketch pads spread out in front of him. Oh my God! Aoife covered her hands with her mouth. She had to get out of here. This was madness. She now had proof that Cian was a thief. She needed to call the police immediately.

As she backed out of the room, Cian looked up. 'Aoife! What are you doing here?' He followed her gaze to the sketch pads. The colour drained from his face.

FORTY-NINE

'You took Orla's key? You broke into my house?'

Cian put his hands on his head. 'I'm sorry, Aoife. I know it's no excuse, but I wanted to destroy the sketches. I don't want Orla to ever see them again.'

'What? That doesn't make any sense.'

He held out his hands. 'I know it doesn't, Aoife. I was desperate. I can't bear it that Orla loved Tadhg. I need to destroy all traces of him so Orla can be completely mine.'

'Oh my God! You killed Tadhg, didn't you?'

'No, I didn't! How could you even think that?'

'You did. You're a murderer.' Aoife pulled the phone from her bag and dialled 999. Cian hurried towards her, both arms held at shoulder height in front of him, palms facing her.

'You don't want to do that, Aoife. I promise you, on my mother's grave, I had nothing to do with Tadhg's death.'

'Tell that to the police. While you're at it, you can explain why you broke into my house.'

'I don't know what you're talking about.' Cian returned to the table and sat down. He leaned back in the chair and gave a slight grin. 'I found these sketches in your office, Aoife. Maybe I shouldn't have looked through your desk, but I was perfectly within my legal rights to do so. Why you would think I broke into your house is beyond me.'

'That won't work, Cian. Your fingerprints must be all over my kitchen.'

'I can guarantee there's not a single fingerprint belonging to me in that house.'

'And are you sure there's no hairs or anything else the police can get DNA from?'

Cian looked uncomfortable. 'You work for me. Why shouldn't you have invited me into your house?'

'Then you don't have anything to worry about, do you, Cian? I'm sure the police won't find it at all strange that your DNA is in my house but there's no sign of any of your fingerprints.'

Cian paused. 'The police aren't going to do DNA tests because you think somebody was in your house. Nothing has been disturbed and nothing is missing. They'll think you're nuts.'

He was probably right, but Aoife wasn't about to admit it. She shrugged. 'It's a chance I'm willing to take.' She dialled 999 again.

'Wait!' Cian stood up but he kept his distance. 'I didn't kill Tadhg, but if you call the police, it's going to cause all sorts of problems. For both of us.'

∽

'What?'

'Our entire working relationship is illegal, Aoife. I should have registered you as an employee and you should be paying taxes on your wages. You'll get us both in trouble.'

'I haven't worked for you for long and it's my first job this tax year. I'm way below the threshold for paying tax.'

'You should still have registered your employment with the tax office.'

'Maybe I should, but it's not tax fraud if I don't owe any tax. Anyway I'm pretty sure I have until the end of the tax year to register.'

'Whatever your situation is, it's illegal to hire somebody and not pay their PRSI contributions and all that other stuff. From the day you started working for me, I was breaking the law. Why would you want to get me in trouble?'

'I don't care about PRSI contributions. I care that you killed Tadhg.'

'I didn't, Aoife. I wanted the sketches. You wouldn't give them to me, so I took them. I admit, I shouldn't have done that, but I didn't kill anyone.'

'I don't believe you and I don't think the police will believe you either.'

'Okay, Aoife. Look, I'll tell you the whole truth.'

∽

Aoife waited. Cian seemed to think his explanation required a lot of thought. Or was he stalling to give himself time to make up a plausible story?

'I don't want the police linking me to Tadhg's death. Not because I had anything to do with it. Because there are other things I don't want them to discover.' When Aoife looked unconvinced, he added, 'I specifically didn't want them seeing Tadhg's sketches because of this.' He held up the sketch of the rectangular box that had reminded Aoife of Tadhg's coffin.

'You don't want them to know that Tadhg made a drawing of a rectangle?'

Cian didn't answer. Clearly it wasn't a rectangle. Now that

Aoife looked at it, the sketch reminded her of something. 'It's the painting you had on the wall. The one you put in your bedroom when Orla decided to invite the art critics for dinner. You don't want the police to see it. It's stolen, isn't it?' She put her phone in her pocket. 'I should have known. That's why you have so much money. You're dealing in stolen art.'

'It's not stolen. Check it online if you don't believe me. It's very famous. It used to be on loan to the Museum of Modern Art in New York until I bought it from the owner.'

'MoMA! It must be worth millions. How could you afford that?'

'Another question I don't want the police asking.'

'But where did you get the money?'

'It's not important. The point is I don't want the police asking that question and I don't want them to see Tadhg's sketch because it might get them thinking on the right track.'

'Wait a minute. Tadhg had several books on modern art. He recognised this painting, didn't he?'

'If he did, don't you think he would have told you or Orla?'

'Maybe he didn't have time. Those art books looked pretty new. Maybe he discovered it the night he died. Is that what happened? Your number is on the list of calls Tadhg made that night. Did he threaten to tell the police?'

'You're letting your imagination run away with you, Aoife.'

'Am I? I'm sure it didn't take Tadhg long to figure out where you got the money for that kind of artwork. He was a lot brighter than me, but even I got there eventually. It's the bank robbery money, isn't it?'

FIFTY

CIAN SHRUGGED. WHEN it was obvious he didn't intend to reply, Aoife said, 'You robbed the bank.'

'Don't be ridiculous. I was a teenager.'

'Your father robbed it?'

'He was desperate. He thought if he could afford to take my mother to Switzerland or the Mayo Clinic, he'd be able to get her onto some clinical trial. Somebody might be able to save her.'

'So Danny wasn't involved?'

'No.'

'And your father robbed the bank the night Danny disappeared so the police would think Danny was the thief?'

'He'd planned to rob the bank the following week anyway. He'd made sure Martin Hanrahan's visits to the bank were on CCTV. Not that he wanted Hanrahan arrested. He just wanted to confuse the police. When Maura phoned to say Danny was missing, Dad saw another opportunity to create confusion. He had no way of knowing if Danny would ever return, but either way it would put the police investigation on the wrong track.'

'You made up the story about the three men breaking into your home and tying you up?'

Cian nodded.

'What did your father do with the money?'

'Nothing. My mother deteriorated so quickly there wasn't any time to get her treatment abroad. Once she died, Dad had no interest in the money. I asked him where it was once or twice. All he would say was "it doesn't matter now". It took me months to find it after he died and a few more months to figure out what to do with it. I buy everything I can with cash, and I try to stay under the radar. That's why I couldn't hire you officially. Some of the cash is in Dad's old hiding place, but I spend a lot of it on art.' He picked up Tadhg's sketch. 'It took me years to build up enough contacts in the art world to find the type of people who trade in art on the black market.' He put the sketch down on the table. 'That was my biggest purchase, and the guy who sold it to me didn't even bat an eyelid when I said I wanted to pay in cash. As soon as I get a good buyer, I'll sell it on. That will give me more money I can safely lodge in the bank.'

'How did you get the paintings into the country?'

'Different ways. If the painting is in Europe, I take the ferry and drive back with it. It's easier to sneak things into a country when you have an entire car to hide them in. It's a little more challenging when I have to buy them in the States. Orla brought back my latest purchase.'

'That time she went to New York? You had planned to send me, hadn't you?'

'Why do you think I risked hiring a secretary? I thought if I created this huge panic, you'd rush off to New York. I'd keep you so busy there you wouldn't have time to wonder what you were doing. I even hoped you'd bring Amy. A young mother with a baby is unlikely to be targeted by customs officials.' He shrugged. 'But Orla worked out just as well. Maybe even better.'

'You've been using Orla all this time. You don't love her at all?'

'Love might be a bit strong. I care—no, I enjoy her very much. She's the most beautiful woman I've ever known. She's also a brilliant distraction. Not even customs officials are immune to her charms. Nobody pays the slightest attention to me when we're together. I could probably get away with shipping an entire art collection in my luggage without anyone noticing.'

'Your father killed Danny, right?'

'No, he didn't.'

'How can you even know? You weren't there.'

'I knew my father. He wouldn't hurt anyone, let alone kill them. He wouldn't even have considered robbing the bank if he wasn't desperate to save my mother.'

'The money mattered to you, though, didn't it, Cian? It mattered enough to kill Tadhg when he discovered your secret.' She pulled her mobile out of her pocket again.

'I told you, I didn't kill Tadhg. If Tadhg figured out where I got my money, he never mentioned it to me.'

Aoife dialled 999.

'Aoife, listen to me. Maybe you're right and Tadhg was checking art books looking for my paintings, but he hadn't discovered anything yet. Are you listening to me? Tadhg knew nothing about me, I swear.'

Aoife didn't reply. The operator answered. 'Hello, I'd like to speak to—'

Cian sighed. 'Do you want me to take Amy again?'

FIFTY-ONE

'WHAT?'

'You heard me.'

'Sorry, I dialled the wrong number,' Aoife said to the operator and disconnected the call. She put the phone back in her pocket. 'You took my daughter?'

'Ah, now I've got your attention. That little episode wasn't the disaster I thought it had turned out to be after all. The only part that worked out was that silly girl accepting my fake ID.'

'What are you talking about? You kidnapped my daughter so I'd stop investigating Danny's death? Why do you even care?'

'I don't. I told you the whole thing was a disaster. I didn't even know you were investigating your father-in-law's death.'

'But the note—'

'The note meant stop investigating Tadhg's death.'

'So I was right. You did kill him.'

'I didn't kill anyone. Tadhg worked for me. I didn't want the police involving me in the investigation. It was bad enough when Orla said my phone number was on the list of people Tadhg contacted the night he died, but then she said you were investigating Tadhg's death. I never would have hired you if I knew you fancied yourself as a detective. I needed the investigation to stop.'

Aoife felt like she was losing her mind. 'You kidnapped my daughter because you wanted Orla to stop her investigation. What sense does that make?'

'You were helping Orla. Orla had made friends with the detective assigned to the case. Anything you uncovered would go straight to the guards. It mightn't occur to Orla that I was involved, but the police were sure to think I was worth investigating. How long would it be before they wondered where my money came from?'

'What kind of a sick scumbag are you? You would terrify my little girl and nearly give me heart failure for something that didn't involve either of us?'

'You know very well Amy wasn't terrified. She had a great time in the park. She's still talking about all the ice cream.' Cian sat down again. He relaxed back in the chair, feet spread out in front of him. 'I don't hurt children.' He smiled. 'But rumour has it that some of the contacts I made in the art world would sell anything. I've even heard they might be into a little child trafficking.'

'You bastard!'

'Now, that's not getting us anywhere, is it, Aoife? I don't want to take your daughter. Keep your mouth shut and you have nothing to worry about.'

FIFTY-TWO

Aoife glanced at the knife block on the kitchen island. She had to get out of here before she attacked the scumbag. She ran to her car, sped out of the driveway, drove a hundred yards down the road and pulled over. Where was she going? She couldn't risk calling the police. Orla! Where the hell was she? She had mentioned visiting her parents the previous week. It was unlikely she'd visit them two weeks in a row. Her friends hadn't seen her. That only left Jack. Of course! She should have thought of that earlier. Orla had called to the halfway house on several occasions insisting Jack accompany her to lunch. If she found out Jack was at home sick, of course she would visit him.

It took almost an hour to get to Jack's house. The entire journey Aoife tried to think of a way out of her difficulties. There wasn't one. Orla might be able to come up with a plan. Although when Orla realised Cian had murdered Tadhg, she'd go off her head entirely. She'd want to go straight to the police. Was that a good idea? If the police raided Cian's house, they'd find the paintings. They'd certainly bring Cian in for questioning, but would they arrest him? If she and Orla both said they were positive Cian was a murderer, would the police even listen? Would they think Orla was a jealous girlfriend trying to get revenge on the man who dumped her?

Aoife screeched to a halt outside Jack's house and hurried to the front door. She rang the bell, hopping from foot to foot, counting the seconds before she could ring again. It began to rain and she pulled up her hood. Three rings later Aoife decided Jack must be out. Almost crying with frustration, she ran back to the car. As she was opening the door she looked back at the house and glimpsed a bald head peeking through the drawn curtains. Waving at the figure, Aoife rushed back to the house and waited.

When Jack opened the door, his few wisps of hair were tousled. He wore black jogging trousers and a black sweatshirt. She'd never seen him dressed so casually. 'Aoife, I'm sorry. I heard the doorbell, but I was in bed, so I didn't answer. What are you doing here? Is everything okay?'

'No, Jack, everything's far from okay. I need to talk to Orla, but she's not answering her phone. Do you have any idea where she is?'

'No. I'm not feeling great, so I haven't seen anyone today. If I hear from her, I'll ask her to phone you.' He went to close the door.

'Jack, can I come in? I need to talk to someone.'

'Now's not the best time, Aoife. I really don't feel up to chatting. I'll phone you in a few days when I'm better.'

He was closing the door when Aoife said, 'I know who killed Tadhg.'

⚜

The door opened again. 'Who?'

'I need to talk to you.'

Jack looked up and down the street. 'This is all I need. The neighbours gossiping that I'm letting young girls into the house when I'm not even properly dressed. Come in.' He led her into the sitting room. 'What's all this about, Aoife?'

'Cian broke into my house today.'

'What?'

'It's a long story, but Cian admitted his father robbed the bank. Cian's been living off the stolen money ever since. He spent most of it on a very expensive painting, which he keeps in the house. It doesn't look like much, but Tadhg commented on it, and when we cleared out Tadhg's room, we found a number of art books. I think Tadhg checked out the painting and discovered it was very valuable. Cian must have killed him to stop him from telling the police.'

Jack stared at her. He reached behind him for the arm of the chair and lowered himself into it. 'Cian stole a painting?'

'No, but he bought it with stolen money. He couldn't afford to have the police looking into his finances. They'd realise he was spending far more than he could possibly earn.'

'Cian admitted this?'

'Not only that, he also admitted kidnapping Amy.'

'Amy's been kidnapped?'

'Not now. It was weeks ago. She disappeared for a few hours. When we found her, there was a note in her pocket telling me to mind my own business or the next time Amy wouldn't be returned. I thought it was a warning to stop investigating Danny's murder, but I was also helping Orla investigate Tadhg's death. That was what Cian wanted to put a stop to.'

'You were investigating Tadhg's death? Why didn't you tell me?'

'It was more of a planned thing really. I never got past checking a few of his phone calls. I gave up my investigations when I found that note.'

'So Cian was behind everything?'

'Yep. I should have guessed when Cian wouldn't let me bring Amy to work. He was afraid she'd recognise him.' Aoife paused. 'Actually, she did recognise him.'

'What?'

'I was taking her to the park on Saturday when we ran into Cian and Orla. Amy held out her hands and said, "Ice cream". I thought she was talking to Orla, but she wasn't. She recognised Cian. She knew Cian was the person who brought her to the park and gave her ice cream.'

'But who murdered Danny?'

'Stephen Mannion. Danny must have discovered he was planning to rob the bank and threatened to expose him.'

'Cian told you that too?'

'No. He said his father wouldn't murder anyone, but Cian can't know what his father did that night. He wasn't there.'

'Well, that's it, then.' Jack looked at her with something approaching awe. 'You're amazing. Do you know that? You solved two murders in one afternoon.' He shook his head. 'I still can't believe it. Have you told the police?'

'Not yet. I need to talk to Orla. I can't risk Cian coming after Amy again.'

Jack put both hands on her shoulders. 'Listen to me, Aoife. You have got to go to the police right now. Amy's with Maura, isn't she?'

Aoife nodded.

'Maura will make sure nothing happens to her. Get the police to arrest Cian and you'll have nothing to worry about.'

'I don't know, Jack. I'm not sure it's a risk I want to take, and I really should tell Orla first. She's practically living with Cian.'

Jack raised his eyebrows. 'She may be your friend, Aoife, but you know very well that Orla doesn't love that man.'

'Maybe not, but she's fond of him.'

'She'll get over it. It's more important that you go to the police right now. This man kidnapped your child. What else is he capable of?'

'What if the police don't believe me? I can't prove anything. Amy saying "ice cream" isn't exactly evidence.'

'Hmm. Okay, phone that detective you know. Get him to help you explain it to the police. Maybe they could fit you with a wire. You could go back to the house and get Cian to admit everything on tape. That would stand up in court.'

'You think the police would take my allegations that seriously?'

'They would if the detective supported you. Ring him and explain what happened.'

'Maybe I should just go back to Cian's house and use my mobile to record him.'

Jack shook his head. 'You can't risk it. It would have been fine if you'd recorded your first conversation, but Cian's not an idiot. He's going to wonder why you want him to repeat everything. The police will tell you how to steer the conversation in the right direction. This is our one opportunity to make Danny's killer pay. We can't take any chances.'

Aoife nodded, remembering far too late that she should have broken her news gently. She had forgotten Danny was the closest thing to a son that Jack would ever have. She took out her phone. She hated the idea of asking Detective Moloney for help, but Jack was right. This was the best way to protect Amy.

The phone went to voicemail. 'Detective Moloney, this is

Aoife Walsh. I know who murdered my father-in-law and kidnapped my daughter. I'm on my way to the local Garda station. Please phone me when you get this message. I need your help explaining everything to the police.'

'You did the right thing, Aoife.'

Aoife nodded. 'This is best for everyone. Although I wish I could have spoken to Orla first and I would have liked her to come to the police station with me. I hate going there alone.'

'You won't be alone. The detective will be on your side.'

Jack got up to let her out. As Aoife followed, she dialled Orla's number again. A low buzzing sound came from beneath Jack's sofa.

⥲

'No wonder she wasn't answering her phone.' Aoife knelt down and pulled the phone from beneath the furniture. 'When was Orla here?'

'Yesterday evening. She stopped by after college to drop off some soup.' Jack smiled. 'She's not a bad nurse. I was quite surprised.'

'Yeah, Orla can surprise you alright.' Aoife buttoned her rain jacket. 'I really don't want to go to the police station on my own. Any chance you could come with me?'

Jack hesitated, then shrugged. 'Maybe the fresh air will do me some good. I'll just slip on a coat. It wouldn't do to let the neighbourhood see me dressed like this.'

Aoife could hear him pottering around the kitchen.

'I always thought there was something odd about Cian,' he called.

'That's what Jason said. Tadhg said it too. I should have listened to them.'

'I'll bet Jason was delighted to have been proved right.'

'I'm sure he will be. I'm going to let Maura tell him.'

Jack came into the hallway and rooted in the closet. 'One good thing came out of all this. At least the police won't be bothering Maura anymore. That must be a relief to her.'

'Yeah, silver linings and all that. Can I help you find something, Jack?'

'I've no idea where I put my coat. Would you mind checking upstairs? It's the last room on the right.'

Aoife ran up the stairs. She pulled the door handle, but nothing happened.

'Did you say the last door on the right, Jack?'

'Yes, is the door stuck again?'

'It seems to be locked.'

'Locked? That's strange.'

A few minutes later, Jack joined her in the corridor, a large bunch of keys jangling from his hand. 'The cleaner was here yesterday, but I can't imagine why she would lock the door.' Aoife stood aside to let him insert the key. Five minutes later, Jack had tried every key twice. None of them worked. 'I'll have to phone Mrs Slattery and ask her what she did with the key.' He took his mobile out of his pocket. 'Try all the keys again, Aoife. Maybe I missed one.'

The second key Aoife tried worked. 'I got—'

The shove sent her flying through the door.

FIFTY-THREE

Aoife landed on the ground with a thud.

'What the—? Jack, what the hell are you doing?' She shuffled into a sitting position and looked around. The room was pitch black. Jack stood over her, but it was so dark she couldn't read his expression. This couldn't be what she thought it was. 'Jack! What's going on?'

'Why did you have to come here, Aoife? You've ruined everything.'

'I don't know what you're talking about. Let me out of here.'

Jack removed a penlight from his pocket and shone it on her face. She blinked and put her hand up to shield her eyes.

'Let you out of here? For God's sake, Aoife, I never wanted you here in the first place. Why the hell couldn't you stay out of my way? The last thing I wanted to do was hurt you.'

Her mouth was dry. 'H—hurt me?' she croaked.

'You can't say I didn't try. I barely spoke to you. I never touched you and I tried not to be in the office when you were there.'

'I—I—what?'

'Give me your hands.' When Aoife didn't react, Jack grabbed her arm and led her to the corner of the room. She could just about make out the shape of a kitchen chair. Jack put one hand on her shoulder and pushed her into a sitting position. It was then she noticed the roll of duct tape in his left hand. He tied her arms to the back of the chair.

'Jack, I don't understand. Why are you doing this?'

'Shh.' Jack pulled her legs in front and bound them with the tape. 'I don't have enough equipment to tie you up properly, so I'm going to have to make do until I decide how I'm going to fix this.'

'Fix what?'

'You, of course. I can't just kill you. I have to make sure nobody can tie me to your death.'

FIFTY-FOUR

'K—KILL ME? WHY would you want to kill me? We're family.'

'Poor Aoife! You're not very bright, are you?'

֍

When he had tied her securely, Jack paced up and down the room. 'Let me think. You didn't tell anyone you were coming here, but your car's outside my door. Anyone could have seen you pull up.'

'Jack, I don't understand what's going on here.'

'Shh. Okay, you came to my house looking for Orla. We had a cup of tea and a chat. You told me about Cian. I convinced you to phone the police. You phoned the detective. Then you had second—'

'Jack, what are you doing?'

'Be quiet, Aoife.' He resumed his pacing. 'You had second thoughts, so I had to spend ages convincing you it was the right thing to do. But how will I explain that your car is still outside my house? I can't drive it away. Someone might see me.'

'I could drive it away.'

Jack laughed.

'I mean it. We could drive away together, and we could walk back after dark.'

'Aoife, please. I'm trying to concentrate.'

She could barely make out his outline as he paced. Finally he returned to look down on her. 'This is what we'll do. You'll phone Maura and tell her you're going into town to meet a friend and you need her to keep Amy overnight.'

'Jack, please tell me what this is about. I'm sure we could work something out if you'd just talk to me.'

'There's nothing to work out. The damage is done.' He removed her phone from her pocket, untied one hand and gave it to her. 'Unlock it, please.'

'No.'

'If you don't do as I ask, I'll phone Maura, tell her you're at my house and that you want her and Amy to join us. Do you want them both involved in this?'

'Involved in what?'

When he didn't answer, Aoife entered the code to unblock her phone. Jack scrolled through the numbers until he came to Maura's. 'Are we agreed? You're meeting a friend in town and you want her to keep Amy overnight. Sound convincing. If Maura even suspects anything is wrong, I'll have to kill her too.'

Kill her? Too! Who was this monster?

Jack switched the phone to speaker. Aoife delivered the message exactly as instructed. When Maura asked where she was, Jack disconnected the call, then removed the SIM card.

'I should have done this to Orla's phone last night, but I couldn't find it. I was afraid to phone it in case she hadn't brought it with her. I didn't want the police to discover I was her last caller.'

He felt in his pocket and pulled out Tadhg's lighter. Aoife watched him walk to the other end of the room. The flame from the lighter was so strong she could see he was burning two SIM cards into a mug. 'Now we're going to sit here and wait until it's dark enough for me to move the car without being seen.'

꿍

'What—what have you done with Orla?'

'Nothing yet. You completely ruined that for me, Aoife. She's the first girl I've taken in fifteen years. You can't even imagine how hard it's been for me. I had it all planned. I was going to take my time and really enjoy it. Then you turned up.'

'You took all those girls? Not Buckley?'

'Oh, it was Buckley. I wasn't even in the country when most of those girls disappeared. And I don't normally take girls from developed countries. It causes too much fuss.' He lit a cigarette. 'War-torn countries are the best. Obviously not ones where I might get killed, but ones where there's occasional guerrilla action. So long as the family is poor, the authorities barely bother to register the death.'

'Did you kill Triona?'

'Poor little Triona. She was the only Irish girl I ever took. I knew it was a bad idea, but I was still young enough to have difficulty controlling my urges. I'd been stuck in Ireland for over a year and I was getting desperate.'

'And you killed Danny.'

'I didn't want to. I made the mistake of getting too close to Danny. I thought of him as my own son. People like me can't afford feelings like that.'

'You told him the truth?'

'No, of course not. Aoife, I used to think you were intelligent, but you're being extraordinarily slow today. I used to have lunch with Danny every Friday. When I took the girl, I cancelled. I told Danny I had to go to a funeral down the country. I'd forgotten I'd given Bridget a key to my house. Danny was cutting his mother's grass, so he decided to do my garden at the same time.'

'He found you with the girl?'

'That was the worst day of my life. It had gone okay with the girl, but afterwards I felt the usual guilt. I'd been up all night with her, I was completely exhausted and there was no possibility of getting rid of the body until dark. There didn't seem any harm in taking a nap. I didn't even hear Danny come in. When the lawnmower woke me, I didn't know what to do. I'd hidden the body in the garage, you see. Danny hadn't noticed it when he took out the lawnmower, so I thought maybe everything would be okay. I decided to go out to him and say I'd been too sick to go to the funeral but now I was feeling better and I'd finish the grass myself. Before I got there, Danny ran out of petrol.' Jack extinguished his cigarette. His hands shook as he lit another. 'Isn't it amazing how things work out? If only I had refilled the lawnmower before I put it away or I'd come up with some other excuse for not meeting Danny.' He sighed. 'But that wasn't our fate. It nearly broke my heart to kill Danny, but what else could I do?' Jack put his hand out and touched Aoife's face. She flinched and jerked her head away. 'Danny didn't suffer. I came up behind him and stabbed him before he even had time to work out what was happening. You won't suffer either, Aoife, I promise.'

FIFTY-FIVE

AOIFE CHOKED BACK a scream. She had to keep Jack talking. As long as her car was parked outside, she had a good chance of survival. Moaney would come looking for her. Maura would tell him she was meeting a friend in Dublin. Moaney would think first of Orla and then Jack. Who else would she want to talk to about Tadhg's death? He would go to Orla's house and eventually he would come to Jack's. When he saw her car parked outside the house, he wouldn't just walk away. Would he?

'You told Elaine you saw Maura and Brendan in Dublin the night Danny was killed.'

Jack smiled. 'That was almost too easy. I rambled on and on about how I wanted to protect Maura and her boys, and I was telling Elaine what I saw in strictest confidence. Of course Elaine would never betray her Uncle Jack. But if the police ever suspect me, I can count on her to tell them what I claimed to have seen.'

'And you were the anonymous caller. You claimed you'd seen Danny with Eimear.'

'I wanted the police to stop investigating Triona's disappearance. It was a lot safer for me if they concentrated on one of the other girls.'

'And it didn't bother you that Danny, who you claimed was like a son to you, would be remembered as a serial killer?'

'Danny is long dead. Nothing can hurt him now.'

'Maura can be hurt, though, and you had no problem framing her for Danny's murder?'

'I hope the police never charge Maura with murder. But if they do—' He shrugged. 'Better her than me.'

'And what about me, Jack? Why are you doing this to me?'

'You think I want to? After Danny, I swore I'd never touch another girl. Shortly afterwards my uncle died and I inherited the farm. It was worth nothing until the building boom, but then everyone wanted the land. It was a prime location, two minutes' walk from the beach and a ten-minute drive to the nearest town. With the proceeds, I set up the charities. I never allowed females on the premises. When I wasn't at work, I was home alone or with Bridget. I was safe. Then you turned up. But I managed to quell any feeling I had towards you. Orla was harder. And when she killed Tadhg—well, that was the end.'

FIFTY-SIX

'Orla didn't kill Tadhg.'

'Yes, she did.'

'She did not. You wrote that email about the drugs and left it in Tadhg's computer.'

'Oh, that! It was an insurance policy. Something else to point the investigation in another direction if the police ever suspected me. Actually, I rather hoped the police would find the email. I'd have liked to see that bitch locked up for Tadhg's murder. After all, it's her fault he's dead.'

'What are you talking about? How could Orla have caused Tadhg's death?'

'The poor boy would never have known about the missing girls if that slut had stayed away from him. That reminds me, I need you to phone the detective again and leave him a message telling him all about Cian's confession.' He paused. 'No, that wouldn't work. They could trace the call. You'd better write a letter. Let me think—yes, you'd better address it to Orla. Say you couldn't face telling her in person. Tell her about Cian's confession, exactly the way you told me. The last thing I need is you disappearing without telling anyone your suspicions. God knows what direction the police investigation would take.'

'How could you kill Tadhg? I thought you loved him.'

'I cared about him. I didn't love him.' He shook his head. 'Oh no. Danny taught me never to love anybody again. But killing Tadhg was still hard. It was such a waste. He could have been my first big success.' Jack took the cigarette lighter out of his pocket and twirled it between his fingers. 'I try really hard with those boys. It's the least I could do to make up for the girls I had to kill, but it's not easy. Some of them are beyond help. Most years I throw at least one of them out of the house for drug use or excessive drinking. That's where I got the pills to plant on Tadhg's body. I'll probably never again find someone with Tadhg's potential.'

There was a long pause. When it was obvious he didn't intend to explain further, Aoife repeated the question.

'Why did you kill him?'

Jack blinked. 'What? Oh! After my birthday party, he came to my office. Did you know he got photos of me from Bridget and had them enlarged?'

Aoife nodded.

'About a month after Danny disappeared, we had a special mass for his safe return.'

Aoife raised an eyebrow.

'I know,' Jack said. 'But Bridget wanted it and I could hardly refuse. All the neighbours came and there wasn't enough space in Bridget's tiny sitting room, so we had it in my house. We lit candles and made a little altar of photos of Danny throughout his life. Bridget took pictures.'

'That was one of the photos she gave Tadhg?'

Jack nodded. 'Yes, me all dressed up in my priest outfit saying mass. Ironic, isn't it?'

'Why was it ironic?'

'If Tadhg hadn't wanted a photo of me acting all saintly, he'd never have discovered how wrong he was about me.'

'I don't understand.'

'I thought I had cleaned the house out before the mass. Obviously the girl's body was long gone. But I hadn't planned to take Triona, you see. It was a spur-of-the-moment thing. I saw her on the street. She recognised me because I had been in the car one time Danny gave her a lift.'

'How did Danny know her?'

'He saw her walking home from the supermarket. Her bags were too heavy and she'd put them down on the ground to give her arms a rest. Danny stopped and offered her a lift. After that he gave her a lift anytime he saw her.'

'Did she get into your car willingly?'

'Oh yes. Danny had told her I was a friend and a priest. She thought I was safe. Once she was in the car, what was I supposed to do? There was a new housing estate nearby and only a few of the houses were occupied. I said I was collecting a friend. I parked in front of an empty house and I choked her until she passed out.' He glanced at Aoife, waiting for a reaction. When she said nothing, he continued.

'I stuffed her in the boot and parked the car in my garage. There's a connecting door to my kitchen, so the neighbours didn't see anything. Of course, the girl started screaming the second I opened the boot, so I had to choke her again.' He banged his first on his forehead. 'So stupid. If only I'd waited a few days and planned it properly. Anyway, I dumped her on the couch in the sitting room and she came to while I was looking for something to gag her with. In the struggle she must have lost her necklace. It was months before I found it behind the TV cabinet. That was the cabinet we moved to set up the altar for Danny.' He sighed. 'When Tadhg had the photo Bridget gave him enlarged, he spotted the necklace beside one of the table legs. He would never have noticed it otherwise.'

'Tadhg knew you'd murdered Triona? Why didn't he go to the police?'

'He knew it, but he couldn't bring himself to believe it. He came to my office after the party and asked me about it.'

'What did you say?'

'I said I had no idea how that necklace ended up in my sitting room. I insisted we had to take the photo to the police immediately.' Jack smiled. 'Tadhg was bright, but he was so vulnerable. He didn't want me to be a murderer, so he chose to believe I wasn't. Once we were outside, the rest was easy. I had taken a knife from the kitchen and some of the drugs I'd confiscated over the years. I stabbed Tadhg as he was getting into the car. Then I pushed him inside, shoved the pills in his pocket and dumped him in an alley.'

'How could you do that? Tadhg loved you. You were the closest thing he ever had to a father.'

'I know. That's what I counted on when I lied about the necklace.' He stubbed the cigarette butt into the mug containing the burnt SIM cards. 'It wasn't as hard as having to kill Danny, but it still destroyed a part of me. Then I remembered it was that bitch who'd shown Tadhg the picture of the necklace. It was her fault Tadhg knew anything about those girls. Tadhg was going to be my success story, but that bitch took him away. I got quite excited planning how I'd make her pay.'

'I was the one who told Tadhg about the necklace.'

'Don't lie for her, Aoife. She's going to pay for what she did to Tadhg and there's nothing you can do to stop it. Every time she mentioned his name, I wanted to punch her in the face. All that bleating on about how much she'd loved Tadhg, but she couldn't have a relationship with a teenager? If Tadhg's family had money, Orla would have overcome her scruples soon enough. What she meant was she couldn't tie herself to a penniless young man with a very uncertain future.'

'Orla might not have known what she wanted, but it was you who killed Tadhg. Don't try to blame someone else. Don't you have any conscience? You're a priest.'

'That wasn't my decision. And I'm only a priest in name. I don't actually believe in God.'

'How convenient.'

'Why, because otherwise I wouldn't do this? I believed in God when I was fifteen and felt the urge to kill. I believed the first time I murdered a young girl. Afterwards I prayed all day every day for an entire week. I begged God to take the desire away. After my second kill I knew God didn't exist.'

'Or you told yourself that because it relieved the guilt?'

'I still feel guilty. I just accept that this is something I can't control. I keep trying to control it, mind, but it gets away from me sometimes.'

'What is it you're trying to control? Your instincts or the risk of getting caught?'

'You're determined to think badly of me, aren't you?'

'I tend to have a low opinion of murderers.'

'I'm a nice guy, Aoife. I take care of the homeless, and I gave Maura a job even though it meant allowing you on the premises, a risk I wouldn't normally take.'

'You do those things so you can convince yourself you're a decent person with an unfortunate condition you can't control. You're scum, Jack. If Maura, the boys you helped, Danny or even your own mother knew what you were really like, they'd despise you.'

Something changed. Aoife saw it in his face. When he stood up, she was certain she had seconds to live.

FIFTY-SEVEN

JACK RAISED HIS fist in the air. Aoife shut her eyes and ducked her head. When she opened them, Jack was once again sitting in his chair. 'You're a silly little girl, Aoife,' he spat. 'And you have no idea what you're talking about.'

'Don't I? I know you believe in God. You pretend you don't so you can do things you know are wrong.'

Jack smiled. 'I knew you had no idea what you were talking about. I used to pray that God would change me and make me a better person. Then I spent a short time in one of those industrial schools and I realised I wasn't half as bad as I thought I was. At least my victims were adults. I never touched anyone under eighteen and most of them were bitches.'

'Because they didn't live up to your idea of morality?'

'Because they knew they could twist men around their little fingers, and they got pleasure from doing it.'

'And that's so much worse than being a murderer?'

'I never said that was why I killed them. Or even that they deserved to die. Killing them is a purely physical thing for me. Some men need sex, I need this. I tried to always choose the less deserving.'

'Tried?'

'Sometimes I could control the desire better than others. And I have to admit there's something very special about killing the pure and innocent.' He had a faraway look in his eyes. 'But I rarely allowed myself that pleasure.' He shrugged. 'Anyway, it was only pleasurable for a short time. The guilt afterwards was terrible.'

'Oh really!'

'Sarcasm doesn't suit you, Aoife. I regret taking Triona more than anything else in my entire life. I didn't prepare and Danny paid the price. I even considered killing myself afterwards.'

'Why didn't you?'

'I'm a coward. And then there was Maura. Without me, who would have given her money each month?'

'That was you?'

'Of course. I robbed her of a husband. It was the least I could do. You see, I told you I was a nice guy.'

⌢

Jack lit another cigarette, leaned back in the chair and puffed with an air of self-satisfaction. Did this monster have any sense of reality?

'You think you're nice? Nice! You killed Maura's husband and then you tried to frame her for his murder.'

'I didn't try to frame Maura and I don't want her arrested.'

'You put her fingerprint on the envelope of cash.'

'Another insurance policy. Obviously the police will never be able to link Maura to the money, so she doesn't have anything to worry about.'

'How did you get her fingerprint on that envelope anyway?'

'That was easy. Remember when you both came to Bridget's house to discuss the funeral arrangements?'

Aoife nodded.

'When Maura tried to sit down, the couch was covered in papers and magazines. I'd stuck several empty envelopes amongst them. I knew Maura's fingerprints would end up on one of them. I was still wearing gloves when I took the papers from her and I watched carefully to see which envelope she was touching.' He shrugged. 'It was child's play.'

'But how did you get Angela Power to post the envelope? Bridget said you never even met her.'

'I didn't. I wasn't even aware she was Brian Connolly's niece until last week.'

'Brian Connolly? The priest who married Maura and Danny? Angela was at Maura's wedding because she was related to the priest?'

'Brian always had a soft heart. He knew Danny's marriage was going to be a miserable affair. Bridget certainly wasn't going to fork out money for flowers or music. That's why Brian asked his niece to sing at the wedding. Apparently, she used to be quite the singer in her day.'

'Since when are singers included in wedding party photos?'

Jack laughed. 'That's typical Brian. He had a real affection for "those poor girls", as he called any girl who got pregnant outside marriage. "No flowers, no music and not a kind word from anyone." He used to force the entire congregation to contribute. Anyone who could sing avoided him like the plague if they knew one of those weddings was coming up. And he practically ordered the women who helped out in the church to cover the place in flowers.' Jack flicked the cigarette ash into the mug and took a long drag. 'Brian was quite a character. Those women adored him, but they were terrified of him too. The morning of one of those weddings they'd arrive really early to do the flower arranging Brian insisted on. They'd try to sneak out before Brian arrived, but he usually caught one or two of them and forced them to take part in the wedding photos. "What kind of wedding photos will that poor girl have to show their children?" he'd say. "A bunch of scowling relatives trying to sit as far away from the 'fallen woman' as possible." I was at one of those weddings.' Jack broke into peals of laughter. 'Aoife, you should have seen their faces. Those poor women were mortified.'

One look at Aoife's face and the laughing stopped. 'Sorry, I shouldn't be telling jokes at a time like this. It's just I hadn't thought of Brian in a long time. He was a great guy.'

∽

'How did Angela end up posting your envelope to Maura?'

'Every now and again, one of my parishioners would get herself pregnant. If she was lucky enough to be able to support herself, she could stay out of the laundries. But, of course, she couldn't go home, and every one of them would have died rather than let their families know they were unmarried mothers. The girl had to come up with a reason why she could never visit her family. Usually she pretended she'd found work in England. I didn't share Brian's sympathy for those girls, but I couldn't turn my back on them. We were a lot alike, really. We were all slaves to our instincts. Some of the girls came to me in confession. I got them to write a letter home each month and give it to me. Then I posted it to Brian. He was glad to help. Brian posted the envelopes from England so the girls' families could see they had an English postmark. We did that for several girls over a period of about thirty years or so. Of course, unmarried pregnancies stopped being a family disgrace long ago, but I told Brian there was one girl in my parish whose family were fundamentalist Christians. He didn't even question it. He just posted the envelope every month, same as he'd always done.'

'But how did Angela Power end up posting the final envelope?'

'Brian took his commitments very seriously. When Angela went to England, she stayed with her uncle for a few months. Later she married and had a family of her own, but she and Brian were always close. He left his few possessions to her in his will. He also left a letter asking her to continue posting my envelope each month.' Jack sighed. 'Brian was one of the finest men I ever met, and he was a credit to the Church.'

'Unlike you.'

'Aoife, you're beginning to annoy me. If you keep this up, I might have a little fun with Orla and force you to watch.'

FIFTY-EIGHT

THERE WAS A long silence. Aoife was afraid to speak but she had to keep Jack talking. The longer they spoke, the longer her car was parked outside his house.

'What are you going to do to Orla?'

'Who knows? Quite a lot if you hadn't interrupted. I had everything ready. I'd changed into these'—he pointed at his sweats—'so the blood wouldn't stain. All I had to do was cover the ground in plastic and then the fun would have begun. But you had to ruin that for me, didn't you? Now it will have to be a rush job like the last one.' He scowled. 'It could have been up to a week before the police took the disappearance of a girl like that seriously, but a young mother—I'll need to have both of you out of here by tomorrow morning.'

Aoife took a deep breath and tried to remember an article she'd read on controlling panic attacks. She had to keep her wits about her. By now Moaney would have the police looking for her. Her job was to keep Jack in this room as long as possible. 'Where is Orla now?'

'Here.'

'Can I see her?'

'The drugs won't wear off for a while yet. She's one hell of a bitch, that one, scratching and biting like a wild animal. That must be how her phone ended up under the couch. I looked for it, but I didn't think there was any rush. As soon as I'd finished with her, I would have searched every inch of the house. I wasn't going to repeat the mistake I made with Triona.'

Was there any way to get through to this monster?

'Do you care about Maura?'

'I feel sorry for her, but I don't really know her.'

'You feel guilty for killing her husband?'

'Of course.'

'So why would you kill her daughter-in-law?'

'I told you, Aoife. I don't want to kill you, but I have no choice. It's fate. Yours and mine.'

'It's not my fate. You can let me out of here right now.'

'You expect me to believe you wouldn't say anything to the police?'

'Not if you let Orla free as well.'

'I'm not sure I could do that even if I believed you. Aoife, I know you're scared, but I promise I'll make it really quick. You don't have to be afraid. I've had lots of practice. I can kill without inflicting any pain at all.'

'Am I supposed to be grateful for that?'

'Believe me, if you knew what I have planned for Orla, you'd be very grateful indeed.'

⌘

Aoife wrapped her arms around her body to stop the shivering. Men like Jack got a kick from terrifying women, and she was damned if she'd provide him with the slightest bit of pleasure.

'And what about my daughter? Are you going to give

her money every month as well? Blood money for killing her mother?'

'I'll make sure she's okay.'

'You stay away from her!'

'I always stay away from girls. Hadn't you noticed? Besides, I'll probably be dead by the time your daughter reaches eighteen. I definitely won't have the strength to kill any more. Hopefully I'll have lost all the desire as well. Physical desires tend to fade with age.'

'Promise me Orla won't suffer.'

'Orla isn't any of your concern.'

'Of course she's my concern. We've been friends since we were four.'

'That bitch has to pay for what she did to Tadhg and for making me kill him.'

'Killing Tadhg was your choice. Nobody else's.'

'That's not true. I would never have chosen to kill him.'

'You did choose to kill him. Just like you chose to kill Danny and you're choosing to kill me.'

'You're wrong.'

'I'm right and you know it.'

Towering over her, Jack's face was so red Aoife felt her heart pound. Jack was old, overweight and under a lot of pressure. If she could rile him a bit more, he might have a stroke or a heart attack.

'Your mother must be so proud.'

Jack's face turned purple, then he took a deep breath, leaned back in the chair and smiled. 'You're brighter than I gave you credit for, Aoife. You're trying to make me lose control. Believe me, that's not going to happen. I've been controlling myself around women since I was fifteen. I can last a few more hours.'

'Was your mother a bitch? Is that why you need to kill women?'

'Be quiet, Aoife. That kind of talk is beneath you.'

'So she was a bitch?'

'She was a good woman who had a very hard life. I won't let you rile me, and I won't let you speak like that about my mother. I'd rather you didn't die in this house, but I'll kill you right now if I have to.'

⤜

They sat in silence for what felt like hours. Jack chain-smoked the entire time.

Aoife coughed. 'Do you have to smoke on top of me?'

Instead of answering, Jack shoved his chair a few inches back and puffed away. Shouldn't the police be here by now? What was keeping them?

Jack checked his watch. Any minute now he'd decide it was dark enough to move her car.

'Jack, I need to go to the bathroom.'

'You can't.'

'You want me to make a mess here?'

'I don't really care. There will be one hell of a mess to clean up tonight either way.'

'You'll have to sit here with it for hours. Won't that spoil your fun?'

Jack hesitated. 'Alright.' He walked to the end of the room. Aoife could see his silhouette open a drawer and remove something. Returning with a long knife that made her shudder, Jack switched off the penlight and put it in his pocket. He flicked on Tadhg's lighter and placed it upright on the ground. Now both his hands were free, Jack cut the tape binding her legs with one quick swipe. Aoife watched him put the knife on the ground and kick it out of her reach. She flexed her legs, trying to get the blood circulating properly. While Jack was freeing her, she'd kick him in the groin or the head, whichever was closer. While he was down, she'd get the knife. She was tensing her muscles, ready to strike, when Jack yanked her feet into the air and she found herself suspended several inches above the seat of the chair. The only thing anchoring her to the chair was her bound arms. Her head flew backwards and the chair tilted dangerously. Jack steadied it with his foot.

'What the hell are you doing?'

'Quiet.'

Using his arm to anchor Aoife's legs against his body, Jack quickly bound her legs with the duct tape. He let her feet drop, but he moved behind her before they hit the ground. Aoife shifted herself into a sitting position. The next time Jack came close, she'd be ready to attack. Jack put one arm around Aoife's neck and used the other to release her hands. Tightening the pressure on her neck, he said, 'Raise your hands in the air.'

FIFTY-NINE

Aoife tried to pull Jack's arms from her neck, but his grip tightened. 'Put your hands in the air, now.'

Aoife raised both hands.

'Put them together as if you were praying.'

When her hands were in place, Jack grabbed them with one hand. Pushing them behind her head so she was again unbalanced on the chair, he released her neck and quickly bound both hands with the duct tape. He picked up the knife, flicked off the lighter, took out his penlight and said. 'Let's go.'

Aoife spluttered, 'How?'

'Hop.'

Jack kept a tight grip on her arm as Aoife hopped to the door. He unlocked it and she hopped into the corridor. Although the light was now fading, it still took Aoife's eyes a moment to adjust.

The bathroom door was open.

'Are you planning to watch? Is that how you get your kicks?'

'I can't let you in there alone.'

'Really? Why? Because I'd climb out that tiny window? Oh no, let me guess, it's fate. Fate has decreed that although murderers on death row get a final meal, I can't even go the bathroom without an audience. Great excuse.'

'Aoife, I'm really beginning to dislike you.'

'I'm sorry, Jack. Am I not behaving properly? Is this not the correct ladylike way to speak to a murderer?'

Jack shoved her into the bathroom and looked around. He checked the window was locked, picked up a few bottles and the razor she had been eyeing. 'You've got two minutes, then I'm coming in.'

'Aren't you going to untie my hands?'

'No.'

'How am I supposed to manage?'

'I don't care. Two minutes.'

He closed the door behind him. Aoife did a circle of the bathroom. All that remained was a clothes basket and soap. She flung the towel into the clothes basket.

When Jack opened the door, she was standing at the sink, her hands dripping.

'I want a towel.'

'What did you do with the one that was there?'

'There wasn't any towel.'

Jack frowned. 'Hold up your hands.'

He ran his hands over her body. 'I don't know what you think you're going to achieve by hiding my towel. Come on. Out.'

'I want a clean towel.'

'You've caused enough trouble for one day.' Jack grabbed her arm and dragged her out of the room.

'My hands are wet.'

'They'll dry. Be quiet.'

He pushed her into the dark room again and switched on the penlight.

She would be prepared this time. When he pulled her legs, she'd get in at least one good kick.

SIXTY

JACK FLICKED ON the lighter again. He dropped the knife on the ground, kicked it out of Aoife's reach and pushed her down on the chair. Standing behind her, he used the last of the duct tape to bind her to the chair by the waist. He switched off the lighter and got out the penlight. Going to the desk at the end of the room again, he returned with two long strips of material, which he wrapped around the leg of the chair and tied in a knot just above Aoife's knees. Her legs were now bound to the seat of the chair. Jack took a few steps back and looked at her.

'It's not great, but it will do until I get back. I hadn't planned on tying up two people at the same time.'

'You told me I could see Orla.'

'You will.'

He left the room without locking the door. Aoife waited to hear the front door shut. A few minutes later, Jack's footsteps came up the stairs again. He was holding another strip of cloth in one hand. She couldn't make out what he held in his fist. 'Open your mouth.' Aoife kept her mouth clamped shut. Jack pinched her nose. Aoife opened her mouth but kept her teeth clenched. Jack took Tadhg's lighter from his pocket. The flame was so strong she felt her cheeks redden. Huh! Did he think she was an idiot? There was no way Jack would set her on fire. He'd burn the house down.

He moved the lighter close to her eyes. 'Open your mouth or I'll burn your face.'

Aoife shook her head.

'Don't be stupid. I promised you wouldn't have a painful death, and although I'm beginning to regret that promise, I'll keep it if you don't fight me. But if you insist, I will certainly burn your face off first.'

✄

Aoife opened her mouth. Jack put the lighter on the ground again. Stretching Aoife's mouth open with both his hands, Jack shoved a stress ball into the opening. It was too large to fit into her mouth completely and about a quarter of it jutted out. Jack took the strip of cloth and bound it tightly around her mouth.

'Ugh!'

'Quiet!'

Jack flicked off the lighter, switched on the penlight and did a circle of the chair, checking her bindings. 'It will have to do,' he muttered. He gathered up his equipment. At the door he said, 'I told you, I always keep my promises. You can see Orla now.'

What was that supposed to mean? Aoife struggled against her bonds. Jack laughed.

'Don't waste your energy.'

He shut the door and the room plunged into darkness. The key turned. A few minutes later Aoife heard the front door close.

Okay, this wasn't the time to think about Orla. Her car would no longer be outside Jack's house, so she couldn't count on the police rescuing her. She was on her own. She had to concentrate on getting free. At least she could breathe, but the stress ball left a disgusting taste in her mouth and the cloth was bound so tightly around her mouth that she couldn't spit it out. She tried to speak. 'Ugh! Ugh!' was the best she could manage. Shouting for help was out of the question, obviously. In any case, Jack's was an end house. He had no neighbours on one side, and the house on the other side appeared to be deserted.

Aoife had tightened every muscle while Jack tied her up. She'd read somewhere that this would create a little bit of give when her muscles were relaxed. She'd also spent most of her time in the bathroom with her hands in a basin of hot water. Surely it had done something to loosen the adhesive? If she could get her hands free, she'd have a good chance of escaping. Aoife was twisting her wrists back and forth, trying to weaken the tape, when she heard a muffled sound.

Orla?

'Ugh.' The sound was louder.

'Ugh,' Aoife replied. She tilted the chair backwards and let the two front legs crash down on the ground to let Orla know she could hear her. The sound was dulled by the carpet. Aoife remembered movies where people tilted their chair backwards, fell on the ground and the chair splintered into pieces. Should she try that? No. The chair felt sturdy. It wouldn't break and she might hurt herself. Working on her hands was their best chance.

Orla made occasional grunts and Aoife responded. It was a very ineffective method of communication, but at least they both knew they weren't alone. Aoife had no idea how much time passed, but it felt like hours before the tape tore a bit. A little while later, her hands were free.

She rotated her wrists. When the feeling had returned, it only took a few minutes to untie the knot around her head. She spat out the foul-tasting ball.

'I'm almost free, Orla. Hang on.'

Aoife assumed Orla's gurgles were enthusiastic support.

Untying the strips of cloth that bound her thighs to the seat of the chair was the easiest part of the process. Now that she could move her legs, Aoife crossed her ankles back and forth, putting strain on the tape binding them. At the same time, she used her nails to claw at the tape around her waist. It took a while, but the tape eventually gave.

As she was no longer bound at the waist, Aoife could bend down and use her hands to claw at the tape binding her legs. Rotating her ankles had weakened the tape a little, but it was a desperately slow process.

When the tape finally gave way, Aoife shouted, 'I did it!' Orla gurgled loudly. Aoife stumbled to the door. She felt along the wall for a light switch. As Jack had used a torch, she assumed the light wouldn't work. It didn't. She followed Orla's gurgles to the opposite side of the room. Orla's terrified, bloodshot eyes met hers.

Orla was tied to what looked like a hospital bed. A large ball was protruding from her mouth. Drool dripped down her chin. Unlike Aoife, her mouth hadn't been gagged. Aoife tugged at the ball, but it wouldn't move. Orla gurgled again. She was tied to the bed by thick ropes. How the hell was Aoife going to get her free?

When Jack had brought her back from the bathroom, Aoife had used the dim light from Jack's torch to check out the room. She had noticed heavy drapes on the wall opposite the door. She would break the window, climb out and get help for Orla. As she moved away, Orla's gurgles became more urgent. 'I'll be back in a minute,' Aoife promised. She felt her way along the wall until she touched the thick velvet material and yanked back the curtains.

She was looking out on an empty field.

'We're in the back of the house, Orla. There's only a field outside.'

Orla gurgled frantically.

'I'm coming,' Aoife replied. She tried to focus on the window. The only light came from the stars, so she couldn't see much. Why were there dark patches in her vision? Then she understood. The windows were barred.

SIXTY-ONE

THE LIGHT FROM the stars helped Aoife find her way to Orla without stumbling. She knelt down beside her. She could now see that the thing in Orla's mouth was a ball gag. She reached behind Orla's head and untied it. Orla sighed. 'Thank God!' she croaked.

Aoife tugged at the thick ropes that bound Orla to the bed. She patted Orla's hand. 'I'll have you free in no time,' she said, but she wasn't at all sure it was a promise she could keep. She couldn't even see what she was doing.

'Light. I need light. Jack kept the room dark to disorientate us, but he'd want to be able to see what he was doing when he was having his fun.'

Orla shuddered.

'Sorry. I'll check the drawer.'

Orla shook her head.

'No!' she croaked. 'No time.'

'Jack wants people to think I'm in the city. I'm guessing he'll be gone at least an hour and a half. We can't have used up more than an hour. Don't worry. We have enough time.'

Orla shook her head. 'No! Could leave car anywhere.' She coughed. 'Could be back any minute. Hurry!'

'It's wasting time fiddling around in the dark.' Aoife hurried to the drawer and yanked it open. It was almost empty. Her hands touched a box of cigars and a light bulb.

Aoife grabbed the chair she had been tied to and used it to reach the light fixture. She hit the light switch. The room flooded with light. Orla gasped. When Aoife's eyes had adjusted, she searched the floor. She remembered Jack dropping the knife on the ground several times and hoped he'd forgotten to pick it up. He hadn't. What he had forgotten was Tadhg's lighter.

Should she use the lighter to burn Orla's ropes? No, too risky. She stuck the lighter in her pocket and ran back to Orla. 'Oh!'

'What?'

'I thought I only had to undo the ropes tying you to the bed. I didn't realise your hands and legs were bound separately. This will take longer than I'd imagined.'

'No time. Hurry!'

Now she could see what she was doing, Aoife felt more hopeful. Because the rope was thick, the knots were much larger than Aoife had realised and untying them was relatively simple. In less than fifteen minutes she had undone all the ropes binding Orla to the table. Orla sat rigid on the bed while Aoife worked on untying the ropes that bound her wrists.

Orla was still panicking. 'Faster! He'll be back!' She pulled at the ropes that bound her hands but only succeeded in yanking them out of Orla's grasp.

'Don't, Orla. You're making it harder. I'll have you free in a few minutes.'

Orla groaned.

The last knot undone, Orla threw her arms around Aoife. 'Thank y—' A low click caused them both to freeze. It was the front door opening.

SIXTY-TWO

ORLA LOOKED DOWN at the ropes that still bound her ankles. 'Oh God!'

They stared at each other in horror.

'The lighter! Set fire to something,' Orla whispered. 'Distract him, then hit him with the chair.' She reached down and gathered up the ropes that had fallen on the floor.

The only thing Aoife could set fire to was the curtains. They were made of heavy velvety material. Would they have caught fire by the time Jack reached the door? She remembered there was a paper sheet on Orla's bed, like those found in doctor's offices. Aoife rolled it into a ball. She hurried to the furthest corner of the room and clicked the lighter. The sheet caught fire immediately. Aoife ran to the light switch and turned it off. The footsteps were now on the stairs. Aoife grabbed the chair and hid behind the door. Orla was still pulling frantically at the ropes binding her legs.

'Lie down!' Aoife whispered.

Orla's popped the ball gag into her mouth and wrapped the ropes around her body.

The key turned in the lock. Aoife flattened herself against the wall and held her breath. The paper she had burned was now a little ball of fire in the opposite corner of the room. The carpet was beginning to smoulder. The door opened.

'What the hell!'

Jack glanced at Orla, who was lying on her back, eyes closed. Leaving the key in the lock, he ran over and stamped out the fire. Aoife crept up behind him. Unable to reach his head, she stood on her tiptoes and used all her strength to bring the chair down on his neck. Jack stumbled but didn't fall. He turned towards Aoife, his expression a mixture of shock and fury. Remembering the only self-defence class she had ever taken, Aoife grabbed his shoulders to steady herself and kneed him in the groin. Jack dropped to the ground, moaning. Aoife turned to flee. She banged straight into Orla.

Gripping one of the ropes that had bound her ankles, Orla shoved Aoife out of her way. Jack was still bent over, groaning. Orla put the rope around his neck and pulled. 'Help me,' she screamed at Aoife.

'Are you insane! Run!'

Orla ignored her. Jack was now on his knees, grasping at the rope around his neck. Orla wasn't strong enough to strangle him. Neither of them were. Jack yanked the rope, pulling Orla towards him. Tossing the rope to one side, his hands tightened around Orla's neck.

SIXTY-THREE

'OH MY GOD! Oh my God!' Aoife ran towards them. What could she do? She remembered Tadhg's lighter in her pocket. Racing to the light switch, she turned it on, flooding the room with light. A startled Jack loosened his grip on Orla, and she dropped to the ground. Panting and wheezing, she crawled out of his reach. Jack followed her. Aoife used the distraction to creep up behind him. As he was yanking Orla to her feet, Aoife flicked on Tadhg's lighter. Jack was concentrating on Orla. Aoife guessed he wanted to apply enough pressure to subdue but not kill her. Aoife moved closer. The flame from the lighter was as strong as any candle, but it went unnoticed in the brightly lit room. Holding the flame against the bottom of Jack's sweatshirt, Aoife waited for the fire to catch.

The material smouldered but didn't flame. She couldn't wait. Orla was now gurgling, her eyes wide with panic. Aoife picked up what little remained of the chair she had used earlier as a weapon and banged it repeatedly on Jack's back.

Jack released his grip on Orla long enough to fling Aoife to one side. Orla fell to the ground. She was trying to get to her knees when Jack spotted her. He lifted his foot and aimed it at her head. His foot was inches from her face when he felt the burn.

Screaming, Jack yanked the sweatshirt over his head and stamped on it to extinguish the flame. Aoife half lifted a wheezing Orla to her feet. The top of Jack's trousers was now smouldering. He kicked off his shoes, pulled off the trousers and ran after his prisoners. Dragging Orla after her, Aoife made it to the door seconds before Jack. She pushed Orla outside, followed her, slammed the door and turned the key.

She hadn't bought them much time. Jack roared and flung his entire weight against the door. It wouldn't be long before he broke through.

Orla's breathing had returned to normal, but Aoife gripped her arm as they ran down the stairs. She turned the latch on the front door. Nothing happened. The door was locked. There was no sign of the key. What now? There was a loud crash and the bedroom door splintered.

It wouldn't be long before Jack broke through the door entirely. 'Sitting room!' Aoife shouted. She remembered admiring a lamp in that room. It had a very solid base. Strong enough to break glass?

Aoife flung the lamp at the window. It made a small hole, but it wasn't big enough for either of them to fit through. She turned, expecting to find Orla behind her. No Orla. A few seconds later Orla appeared. She was carrying a knife block. She threw the knives on the ground, removed her jumper and, wrapping it around her arm, used the knife block to break away just enough glass for them to squeeze through.

There was a loud crash. They heard Jack thundering down the stairs. Aoife jumped through the hole and turned to help Orla. Orla had disappeared.

SIXTY-FOUR

JUMPING BACK INTO the sitting room, Aoife picked up the knife block and ran into the corridor. A purple-faced Jack was pounding down the stairs. Orla stood on the bottom step, waiting for him. She clutched a kitchen knife in one hand.

'What the hell are you doing?' Aoife roared at her.

Jack slowed to a walk, his eyes on Orla. 'Get out of here, Aoife.' Orla's voice was calm and low.

'You're not strong enough, you idiot. Do you want to get us both killed?'

Never taking her eyes off Jack, Orla said, 'This is between Jack and me. Leave now.'

'For God's sake,' Aoife muttered. She flung the knife block at Jack and was surprised when it caught him in the cheek. She'd been aiming for his head.

Jack screamed and covered his face with both hands. Aoife grabbed Orla's hair and dragged her into the sitting room. Orla tried to shake free, but Aoife's grip was vice-like. She wasn't letting go.

'Get off me,' Orla shouted.

Aoife ignored her. She pushed Orla through the hole in the window and jumped after her. They ran down the driveway.

Out of the corner of her eye, Aoife saw Orla turn and run back towards the house.

As Aoife turned to follow, Jack appeared at the window. He was smashing the knife block against the glass, making a hole large enough so he could fit through. He was coming after them. Giving a howl of fury, Aoife tore after Orla, grabbed her by the arm and swung her around.

Orla pulled away. 'We have to kill him.'

Aoife tried to grab her arm, but Orla had now fully regained her strength and was determined to get vengeance. She pushed Aoife aside.

'He killed Tadgh!'

Aoife grabbed Orla's hair and gave it a hard yank. 'My baby is not going to be without a mother because of your stupid need for revenge, you idiot. Now come on!'

There was a loud crash and Jack came storming down the driveway.

SIXTY-FIVE

THEY HAD BARELY reached the footpath when Jack caught up with them. He grabbed Orla by the arm and stuck the tip of a knife into her spine. Aoife paused. Should she shout for help? Would that get Orla killed?

Jack looked up and down the quiet cul de sac. Keeping his voice low, he said, 'Turn around quietly and walk back to the house.'

Aoife took one step behind him.

'Keep moving.'

She would delay this as much as possible. Very slowly she took another step. Jack turned to watch her. He put one arm around Orla's shoulder and held the tip of the knife against her throat. His back was to the street. Aoife saw an elderly woman approaching. She took another step backwards, then a second, her eyes focused on the woman.

Jack heard the footsteps. He slid the knife into his pocket, pulled Orla into a tighter hug and turned.

'Evening, Mrs Tuohy,' he said.

'Oh my God!' The woman dropped her shopping and covered her hands with her mouth.

'Oh, don't worry about the window.' Jack gave a wide,

friendly smile. 'I had to break it because I lost the key to the front door. I'm getting more absent-minded every year.'

The old woman didn't reply. She took a few steps backward, eyes wide with shock.

'It's alright, Mrs Tuohy. These are my nieces. We're going inside now for a nice cup of tea. Would you like to join us?'

Aoife opened her mouth to protest. A stifled grunt from Orla caused her to stop. She took another step backwards.

A young woman approached from the opposite direction, a girl of about four or five skipping beside her. The woman followed Mrs Tuohy's horrified gaze and came to an abrupt stop. 'What—' She picked up the child and ran across the street. Putting the girl on the ground, she reached for her phone.

Jack frowned. 'Mrs Touhy, what's the—what's the matter?'

Mrs Tuohy's hands still covered her mouth. She appeared unable to speak or move.

The young woman could be heard talking into her phone. 'Mummy, why isn't that old man wearing any clothes?' the little girl asked.

Jack looked down. 'Oh my God! I can explain, Mrs Tuohy. There's nothing to be frightened about.'

A siren wailed in the distance.

Jack released Orla, looked desperately in all directions and ran towards the house. As he passed Aoife, she put out one foot and tripped him.

SIXTY-SIX

TWO GUARDS LED Jack to a waiting vehicle. Aoife looked away. She never wanted to set eyes on that bastard again. She hoped the police could get him to admit where he had hidden Triona's body. It was the least he could do for her family. But he wouldn't. Jack and his ilk were all the same. Like Buckley, he'd go to his grave insisting this was all a huge miscarriage of justice.

A crowd of neighbours had gathered on the street, and two policemen were attempting to disperse them. A young guard who looked like he was barely out of his teens was given the task of looking after Aoife and Orla.

'I'll drive you both to the hospital. Best have you checked out.'

'I'm fine,' Orla and Aoife said together.

'We'll let the hospital be the judge of that,' the young guard said.

When they were seated, Aoife phoned Maura and filled her in briefly on what had happened.

'Jack? Jack's been arrested for killing Danny? But Jack was practically a second father to him. I can't believe it! Jack? After everything he did for us. And he was the one who sent me the money?'

Maura was so shocked she didn't seem to fully take in the

trauma Aoife had suffered. Eventually she said, 'I'll collect you from the hospi—oh my God! Bridget! I'll have to phone her. No, that would finish her off altogether. I wonder if I have a number for Elain—'

'You take care of Bridget,' Aoife said. 'I'll take a taxi from the hospital.' She wouldn't, of course. It would cost a fortune, but Maura was in no state to think of that. 'I'll come by and pick up Amy on my way home.'

'Right, okay. Now I don't have Elaine's number. She's moved several times since Danny died. I don't think Michael's moved. I wonder where Danny would have put his number.'

As Aoife was hanging up, she remembered she had forgotten to thank the young woman who had phoned the police. 'Do you have her details?' she asked the young policeman. 'Can you please tell her how grateful we are?'

'Sure, I'll tell her. Good thing we were in the area. That mad lunatic would probably have killed all five of you, even that little girl. We've been keeping an eye out for you all day. The bulletin said to concentrate on the city centre, Dun Laoghaire and Kildare. None of them are on our beat, so we weren't involved in the search, but we were on the alert anyway. We were about to go on our break when that young woman phoned 999. You couldn't have timed your escape better.'

'You were looking for me?' Orla said. 'My apartment is in Dun Laoghaire. Did Cian report me missing?'

'Not you. We didn't realise you were in any trouble. It's Aoife we were searching for. Some detective asked all the stations to keep an eye out for her.'

'Oh, that must be Detective Moloney. Did you tell him you were going to visit me? Aoife, why are you looking at me like that?'

'There's something I have to tell you, Orla. It's about Cian.'

SIXTY-SEVEN

THE HOSPITAL RELEASED Aoife. Orla was to be kept under observation until they had the results of her blood tests. There was no knowing what drugs Jack had given her.

Nurses and doctors fussed around them, but eventually they were alone.

They looked at each other for a few seconds, then Orla said, 'We must be the world's worst judges of character.'

Aoife tried to smile.

'I know. It's not funny, but if you don't laugh at these things, you'll go off your head. I never would have believed Jack was a serial killer. Even in the beginning, when I thought he was a bit odd, I never suspected him of murder. And Cian!'

'We couldn't have been expected to know, Orla. Jack spent a lifetime building up a front, and Cian had been working on it for a few years too.'

'Tadhg knew. Well, not about Jack obviously.' She bit her lip. For a moment Aoife thought she was going to cry, but Orla was determined to put a brave face on everything.

'You know, Cian's been getting on my nerves since Tadhg died. I knew I wasn't myself, and I thought when I felt normal again, I'd want to be with Cian, but deep down I knew that wasn't likely. I'm glad he's out of my life. I suppose he can't be charged with bank robbery, but he must be an accessory, surely? And he'll definitely be charged with kidnap—'

There was a loud commotion, and Orla's parents almost skidded to a stop outside the hospital room in their rush to see their daughter. They threw their arms around Orla, both talking at the same time. Mid-sentence they noticed Aoife, rushed over and hugged her, telling her again and again how grateful they were that she had saved their precious daughter. Immediately forgetting Aoife's existence, they flung themselves on Orla again, demanding she tell them every detail of her ordeal. They interrupted her every few minutes with gasps, shudders and the occasional shriek.

∽

Aoife's head pounded. She dug her nails into the palm of her hand to try to stop the tears that threatened to fill her eyes. It didn't work. Blinking was more effective. She had to get out of here. Watching Orla's parents fuss over their daughter was too much. She didn't need reminding of how alone she was in the world. It wasn't as if she was likely to forget there was nobody she could turn to for support. Maura was consumed with her own issues. Orla had a family to help her through the bad times and, knowing Orla, once she recovered, she'd never want to speak about it again. Aoife would have to work her way through this alone. There wouldn't be anyone to help when the nightmares came.

She must have sighed too loudly because Orla glanced at her. Aoife took the opportunity to mouth goodbye and slip outside.

∽

Aoife was almost at the taxi rank when she saw him. She hadn't been aware of it, but now she realised that in the back of her mind she'd been hoping he'd collect her. He walked towards her slowly, unsure of her reaction. All her anger towards him, all the feeling of betrayal disappeared. She almost ran the last few steps. He put his arms around her. Neither of them spoke. There wasn't any need. The tears flowed freely now, but this time they were tears of happiness. Everything was going to be just fine. Much, much better than fine. Perfect.

They held hands as they walked up the driveway. Maura must have been watching out for them, because the front door opened before they reached it. 'Aoife, thank God you're alright.' Her eyes widened when she noticed their clasped hands, but she recovered quickly. Stepping back to allow them to enter, she said, 'Detective Moloney, please come in.'

Hi,

Thank you for choosing my book. If you enjoyed it, I would be very grateful if you could spare a moment to click on the link provided by Amazon. Any review, however short, would be very welcome.

Only Lies Remain is my second book. My first thriller, ***Girl Targeted***, covered an earlier time in Aoife's life. It is available on Amazon and is now free on Kindle Unlimited. Check it out here: *https://amzn.to/2Gyy56G*

If you'd like to get in touch, you can find me, and all my social media links, at my website https://valcollinsbooks.com/. You can also sign up for my newsletter there. I'd really love to hear from you.

Val

ACKNOWLEDGMENTS

THANK YOU TO my editor, copy editor & proofreader and my designer. It's my second time using Debz Hobbs-Wyatt, Eliza from Clio Editing and Patrick Knowles. As usual, they all did a marvellous job.

Thank you also to Elizabeth Psaltis and Beverly Bambury who helped with marketing and promotion.

I would also like to thank my friends:

Tina – The first person outside my family to read my book. Tina, as always, provided great support and advice.

John – For the second time, John allowed me to pick his brain about the workings of the Irish police force. Without him I would have to leave detectives out of my books entirely.

Yvonne – My expert on child vocabulary and quite a good story consultant.

Most of all I am very grateful to my family, those who are still with me and those who are gone.

Made in the USA
Columbia, SC
28 December 2019

85819252R00190